SARA LEWIS HOLMES

THE
WOLF
HOUR

ARTHUR A. LEVINE BOOKS
An Imprint of Scholastic Inc.

Library of Congress Cataloging-in-Publication Data

Names: Holmes, Sara, author.
Title: The wolf hour / by Sara Lewis Holmes.
Description: First edition. | New York : Arthur A. Levine Books, an imprint of Scholastic Inc., 2017. | Summary: Magia and her family live in the shadow of the Puszcza, an ancient and magical forest rich in stories and mysteries, where wolves can talk and read and unwary humans who enter its boundaries never come back—but despite her beautiful voice Magia longs to be a woodcutter like her father and learn the secrets of the Puszcza.
Identifiers: LCCN 2017016626| ISBN 9780545107976 (hardcover : alk. paper) | ISBN 0545107970 (hardcover : alk. paper) | ISBN 9780545107983 (pbk. : alk. paper) | ISBN 0545107989 (pbk. : alk. paper) | ISBN 9781338185805 (audio) | ISBN 1338185802 (audio)
Subjects: LCSH: Magic—Juvenile fiction. | Forests and forestry—Juvenile fiction. | Wolves—Juvenile fiction. | Fathers and daughters—Juvenile fiction. | CYAC: Fairy tales. | Magic—Fiction. | Forests and forestry—Fiction. | Wolves—Fiction. | Fathers and daughters—Fiction.
Classification: LCC PZ8.H735 Wo 2017 | DDC [Fic]—dc23
LC record available at https://lccn.loc.gov/2017016626

ISBN 978-0-545-10797-6

10 9 8 7 6 5 4 3 2 1   17 18 19 20 21

Printed in the U.S.A.   23

First edition, October 2017

Book design by Carol Ly

For my mom and dad,
who introduced me to stories

Once upon a time there was a Wolf. When he wasn't anymore, there was another one. And another one. How could this be? A Wolf without end?

Welcome, my little lambs, to the Puszcza, where even wolves must live and die by the rules. It's an ancient forest, a keeper of the deepest magic, and there, fairy tales of the darkest kind are real. Some even call them spells, for if you're unlucky enough to be caught in one of them, you must play your part, all the way to the bitter end.

Psiakrew! you say. You're trying to frighten me! Besides, fairy tales contain silly things like talking Wolves and clever Pigs and ugly Witches. Ridiculous, but not dangerous.

You're right, of course, if you mean the pantomimes recorded in books. But those printed words are like the sparse, thin-limbed trees at the edge of the forest—nothing compared with the thick-boughed, magic-laden, spell-fraught depths of the Puszcza.

Here, clever Pigs can follow every word of their mother's advice, and still have their lives blown down around them.

Here, an ugly Witch can offer sweet things to a brave Girl, and both can leave as empty as they came.

And here, a talking Wolf can tumble down a chimney, neat as a bale of hay, into a pot over a hungry fire. No matter how many fancy words he knows.

So I don't blame you if you want to look away, little lambs. Look away until the wild jig of boiling water has loosened the scrubby fur from the wolf's flesh, and released his pike-sharp teeth from his soft pink gums. Look away until all that's left are bones.

Smooth, twinkling-white wolf bones.

But if you desire a life beyond the ragged edges of the forest, and if you wish to see how the living are plucked from the dead and the mad cleaved from the sane, and—most of all—if you're ravenous for another heart to beat in time with yours, come into the Puszcza.

There lived a talking Wolf.

A brave Girl.

And a Witch who told fairy tales.

You can believe those tales if you like, my lambs. You can be amused by the clever pigs who pop up from time to time. But never forget that in the Puszcza's deepest reaches, it is always as dark as the hour between night and dawn. Always the hour more people come into this world and more people leave it than any other. Always the hour the old folk call the Wolf Hour. If you lose your way then, you will be lost forever, your Story no longer your own.

You can bet your bones.

· PART ONE ·

The thick-needled branches of the Puszcza were clotted with late November snow. Magia stood at the forest's edge, a small axe warm in her palm. Nearby, her father crouched over a felled tree, a woodcutter's red stocking cap pulled to his brow.

The *dąb* had made a thunderous noise as it plummeted to the earth, kicking snow into the air and coating Magia from her unbound hair down to her scuffed and patched boots. Snow flecked their wood cart, too, and the canteen of *kwas chlebowy* slung over one of its curved handles. Magia craved a sip of the deeply hued liquid, which smelled of raisins and rye. But not yet. Not until the cart was filled with wood. And not until she'd asked Tata for what she wanted most.

For now, she brushed herself off and bent next to her father. Together, they stripped the tree of its straggly branches.

Swing, *chop*. Swing, *chop*.

Magia didn't have to look at Tata to know she was

wielding her axe correctly. She could tell by the easy way the *dąb* branches fell to the earth, with clean breaks at the tree joints. And by the rhythmic sound of their two blades, which they swung in time to the song they sent up as they worked.

My wood feeds the fire,

sang Tata, his voice as strong and rough as bark.

The fire feeds the pot,

answered Magia, her voice as vigorous and sweet as rising sap.

Then the two of them finished together:

The pot feeds my family

And my family's all I've got.

Soon, between their singing and their chopping, the downed tree was nothing but a thick, branchless trunk.

"Hades!" said Tata as they stood up, their faces flushed. "An old man must've moved into my body while I slept last night!" His bones cracked as he stretched.

Magia hid her smile. Tata didn't use words like *Hades* inside the house. "Tell that old man to stay home tomorrow," she said teasingly. "He could snore by the fire while I wear his red hat and cut wood all day."

Tata laughed, as she'd hoped he would, but what he said next made her heart sink. "And after the wood was cut, who would check the traps in the Puszcza, my little sprout?" He gestured to their wood cart. Three black-furred rabbits hung limply from its iron-ribbed sides.

Magia looked away from the cart. She didn't like seeing the blood congealing at the rabbits' snapped necks.

Tata continued, "And what would Mama say if you missed your first singing lesson? You've been practicing so hard together!"

It wasn't that Magia minded practicing with Mama. Or singing so that Mama could ease into sleep when the baby squeezed inside her. It was too soon—weeks and weeks yet—for the baby to come, and Mama had to be still so it didn't. But Mama wanted more. Mama wanted—

Tata had begun the cold, deliberate task of dividing the tree into larger logs. Magia took the stripped branches, broke them down, and bundled them into neat stacks of kindling. Of course, no wood from the Puszcza's edge was going to burn as long as what Tata normally brought from its mysterious depths.

Magia paused in her bundling and gazed into the dark reaches of the forest. Tata might call her a little sprout, but she knew where she wanted to be. The chill breeze swirling from the forest's borders made brambles in her unbound black curls and filled her nose with the wild smell of heavy-limbed *świerk* trees. She drank in the sight of *dąb* after *dąb* after *dąb*, tall and snow-coated, until her eyes could follow them into the depths no more. And then she listened to how, with each windy gust, the branches of the Puszcza clasped one another in a chattering embrace, then sighed apart, drowning out all other noises.

"Tata," she ventured, "you know how Dorota wants to be a healer?"

"God make her brave," said Tata.

"And Jan wants to be a soldier?"

"God keep him close," said Tata.

"Well . . . ," said Magia. "I want to be a woodcutter. And go into the Puszcza like you."

Tata didn't stop swinging his axe. Or look at her. Magia swallowed hard to loosen her tongue.

"*Tak*, Tata, I know," she said. "I would have to learn so much. You could teach me! Teach me which trees give the longest-burning wood and which to let grow for another year and even . . ." She tied the pile of sticks in her lap together with a quick jerk of string. "And even . . . show me how to set your traps. I already know when they're full." Even though Tata wasn't looking at her, Magia gestured to the sky. "Today, before you came out of the woods, the *kanie* were circling. And making noises like this . . ." She put her lips together and puffed a wavering song like a piper out of breath. "They only do that if there's nothing to eat. I knew you were clearing your traps before they could."

Tata kept chopping.

Magia went on. "And I know when a tree is rotten inside." She pointed to a towering *dąb* three trunks over from the one Tata had felled. "That one, with the pockmarks."

Tata nodded without looking up. He'd seen that tree, too.

"And today . . ." Magia knew this was the boldest, bravest thing she had to tell Tata. "Today I went to the village and got your last orders for you!"

Now Tata did look up. He leaned on his axe. Magia smiled a sly smile. "Pani Wolburska and Pani Gomolka fussed and complained about the cost, of course, but I told them they were your best customers. And they both want two coins' worth!"

"Two coins," said Tata, nodding slowly. To Magia's delight, he smiled slyly back at her. "Sometimes, people surprise you." But then his smile faded. "Oh, Magia," he said, "of course I love working with you. But you have a voice that lifts hearts, and a mama who believes you can enchant the wider world. Before you wish to be like me, you should listen to her."

"Tata, I do listen. Every day. And I sing for her anytime she asks!"

Tata sighed. "That's not what I meant," he said, as he carried logs to the cart. "I can give Mama firewood, and rabbits, and as many kind words as I can. But you—you and Dorota and Jan give her reasons to be happy. She has big dreams for each of you. You should heed those, not follow the lonely path of a woodcutter." Tata's voice grew deeper as he leaned closer to her. "Besides, going into the Puszcza is not like working near its edges. For one thing, you would be bound to wear an ugly hat like this one."

Magia opened her mouth to protest, but stopped, her words caught in her throat. Tata had taken off his red hat, and he was holding it out. To her.

"Go on," said Tata. "Once you see how this hat feels, perhaps that will be the end of it."

Magia's heart bumped even harder as she slowly took the stocking cap. Tata was wrong, she thought. His hat wasn't ugly. Plain, maybe, but the stitches were even and true. And it was a lovely red color, unlike anything else she'd ever seen.

Red was rare near the Puszcza. Sometimes, red berries grew wild in the paupers' cemetery. And once, on the back stoop of a customer's porch, she'd seen a line of red ants, devouring a piece of plum-stuffed *pączek*. But no one in the village painted their house red, or wore red. Red was the color of fire and pain and trouble. It was only for those who chose to leave the company of people and go into the deepest woods. Like Tata. Like her, one day.

Magia tugged Tata's hat onto her head.

Ech.

The hat looked smooth, but it felt rough, like straw. The jagged edges of it made her whole scalp prickle.

Maybe if she started walking, the hat would hurt less. She took a shaky step toward the forest.

Ech. Ech! Now her head burned and itched. It was as if she were that *pączek* and the ants were swarming her!

Tata looked at her intently. Was he trying not to laugh? Or cry? Everything, from the bristling short hair on his now-bare head to his quickened breath, seemed to be waiting for her reaction. Tears began to sting Magia's eyes.

"You see?" Tata said quietly. "Even on your pretty head, a woodcutter's hat acts ugly. It must, or its wearer might be lulled into staying in the Puszcza forever."

"But, Tata . . . ," Magia said, her words scratching out of her throat as if they were as prickly as her scalp. "The hat feels like it's *eating* me!"

"That's what I told my father, too," Tata said as he came up beside Magia. He had her small axe in his hands.

"He'd given me this axe, and I wanted to be the best wood-cutter this forest had ever seen. When I had a taste of the red hat, though—oh, how I yelled. I think I even cried."

Tata was trying to help her with this story, Magia knew it. But it was hard to listen to what he was saying when the tips of her ears burned. And when her eyes stung from the effort of keeping her mouth from quivering.

And yet, the harder the hat bit her scalp, the more the forest seemed to call to her, until she felt her feet tingle with longing to move. She wanted to run into its depths and she wanted to tear the hat from her head. But she could do neither.

"It was only two or three slow-leaking tears, mind you," Tata was saying, his voice soft. "How my mama heard those drops fall, I don't know. But when she found me, she scolded me: 'Hush your crying, Piotrek! Would you rather be eaten by a hat—or swallowed by the Puszcza itself?'"

"Why do you do it, then, Tata?" Magia asked, her fists curled into tight balls. "Why do you cut wood if the Puszcza is deep, and the hat is hard to wear?"

Tata considered her question. She'd asked it before, of course, but he'd said things like: *We must chop wood for everyone. It's what we do.* Or: *My father was a wood-cutter, and his father before him, and his before him, as far back as we remember.*

This time, though, his words felt clearer and more honest. He spoke them next to her, as they faced the woods together.

"In the Puszcza, everything sings to me. The trees, the animals, even the dirt on my boots—it's as if we are made of the same stuff. My father said it was because in the Puszcza, we're woven into a larger story, one that we barely know we are part of otherwise. We are close to the wildest magic there is. That alone, to me, is worth a lifetime of living safely inside the city's gates."

Yes. That was what she wanted, too. Magia uncurled her tense fingers, one by one, and breathed in the unmistakable smell of the Puszcza—a porridge of decaying undergrowth and spicy *sosna* needles that even snow couldn't mask—until she was calm and still.

"But if the Puszcza is a story, my eager bud, it's easy to get lost in the telling. My hat, as painful as it is, keeps me from losing my way. Without its stings and jabs, the Puszcza might swallow me up. Or I might even fall prey to those who would manipulate the forest's magic to their own ends."

Magia nodded. She'd heard tell of *wiedźmy*, those who dallied in the forest to steal the Puszcza's power for their own greedy selves. Like foxes sucked yolks from eggs, leaving the empty shells to rot.

"But, Magia," Tata continued, "a red hat isn't enough." He turned her around to face him, and held her eyes with his serious brown ones. "You must learn the paths of the forest, and how to find the direction of the sun when there's no light overhead. You must be so certain of your true story that you always end up where you want to be."

Now he pointed away from the forest, and across the bleak snow-dusted meadow of sunken dead grasses and snarled scrub. At its end, a thin stream of wood smoke snaked up through the leafless tips of a stately trio of *buk* trees. Below the smoke sat the plain, square-shouldered shape of their home.

"Me? I always want to find myself at Mama's dinner table."

At this, he grinned and tugged his hat from Magia's head. *Ahhhhh.* How sweet the cold wind felt as it nipped her scalp! Magia shook out her hair, her neck, and even her arms, down to her fingers.

"So it's the smell of Mama's *bigos* that makes you come home," she said. "Not the hat."

Tata laughed as he tucked his stocking cap into the pocket of his flapping coat. "*Tak,* Mama's stew is delicious. Mama makes me smarter. And happier. And a bit fatter." He patted his belly where the coat didn't close. Then he reached for the canteen of *kwas chlebowy,* and took a long, filling swallow. "But I'm going to have to wait on rabbit stew today. These logs won't deliver themselves. You can run home, though. No need for us both to be icicles."

Magia looked at the village beyond their house. Most of their customers lived in that nameless place, hoping one day to afford to move inside the protection of Tysiak's iron gates. But even there buildings huddled like frightened animals. Tysiak wasn't for her. Neither was the village. Or any place with more people than trees.

Magia took the canteen from Tata. Had a long swig, too. Wiped her mouth with her hand. "Take the rabbits straight to Mama," she said. "I got the orders this morning. I can deliver the wood for you, too."

"I don't know, Magia," said Tata, "the cart is heavy and—"

Magia interrupted him. "Yes, it is. But it will get lighter as I deliver the orders. I can do it."

Tata looked between her and the village.

"Please, Tata?" said Magia. "You said the woodcutter's life was a hard one. Shouldn't I find out how hard it is *now*?"

He grimaced. "My stubborn nut . . . I need a promise from you first."

"Yes, Tata, anything," said Magia. She reached for the cart.

"You may deliver wood today, but until the baby comes, I want you to stay close to your mama. She needs your help these last few weeks."

Magia wiggled the cart loose from a clump of ice and frozen meadow grass. Tata had said "until the baby comes." Which meant that *after* the baby came . . .

"I promise," she said. "I promise I will listen to Mama." She took a hand off the cart and put it inside Tata's larger one. "But I don't want to burrow inside like the Panie do, telling tales of the Puszcza without ever going there. I want to have my own red hat and go as deep into the forest as I like, every day. Will you teach me, Tata? Will you?"

In answer, Tata only squeezed her hand, but as he reached for the rabbits and slung them over his shoulder, Magia saw him smile.

At that, Magia grinned, too. "Don't snore too loudly by the fire," she said. She put both hands on the cart and steered it toward the village.

By the time she got there, her hands were raw from wrestling with the bucking and sliding handles. Her knees were bruised also, for they had banged into the cart each time it had balked. And, as she'd feared, the Panie were not pleased to see her.

"You again?" Pani Wolburska said, her voice grating Magia's ears. "Where's your tata?"

"Home," Magia said simply. "I'm delivering today."

Pani Wolburska pushed her nose a notch farther out the door. Spiderwebs clogged the corners of her porch. "I'm surprised your father lets you outside alone. Didn't you hear the wolves howling this morning?" She drew her shawls, dense as a thicket, closer. "It's going to be a long, bitter winter."

Wolves? thought Magia. That would be exciting— but there had been no tracks or scat near the Puszcza today. She didn't argue, though, only placed each wedge-shaped log under Pani Wolburska's steps, sending bristly-legged spiders fleeing into the blackened crevices. Maybe her silence and hard work would soften Pani Wolburska's tight mouth.

The woman glared at her. "Don't have a word to say to me, is that it? In my day, a *dziewczynka* heeded her elders. I'm telling you, I heard wolves. The Puszcza will swallow us all this winter!"

"Oh, I wouldn't worry," Magia called up to the porch, "the Puszcza isn't as hungry as all that! Besides, you'll have our wood to keep you warm!"

Then Magia heard the unmistakable thump of Pani Gomolka's walking stick. The old woman hobbled past her and climbed Pani Wolburska's stairs, one slow step at a time.

"*Tsshsk*," said Pani Gomolka, glaring down at Magia. "What do you know? You haven't lived as many winters as we have!" Then she said to Pani Wolburska, "Where's this girl's tata?"

Magia sighed. "I'm delivering today."

"Are you?" said Pani Gomolka, with a sniff. "This morning you said we were your tata's best customers. Why doesn't he deliver wood to us himself? Why does he send his youngest, dressed like a burst sausage?"

Magia's shoulders stiffened. Her brother's hand-me-down pants might drag on the ground, and snow might creep into the space where her sister's old sweater didn't cover her neck, but her axe fit her hand exactly right.

Pani Wolburska chimed in: "Oh, she won't be the youngest much longer. Then she'll have to stop playing with her toy axe and stay home and help her mama. All *dziewczynki* must."

"True. True," added Pani Gomolka. She thumped her stick. "Of course, as my *babcia* used to say: Girls do have choices." She glanced at her neighbor with a sliver of a smile. "They can prick their fingers on needles . . ."

"Or stab them on *pins*!" Pani Wolburska finished. The two of them laughed as if this were funny.

Then Pani Wolburska leaned over to Pani Gomolka and said in a low voice, "We're wasting our breath, you know. This one has no ears for her elders. And she has the manners of a turnip. I doubt she'll even sweep our porches."

Sweep their porches? Did Tata do that for them? "I can," said Magia, coming up the steps. "But . . . this one looks clean to me," she said. Which was mostly true, if you didn't count the spiderwebs.

"Of course my porch is clean!" huffed Pani Wolburska.

Pani Gomolka looked at Magia as if Magia were a brainless *gapa*. "We had to come out of our houses to talk to you," she said slowly. "Now look at the footprints we've left! That's all a *wiedźma* needs to spoil someone. She measures the print with some string . . . and then she burns it. *Pfffffff!* You're cursed."

Magia looked from one pinched face to the other. It seemed silly to sweep marks that would reappear the next day, but she would please these two for Tata's sake. Then she took the broom Pani Gomolka thrust at her.

· · ◆ · ·

Finally, hours later, Magia was finished. She'd delivered all the wood, swept all the porches, and collected all the small packets of coin the Panie and Tata's other customers had tossed into her cart. She could head for home.

Before she was out of earshot of Pani Wolburska and Pani Gomolka's houses, though, Magia stopped to look at their shuttered windows. Today she'd tried on Tata's red hat. She'd gazed into the depths of the Puszcza. She'd done everything Tata had asked of her and more. She wasn't *playing*.

She smiled softly. Maybe there had been no sign of wolves near the Puszcza, really. But the Panie didn't have to know that. Magia tilted her nose to the clumpy snow clouds darkening overhead. Then she loosed a long howl to the sky.

Aw-whooooooooooo! Aw-whooooooooooo!

The sound rolled out of her throat with a satisfyingly wild thrumming. There. Now the Panie wouldn't poke their noses outside for a week! Magia closed her eyes and grinned.

· ◆ ·

Later that evening, Magia squatted as far away from the hearth as possible while Mama, from her bed, gave orders to Dorota for butchering the rabbits. Mama was yellow-haired and tall, with a face as delicate as a crescent moon. She was ordinarily as thin as a new moon, too, but the baby had made her wax full. Her words came in spurts as she lifted her head to see what her eldest was doing, and then winced, as if pains laced her belly, before settling back into the blankets Tata kept piling around her. Finally, Mama shooed him away.

"You did your work; let me do mine," she said.

Tata obediently went to poke the logs in the fireplace, but Magia could see him looking back into the bedroom. There were only two rooms in the whole house: Mama and Tata's room, where Mama lay now; and this other, slightly larger room where the children slept at night. During the day, it was used for everything else, like cooking and studying and praying and visiting—if they ever had visitors, which they didn't much. Right now, it smelled of Dorota's sweat and fresh rabbit meat.

Magia put her head down and twined the string of onions Mama had given her into a fat braid. Or she tried to. Her hands hurt from all the chopping and pushing and stacking of wood and sweeping she'd done today. The onions, freshly dug and sleek, kept escaping and bouncing to the floor at Jan's feet.

"Help!" said Jan playfully. "I'm under attack!" His sun-bright hair, so much like Mama's, flopped against his ears as he kicked an onion back to her. But he didn't stop carving the chess piece in his hands.

Magia grabbed the loose onion. Inside work always made her feel all knuckles and thumbs. She ground her teeth as she remembered the words of the Panie. Girls had no choices but needles or pins, did they?

Magia looked at her sister. Dorota's black dress was neat and clean. Her braids, as always, dropped straight from her ears as if they were candles, drying. Nothing about her was out of place. But her face was hot and blistery red from the fire. As Magia watched, Dorota sighed, fished a rabbit leg back out of the pot, and peeled off a tag of forgotten skin. Nearby, the dresses and shirts of city folk waited for her in an overflowing basket of mending.

Magia bent over the onions and jerked them roughly into place. As soon as she was done, she got up and found her axe. Steadily and slowly, she polished the blade to a high gleam. She didn't look up until Tata called everyone to take a bowl of stew into the bedroom, for Mama wasn't supposed to get up, not even to the table. They ate, knee to knee, around her bed.

After dinner, Mama waved her hands when Dorota tried to clear the bowls. "Dishes are a duty, but music is a delight," she declared. "Let Magia sing first."

From under her pillow, Mama drew out a yellowing rectangle of cloth. She'd cut it from the skirt of a threadbare apron months ago, when the baby had first begun to rebel against her. On it, she'd instructed Magia to ink a line of rectangles, all pressed together, and all the width of Magia's finger. Then, in groups of twos and threes, she'd shown Magia how to overlay the shapes with smaller rectangles, and shade them until they were a solid black.

"What is it?" Magia had asked.

"A piano," Mama had said. "In Białowieża, when I was a girl, every fine house had a piano. And every girl learned to play one."

Now she said in a wistful voice, "When I was little, at this time of the evening, you could hear musicians warming up their instruments in the concert halls, their notes popping into the sky along with the stars. Here, we don't have such halls, but we do our best."

She spread the cloth flat on the edge of her bed near Magia's chair, and then put one hand, softly, over Magia's hand. "I know it's been hard, my love, to sing along with such a poor instrument." Under the covers, a rippling wave roiled her belly, and her face whitened as the baby kicked. Her eyes latched on to Magia's with the same fierceness she'd used to wave away Tata's fussing, but her fingers were cold and clammy. "Tomorrow, you'll be glad you're prepared," she continued. "Tomorrow, when you have the attention of the best teacher Tysiak has seen in a long while . . ."

Her voice trailed off as her belly contracted again. Then, slowly, she released Magia's hand, curved her fingers against the cloth piano, and nodded at her daughter to begin.

An old apron couldn't make sound float into the air, of course, but Mama said a singer should learn to sing in time with a musical instrument. As long as Magia watched Mama's fingers, she could make her voice match Mama's rhythm.

Ah-la-la, Magia sang.

Ah-la-lo

Ah-la-la

Ah-la-lo

As she sang, she could see fatigue creep into Mama's half-lidded, sunken eyes. She could stare at Mama's swollen legs, which seemed like giant logs under the too-thin quilt. Magia thought, for an instant, of the pockmarked tree she'd pointed out to Tata—but that was silly. Mama wasn't rotting from the inside. She was tired from growing a baby.

Still, Magia was glad when the song was over and Mama rolled up the piano with satisfaction.

"Could we have a story now, Mama? Please?" Jan said. He was holding his finished chess man in his fist.

"Only a short one," said Tata, eyeing Mama's pale face.

Mama nodded and cleared her throat. "This is a story told to me by my mother," she said softly, "who heard it from her mother, who heard it from her mother, who heard it from hers, and hers before that, all the way back to a *dziewczynka* who saw this story happen with her own eyes."

Magia shifted in her chair. Mama's stories always began this way. And Magia always wished she could meet that *dziewczynka,* the girl who had seen everything happen. How had she been so lucky?

Mama continued in her low voice. "This tale is about three little pigs who moved into the Puszcza, not knowing they should be careful. The first two pigs were in a hurry to build their shelters, so one built a house of straw and one, a house of clay. Which did them no good, for those houses were weak, and soon blown down by a wolf's huffing and puffing."

"Huff!" said Jan.

"Puff!" said Magia, shivering. She'd heard this story before.

"Meanwhile," said Mama, her voice growing stronger, "the third pig had *prepared*. He'd taken his *time*." She looked at each of her children. "This pig built a *solid* house of brick. The wolf couldn't blow it down, no matter how hard he huffed and puffed."

"Huff!" said Jan.

"Puff!" said Magia, even more quietly.

"Finally," said Mama, "the wolf tried to get in through the chimney."

Magia winced. She hated this part.

"Of course," Mama said, her voice rising, "the wise pig had *prepared* for this, too. He had a giant pot of water at the boil!"

"No more huff," whispered Jan to Magia.

"No more puff," said Dorota, with satisfaction.

Magia gripped her chair with her hands.

"Imagine the wolf's surprise at being dinner!" said Mama. "They say you can hear his howl on the wind to this day."

Magia glanced over at Tata, who was oiling the handle of his axe as he listened. Today, he'd talked of a bigger story. A story he felt part of in the Puszcza. She wished he would tell her more about *that*.

"So, the moral is . . . ," Mama said.

"Don't howl," said Dorota.

"Guard every entrance!" said Jan.

Mama smiled. "No, no," she said. "It's be *prepared*." Her face flushed with the effort to speak firmly. "My mama always told me that each of us is born with magic in our bones, and we must prepare to live as if that is true. That's why I'm proud that Dorota endures endless mending, for one day, she will mend people." At this, Dorota sat up straighter in her chair. "And I'm proud that Jan knows how to make beautiful things, for even if a soldier is strong and brave, he must value the beauty of what he is guarding above all else." Jan twirled his wooden knight in the air before making it bow, deeply, toward Mama.

Then Mama's face lit up as she turned to Magia. "And I'm proud that Magia will soon learn to make the most of her beautiful voice. My youngest thinks it is a small thing to be able to sweeten the air with honeyed notes, but her voice will open doors to her in Tysiak and beyond. Perhaps all the way to the concert halls of Białowieża."

Magia's stomach tightened. She liked to sing, but she didn't want to live inside a city's gates. That would be both needles AND pins.

Mama, though, had dreamily closed her eyes. Slowly, the family got up from their chairs and crept into the other room. Magia stood more slowly than the rest. Oh, how her legs ached. Oh, how her fingers stung where the splintered broom had raked them! And, she thought, she smelled of onion.

"What's wrong, my *siekierka*? Are you tired from helping me today?" Tata said. "Or did the Panie gnaw you to bits?"

Magia stealthily dumped a scrap of rabbit skin into their fire. The flames snapped and glowed as red as Tata's hat. She had done a woodcutter's work today. And now Tata had called her by her favorite nickname: little axe. She smiled at him.

"No, Tata. I feel wonderful," she said.

Meanwhile, in the Puszcza . . .

"Once upon a time," Biggest would say, "there were three little pigs."

"Three little pigs and their wonderful, amazing, brilliant mother!" said Middlest.

"Yes! Yes! She's the best! Tell it right!" insisted Littlest.

"Fine," said Biggest, and began again. "Once upon a time, there were three little pigs—and their wonderful, amazing, brilliant mother. One day, the wonderful, amazing, brilliant mother said to her three young ones:

" 'It breaks my large, warm heart, but I can no longer afford to feed you, my piglets. Run off now, to a nearby meadow, and make strong and steady and stalwart homes of your own.'

"But the three piglets, who thought they knew better, decided, instead, to explore the Puszcza."

Here, Littlest would always start to weep.

"Land was cheap there," Biggest would admonish him. "We were able to afford larger dwellings."

But Middlest would respond, every time: "So what? We should never have listened to you! It's *your* fault!"

But, in truth, it had been he and Littlest who had snatched up the first materials they spotted in the forest—pine straw and mud—to construct their houses. Two no-good, not strong, not steady, and completely stalwart-less houses.

As for Biggest, he'd been perplexed. He'd said *land* in the Puszcza was cheap. Not that they should build cheap houses. But he was accustomed to being the only pig with half a brain, so he ignored his brothers and erected a house of bricks. It took him days. When he was finished, he informed his brothers that their brilliant, amazing, wonderful mother, who had remained, alone, outside the forest, should now come for a visit—and judge which dwelling was the best.

When the three pigs went to invite their mother to view their houses, however, they didn't find her. Instead, in the meadow where once Mother Pig had frolicked with them, a woman sat with a book. She was scratching words into it with a long feathered pen.

"Where is our mother?" squealed Littlest.

"What are you doing with that pen?" said Middlest. He shuddered as the strange woman squeaked the feathered quill against the book's smooth pages.

"I can't believe you don't know what a pen is for," Biggest scolded his brother. "Didn't Mama tell us that we should never let ourselves be captured by one?"

"I thought she said: Never let yourselves be captured *in* one," argued Middlest.

"I want my mama!" yelled Littlest.

The woman looked up from her writing. "Oh, my dear piglets. How sad your mother was that she couldn't afford to feed you anymore. How sad she was that you were forced, so young, to build your own houses. And how very, very sad she was that she couldn't keep you *little* piglets forever. So I offered my help."

"What if we don't want your help?" said Middlest bravely. He was used to arguing with Biggest, and would do it with anyone.

"Now, now," said the woman, licking the point of her pen with her tongue, and eyeing Middlest. "Your wonderful, amazing, brilliant mother is safe with me — at least for the time being — but she is counting on you. She's left instructions. If you follow them, all will be well." Then she turned the book she'd been writing in toward them and showed them exactly what they must do, if they wished to remain Mama's little pigs forever.

The three pigs gasped.

"No," said Biggest. "Pigs are civilized animals. We have no business doing *that*."

His words made no difference. For the woman wasn't a woman at all. She was a *wiedźma*. And now, none of the pigs knew how their story would end.

The next morning, Magia had to remind herself that she'd promised Tata she would listen to Mama. Even if that meant she had to be encased in Dorota's itchy hand-me-down wool tights. Worse, her arms were trapped in the narrow sleeves of a steely blue dress. Even Magia's flowing hair had been secured to her scalp in two braids like Dorota's, leaving her ears exposed to the raw air and the loud noises of Tysiak.

Magia grimaced. Why was her sister squeezing her fingers? Magia couldn't run anywhere. She and Jan and Dorota had already walked past the watchful eyes of the guards at Tysiak's massive iron gates, and now they were surrounded by the taller, many-windowed houses that made up the center of the city. Now they were crowded by people parading too close to them, some on foot, and some atop the fat, swaying sides of slow-moving horses. Now there were hooves clopping and mouths chattering and heavy-heeled boots clicking. Magia could smell the warm leather of *konie* saddles, and the stink of fish oil used to ward off illness, and the overly perfumed handkerchief a woman hastily put to her nose as she stepped around them where they stood, in front of a stern-looking, steep-gabled house.

Ech. Magia didn't understand why they couldn't get this over with. They were expected, weren't they? But Dorota said the lesson was at ten o'clock, so ten o'clock would have to strike before they approached the door. That was how people who lived in Tysiak did things — not by the sun and sky, but by the clock.

Magia looked up at the music teacher's house. It had seven wide steps, which were framed by wrought-iron railings, and beside the brass-handled door hung a newish-looking sign, which read:

MELODIC RARITIES

· ♦ · ·

TEMPORAL TREASURES

· ♦ · ·

All Callers by Appointment Only

"What does that mean?" Magia asked.

Dorota looked at the sign. "Melodic means musical. She must sell unusual musical instruments, I guess, as well as teach lessons."

"I know that," said Magia. "I was asking about the other words. What are temporal treasures?"

"I don't know," Dorota said, frowning. "Something to do with time? Or—"

She stopped talking, because from the music teacher's house came a low keening. Magia turned her head to peer up at the windows, but she could see nothing. Someone in there was singing a wordless, haunting song.

The music reminded Magia of the time of year—almost here—when daylight dwindled to a few hours a day, and Tata had to be quick about his visits to the Puszcza. When the *jesion* trees, ghostly with their white bark, were swallowed by heavy snow. When most animals that lived in the forest sought shelter. Except, the music said, this someone . . . this something . . . had no shelter. Had no hope. And had no words to say what it most wanted to say.

"Do you hear that?" said Dorota. "Someone is singing about summer, and fresh berries . . . and the most perfect, cloudless sky. Isn't it beautiful?" Her face looked lovely and serene as she smiled at Magia, her firm grip on Magia's hand loosening.

"Yes," said Jan. He jiggled the coins in his pocket as if playing along to the melody. "Why, I could march to Białowieża and back with that tune in my head!"

Magia gaped at her brother and sister. What were they talking about? The music was beautiful, yes, but it was also painful and terrible and fierce. Listening to it made her feel as she had yesterday, as restless and hungry as the *kania* that wailed fruitlessly overhead. Before she could say so, the music stopped and the city clock began to strike the hour.

"That's it, then," said Jan, as the clock finished its tenth clang. "That lesson's over. Time for ours." He looked at

Magia, who was trying to shake the sound of the song out of her head. "Sorry—yours." He bounded up the steps, and lifted his hand to knock at the door.

It opened under his fist to reveal a florid man in a fine suit of clothes, complete with a feather-garnished hat and ribbed stockings. Magia stared. This well-dressed, well-fed man couldn't be the achingly hungry voice she'd heard singing, could he?

But there was no one else with him. Instead, the man was holding aloft a birdcage, the bars shrouded with a dusky cloth. He pushed past Jan without a word, all important elbows and striding, heavily booted legs. Magia, still on the stairs, tried to move back, but the cage bumped her shoulder.

"Watch where you're going!" cried the man. His voice was as muddy and coarse as his pulpy face.

Before Magia could say a word in reply, the cloth shifted, and she glimpsed not a bird in the cage but a—white stick? It was shaped like one of those whistles Jan sometimes carved, only longer and decorated with more holes. It arched and flexed, as if a chill breeze were blowing over its body, and from it came a low, wavering song. Instinctively, Magia reached a hand to it. Was this what they'd heard? Why, it was—

"What do you think you're doing?" said a voice.

Magia blinked. A woman stood in the doorway of the house. Her hair was the color of three-day-old dishwater, and her skin was equally drab, like the underside of a mushroom. Only her gown had any hue to it, and it was the chalky shade of ashes. She was no taller than Magia herself, and thinner by a full stone. How long had she been there? And why was she staring as if Magia were a beetle trapped inside a bottle?

The man jerked the cage away from Magia's hand, and made a show of adjusting the drape over it. "This *gapa* is trying to spoil my purchase, Miss Grand, that's what she's doing!" he said.

Magia couldn't believe it. This was Miss Grand, the famous music teacher?

"She couldn't spoil it if you weren't still here," Miss Grand said to the man, but her sunken eyes stayed on Magia. "I told you to take that home."

The man huffed in displeasure. "I wonder that any brainless girl might damage my daughter's gift. If it is damaged, I should get my money back."

Miss Grand's eyes snapped from Magia to the man. "My, my," she said. "Such concern over nothing." She waved a hand in the air. "Return to your house. Give your daughter the flute you've cleverly bargained for. Then everyone will see that you treasure her above all else, and wish to keep her safely at home." She regarded him with a tight smile. "You do wish to keep her safe, don't you?"

The man's face crumpled, as if the anger holding it stiff had burned away. "Yes," he said. "Yes. That is what matters. Thank you, Miss Grand! Thank you!" Then, with a flourish of his feathered hat, his boots clicked down the steps and into the swirling street, where he elevated his precious purchase above the heads of the lesser folk.

Magia stole a quick glance at her brother and sister. Had they followed this conversation? How could that strange instrument—that flute—keep anyone safe? But Jan and Dorota were looking at Miss Grand, who regarded the three of them as if they were mouse droppings in cream.

"Now," she said, her smile gone with the man, "I won't ask again: What are you children doing here?"

Jan jumped forward. "We're here for a lesson," he said. "We have an appointment."

"I see," said Miss Grand, her voice dry. "I don't recall receiving payment for you."

"It's not for him," said Dorota as she drew Magia up the steps with her. "It's for our sister. Give the teacher the coins, Jan," she added.

Jan fished them from his pocket and thrust them at Miss Grand. "We have an appointment," he repeated. "At ten o'clock."

Miss Grand slid the money into the pocket of her gray gown. "Well, then," she said, "you're late."

She turned and went back inside. Dorota, Jan, and Magia could do nothing but scramble after her through the dim front hall. They shuffled to a stop, dumbfounded, in the teacher's parlor.

For as drab as Miss Grand was, her house reeked of rosy color. Magia stared at the pair of pink, long-benched sofas that stood too far apart, like reluctant dance partners; then at the stiffly upright, matching chairs that hovered awkwardly at the corners of the room. She marveled at the windows, which were smothered in pink cloth, and gaped at the portly pink teapot on display, which was ringed by a double hedge of teacups, each cup painted with vivid pictures of thick-thorned roses. The teacher must've brought these things from Białowieża or beyond; no one sold such daring decor here.

Magia inched farther into the parlor. Mama had told them that in the city, plants could be kept inside, confined to wooden boxes, but Magia hadn't believed it. Nor had she believed she would ever see such thick and colorfully bound books! A row of ten or more of them lined a shelf between the stately windows. Mama would give anything to have such books. Magia leaned forward to see the titles.

"Are you going to poke your nose into everything?" Miss Grand said.

Magia flinched. "No," she said quickly, turning. "I wanted to tell my mama what books you have. She likes stories."

"I see," said Miss Grand. "What about you? Do you like stories?"

"No," said Magia. "I like cutting wood. I'm going to help Tata. He's going to teach me everything he knows about the Puszcza."

Why had she said that? Or even mentioned the Puszcza? People inside the gates didn't like to be reminded of how close they lived to the wildness of the forest. And now Miss Grand was staring at her again. Magia knew Mama had made her presentable, but something about the way this old woman was standing too close, and breathing on Magia's face, made her feel that the teacher was sniffing for something raw and unsightly in her.

Finally, Miss Grand pressed her lips together and gestured to an imposing musical instrument that filled the opposite corner of the room. Even though it, too, was pink, it matched Mama's description of a piano. Its top was propped open so Magia could see a raft of tautly tied strings inside.

"What are you waiting for?" Miss Grand said. "Stand over there, and we'll see if you're worth my time."

Magia reluctantly walked across the parlor. Behind her, she could hear Jan's shoes squeaking as he paced between the twin sofas. Dorota positioned herself near the heavily draped windows. Miss Grand lifted the lid from the piano's keys, and with one gnarled finger, punched out a note. The strings of the piano trembled.

So that was what a real piano sounded like. Was the teacher going to play a melody while Magia sang? Which melody?

But Miss Grand simply pinged the note again, more sharply. "Do you have ears? Nod if you can hear me."

Magia flushed. Slowly, she clasped her hands together, lifted her chest, opened her mouth, and—

"Stop!" the teacher snapped. "I haven't set the time yet!"

Miss Grand held up a pink porcelain pig, as gaudy as her parlor. The pig's cheeks were daubed with two perfectly round, rosy circles of paint, and its ears, which curled from its head like huge, unfolding leaves, were also stained a vivid pink. The pig's tail was coiled up, an errant blob of deeper pink icing on the broad cake of its backside. In the tail's grip was a skinny, upright brass bar.

Miss Grand closed the piano's top so she could put the pig on it. "You will sing exactly as my metronome tells you to," she said to Magia. "No faster, and no slower."

She pushed the free end of the brass bar to the right and released it. Immediately the pig began to click loudly, while the bar jerked left and right, left and right, as if the pig were using its tail to wave good-bye. *Tik tak. Tik tak.* Magia's heart quickened to match its pace. Mama had told her about metronomes, but she'd never used one.

"You may begin," said Miss Grand. "Scales first."

Magia couldn't look away from the pig. Why, it even had painted-on hair! Above its closed, heavily lined eyes, blond bangs swirled like melted butter.

"Is there a problem?" said Miss Grand. She'd settled into one of the prim pink chairs, her arms and legs tucked tightly to her sides. "Do you not know how to sing scales?"

No, Magia knew her scales. She kept one eye on the pig to make sure she was not too fast or too slow. *"Lo!"* she sang. *"Lo, lo, lo, lo, lo!"* stepping up the scale. It was harder than matching Mama's fingers, yes, but no harder than singing in time to her own axe, rising and falling.

When she was finished, Magia allowed herself a glance at the teacher. Surely that wasn't too bad for her first lesson?

To her surprise, Miss Grand was idly fingering one of her rosy teacups, as if Magia was boring her utterly. *Tik tak* went the metronome. "Again!" said Miss Grand, not even looking up. "Stay with the beat this time!"

With great effort, Magia kept her voice steady as it rose and fell on the notes of the scale. This time, she looked directly at the pig, trying harder than ever to match its—

Magia blinked. Blinked again. When she'd hit that last high note, the pig's eyes had . . . *opened.*

Was that supposed to happen? Magia stole another glance at Miss Grand. All the teacher did was say:

"Again!"

Magia looked back at the pig. Now its eyes were closed as before. Magia dutifully opened her mouth and repeated the notes. This pig might be moving stiffly, but she could join its rhythm.

There it was again! On her last note, the pig's eyes had definitely *blinked open.* And the painted china flowers glued to its back trembled, as if the pig had stood up from a long roll in a summer meadow.

Magia didn't bother looking at Miss Grand this time. It took all of her concentration, but she kept the notes flowing up and down the scale as she stared at the pig. Soon, to her delight, her singing lifted the pig's hooves. It was a hesitant jig, but a jig nonetheless.

Magia felt a stab of glee, followed by a twinge of bewilderment. Mama hadn't told her a metronome could do this. Maybe she'd thought Magia would discover this secret at her first lesson.

Magia dropped her stiffly clasped hands to the piano, letting her fingers graze the smooth keys. They quivered as the vibrations of her voice filled the room. What would happen if she sang a little louder, a little freer? If she sang notes as strongly as she could swing her axe? Could she help the pig dance faster?

She began the sequence of notes again. To her delight, the pig's hooves rose and fell as quickly as her notes. Soon, it was as if she and the pig were jigging together. No, more than that. It was as if Magia's voice was making the whole world whirl and leap. She wasn't following the metronome—the metronome was following her! She and the pig could sing anything together. Why, if she wanted to, she could make that pig as alive as—

Suddenly, a voice swore in words that even Tata didn't use. Then something close to Magia thudded and shook, and her notes choked to a stop. The pig abruptly stopped dancing, too. Then, unable to control the still-moving rod in its back, its eyes closed and it toppled over.

Magia looked down. *Fire and sticks!* Miss Grand had slammed the lid to the keys on Magia's fingers.

She gasped as the numbness in her hands snapped into a searing pain. The twitching pig was still clicking on top of the piano, writhing and jerking, as if in time with her throbbing fingers. Somewhere far away, she could hear Dorota yell, "What did you do?"

"Stop interfering, you brainless *gapa*!" shouted Miss Grand. "Stop!"

The metronome still ticked. Magia heard Dorota's feet—or were they Jan's?—moving toward her, but pain was driving blinding tears into her eyes. *Stop? Stop what?*

Then the metronome shuddered, and—

Crrkk!

The pig spun off the piano, hitting the edge sharply. Almost at the same moment, Miss Grand keeled over, too.

"Mercy," gasped Dorota. She ran to Miss Grand. Lodged in the teacher's forehead was a triangle of sharp, vivid pink china.

The pig's ear!

Fear washed over Magia. Was Miss Grand dead? She hadn't meant to break the pig! She'd made it dance, it was true, but she hadn't meant for the dance to end so suddenly! The china body of the pig now lay, one-eared, on the pink rug. Beside it, Jan had slid his arm under Miss Grand's motionless body, lifting her slightly so Dorota could inspect her wound. "You'll be all right, Miss Grand, won't you?" he said. He used his sleeve to halt the trickle of blood that oozed into the teacher's straggly gray eyebrows.

Magia's fingers throbbed as she wiggled them out of the piano lid. *Oh, Mama,* she cried in her head. *I was prepared! I was! How could this have happened?*

"Cold water," Dorota said swiftly. "Get cold water."

Magia headed for the front door.

"Not from a well!" said Dorota. "The kitchen!" At Magia's blank look, she pointed toward an arched doorway. "We're in town! She'll have an inside water pump! Go! NOW!"

Magia stumbled toward the opening. She ran down the hall and pushed the swinging door at the end of it. A long counter ran the length of the room. An oval basin was set into the counter, and a curved metal arm hung over it.

When Magia touched the pump, it was comfortingly cool. She pressed her hands against the cold metal, and gasped as tears threatened her eyes. A line of blue bruises was already forming along her knuckles.

Miss Grand wasn't dead, Magia assured herself. Dorota wouldn't have sent for water if she was. Besides, the nasty woman had hurt *her* first. If she hadn't slammed the lid on Magia's fingers, she could've caught the pig and it would never have rolled off the piano! Magia sniffed back her tears and wiggled the pump handle. A stream of water flowed out and out and out.

Psiakrew! She had nothing to put the water in!

In the dim light, Magia saw a set of heavy shelves built into a back corner of the kitchen, rising ladderlike from floor to ceiling. Her boots softly thudded against the black slate slabs of the wide floor as she walked over to them.

But the shelves held no buckets or jars. Only cages and cages like the one Magia had seen on Miss Grand's steps. In each one gleamed a ghostly white flute.

Magia gaped. The instruments glimmered in the dull light, their slender forms pierced by rows of shadowy holes. She leaned closer, her starched dress pulling under her arms. As she did, the flutes shuddered. A desolate wailing filled the kitchen.

Magia's heart squeezed inside her chest, so hard that her fingers tingled.

"Magia!" yelled Dorota's voice from down the hall. "What are you doing? I need water!"

Startled, Magia stepped back from the shelf. How could she have forgotten? If Miss Grand wasn't dead before, she might be by the time . . .

Magia's gaze swept around the kitchen. There! Hanging from hooks near the cavernous kitchen fireplace was a series of tools, including an enormous soup ladle. Magia quickly filled it with water and, holding her hands steadily around it, fled from the kitchen.

When she burst into the parlor, Dorota had removed the shard of china from Miss Grand's forehead, but the teacher's body was still limp in Jan's arms, her feet splayed on the floor. Magia's fingers trembled as she knelt and put the ladle straight to Miss Grand's lips. The woman's eyes opened.

"Oh, thank goodness!" said Magia. "I thought I'd killed you!"

Miss Grand knocked the ladle out of Magia's hands. Magia gasped as she leapt to her feet, but the icy water had already soaked her stockings and seeped into her dress.

"You were to do as I told you!" Miss Grand said. She pushed Jan and Dorota away and sat up. "Who do you think you are, setting your own time?" Blood oozed angrily from the wound on her forehead.

Dorota looked from Magia to the teacher. "There's no need to yell," she said. "It's only making your wound worse."

She reached forward to dab at the red line on Miss Grand's forehead, but the old lady slapped her hand.

"Stop touching me," said Miss Grand, "or I'll call for the guards. Your sister's already broken my property."

Dorota stood up and stiffened her back into a rod as rigid as the pig's bar had been. "What happened was an accident," she said. "At least on my sister's end of it."

"That wasn't an accident," Miss Grand said. She shoved herself to her feet and confronted Magia, her eyes bright with that odd, hungry look again. "Where did you learn to sing like that?" she demanded.

Magia knew Miss Grand didn't mean the scales Mama had taught her. But what could she say? She'd made the pig dance; she knew she had; she just didn't know how, or why.

"Mama taught me," Magia said. "She said you would teach me, too. But you—" She swallowed. She shouldn't say anything more. But her fingers stung and her stockings were wet and the memory of the flutes' moaning filled her head. "You take money for nothing!" she said. "You weren't even listening to my notes."

Miss Grand's eyes narrowed as she bent down to retrieve the pig. "This . . . ," she said harshly as she shook the fat china body at Magia, "this is not nothing! And now that you've damaged it, you will pay."

Dorota and Jan were suddenly flanking Magia, their bodies warm against hers. "And what about my sister's fingers?" said Dorota, her voice dangerously quiet. "They may be broken. Who will pay to take care of them?"

When Miss Grand snorted in disdain, Dorota grabbed Magia's arm. "I thought so," she said. Then she nodded to Jan, and before Magia could think, her sister and brother were hurrying her out of the parlor.

At the front door, Dorota turned and regarded Miss Grand. "If your metronome is broken, you must've set it wrong," she said in a withering voice. "And if you ever come near my sister again, I'll break *your* ear off."

She and Jan hustled Magia out the door and down the steps into the cobbled street. Immediately, Magia was again surrounded by noise. Hooves! Feet! Voices! Why, there was even a man yelling for no reason at all, except that someone in front of him wasn't getting out of the way.

Dorota stopped several paces down the block. Crowds of people jostled the three of them, as if they were jutting rocks in the path of an angry stream. "Give me your fingers," she ordered Magia curtly, but her face showed no trace of the lash of fury she'd used on Miss Grand.

"They're not so bad," said Magia. "I held them against the pump in the kitchen." Still, she had to lean against Jan and bite the inside of her cheek as her sister gently examined her bruises, wiggling each finger to make sure none of the bones would need to be set. She blinked, hard, and glared back at Miss Grand's door. So many things were strange in that house. The flutes, Miss Grand's boredom, and what about the metronome? Had Jan or Dorota seen it dance as Magia had? She wanted to ask them, but if she did, she'd have to admit she'd made it jig on purpose. Instead, she said in a low voice, "Do you know what was in her kitchen? No food. Just more of those flutes!"

"No food?" Jan looked back at the house, too. "Maybe she eats children," he said. When Dorota and Magia stared at him, he shrugged. "*Nie*, so she probably doesn't—but you have to admit: She's ornery enough to do it." He grinned at Magia, trying to make her laugh.

"Jan," Dorota scolded. "Magia's frightened as it is."

Magia wasn't frightened. Yes, it made her chilled and hot at the same time to think of the keening flutes caged in the cave-dark of the music teacher's pantry. But Miss Grand's greedy eyes on her had been worse. As if she'd wanted to plop Magia into a cage, too, and keep her there.

"Besides, who cares what that woman eats?" Dorota wrapped her own scarf around the worst of Magia's bruises to cushion them. "She's the rudest person I've ever met. Let's go home."

Once they were through the city gate, and past the village that huddled outside it, Magia's steps slowed. She didn't want to face Tata. She'd wasted his three coins. She'd behaved foolishly. And worst of all, she'd have to see Mama's face crumple with disappointment.

"Don't be a cabbagehead," said Dorota, when Magia confided her fears. "Jan and I saw how awful that woman was. And we don't have to tell Tata and Mama everything," she added. "We can say you . . . you didn't sing well enough to be invited back."

Magia breathed a sigh of relief. Sometimes her sister was so sensible it was shocking. Even if Dorota then showed her displeasure with the whole situation by taking back her scarf, turning on her heel, and marching toward home alone.

As Magia and Jan walked more slowly, Jan nimbly plucked something from his pocket. "I guess we'll have to hide this, too, then," he said. He waved a chipped piece of pink china in front of Magia's eyes. The pig's ear.

"Want it?" he said, holding it out. "It can be a medal. For bravery."

Jan was grinning like he'd managed to steal a crown jewel, so Magia smiled weakly and slid the little chip into her dress pocket. She wished Jan wouldn't make it sound like she'd done a heroic thing. All she could hope for now was that Dorota would have everything explained to Tata by the time Magia got home. Maybe he wouldn't be angry. Maybe she could still help with delivery today. Maybe—

Magia's feet ground to a halt. Across the snow-swathed meadow that stood between the village and the Puszcza was a girl. A staggering, swaying, half-dressed, shrieking girl.

"*Wilk!*" squawked the girl as she stumbled toward Magia and Jan. "*Wilk!*"

She slid in the snow and fell stiffly at their feet, her eyes rolling to the sky. Spittle coated her lips, and her arms ratcheted uselessly in the air, as if she were reaching for something that wasn't there.

Without thinking, Magia reached for Jan's hand, and her bruised knuckles bumped into his side. "Ouch!" she yelped.

"For heaven's sake, Magia, be quiet!" whispered Jan. "Didn't you hear her? There's a wolf about!" Without dropping his eyes from the surrounding forest, he stepped over to the nearest tree and snapped off a branch as a makeshift weapon. His head swiveled as he scanned the terrain near them.

Magia bent over to tend to the girl. She was clearly alone, as a single line of footprints zigzagged behind her — no wolf tracks anywhere. She seemed to have staggered and fallen, over and over, in the snow, hurting herself on the twisted brambles beneath. One side of her plain black dress was shredded up to her waist, and her boots were unlaced. The skin on her exposed flesh was as pink as a flower.

"He ate me!" cried the girl again. "He ate me!"

"She doesn't know what she's saying," said Magia, looking up at Jan. "Look at her! She's so mad she's choking on her own words!"

It was true. The girl's tongue was now flopping inside her mouth soundlessly. Magia suddenly felt queasy. If only Dorota hadn't gone ahead. Her sister was good with sick people; she wasn't.

Jan didn't put down his stick, but he knelt on the other side of the girl. Her bark-brown hair, still plaited tightly on one side, had come apart into rough, lanky pieces on the other. Her chest twitched as if she were drowning. Worst of all, the whites of her eyes were streaked with blood, making them look like two monstrous burst blisters.

Carefully, Jan slid an arm under the girl. "You're right," he said to Magia quietly. "She's mad. We should take her to the gate guards. They'll know how to find her mama and tata."

Together, Magia and Jan lifted the girl off the ground, although her feet dangled uselessly as they tried to get her to stand between them. In the end, they had to grasp her under her thin shoulders, one on each side, and steer her back toward Tysiak, her head bobbing and twitching and dropping to her chest as they moved. Every few steps, her mouth would open, and Magia would think she was going to cry out her warning about a *wilk* again. Nothing but nonsense came out.

She was no better by the time Magia and Jan, after long, torturous steps, managed to coax and drag her to the door of the brick guardhouse near the gates.

"Where did you find this girl?" said the sergeant, addressing only Jan as they struggled to hold the girl upright. "Did she say anything to you?"

Jan shook his head. "We found her on the path from the Puszcza. She talked of a *wilk*, sir. But we saw none."

At this, the girl, who had been simply babbling, now snapped her head to Jan. "*Wilk! Wilk! WILK!*" she screamed.

Jan flinched at her fury. From the nearby streets, a few curious onlookers stopped to stare. Another guard came out of the guardhouse's iron-framed door. He also had a black uniform, but it was decorated with shiny buttons and gold braid. The captain.

"What's going on here?" he demanded of the sergeant. "Who is this girl?"

"Yes!" Magia heard someone say. "Who is it? Whose daughter is she?" The growing crowd inched closer, rumbling.

At their approach, the girl only screamed louder. "*Wilk! Wilk! WILK!*" Then she broke away from Magia and Jan and flung herself against the wall of the guardhouse. Her shoulder blades pressed to the bricks, and her eyes darted around the crowd as if she thought they might do her harm.

"I don't know her, sir," the sergeant said, his face blanching under the shrill noise of the shrieking girl. "But a girl was reported missing two days ago. This boy says he found her on the path. Stark mad, she is."

Magia frowned. Jan had clearly said "*we* found her . . ." Why was this man pretending Magia wasn't there? At least someone in the crowd had wits: A young boy hurried off, to get the girl's mama and tata, Magia hoped.

"You found her on the path?" said the captain. He looked from Magia to Jan and back again. His face creased with suspicion. "Not *in* the Puszcza?"

"Yes, sir," Magia said eagerly. At least this man knew she existed. She copied her brother's sober, respectful tone. "And yet . . . if you'll look—in her hair—there are *sosna* needles. That tree only grows in the Puszcza."

At this, the onlookers, who had swelled into a knot of rustling, murmuring bodies, pressed closer to the mad girl. Their rumbles gave way to voicing their fears in earnest.

"So the poor *dziewczynka* WAS in the Puszcza! Why don't those foolish girls ever learn?"

"It's not as if their tatas and mamas don't warn them! They should stay close to home!"

"And what about this other loudmouthed girl? How does SHE know about *sosna* needles and where they grow?"

Suddenly, Magia heard a voice she recognized. "That wild one? That's the woodcutter's daughter." Pani Wolburska emerged from the crowd, shifting her shawls so she could point at Magia.

"Never saw her that clean before!" another familiar voice scraped. The harsh words were followed by the unmistakable thump of Pani Gomolka's walking stick. The two women stood together, gawking at Magia in her dress, their wary eyes alive with excitement.

Now the crowd turned to the Panie as if they were wise beyond measure. "I heard the same thing happened to a girl two villages over," said Pani Gomolka. "The Puszcza reached out and sucked her in, and now the poor thing's tongue is as useless as the one in a monkey's head!"

"Better she'd not come back, then," Pani Wolburska said, her voice breathless. "Some lost things should stay lost."

Why were the Panie gossiping about what had happened two villages over? There was a mystery right here in front of them. "Sir," Magia said to the captain firmly. "There's also the fact that the girl's skin is pink."

"What?" said the captain, looking embarrassed. Perhaps he thought no one should notice the girl's torn dress.

Magia ignored his discomfort. "If she's been missing for two days," she said, "dressed like that in this cold, her skin would be white from frostbite. Perhaps she was wearing a coat at some point? If we made a search, and could find that, then we might know for certain where she's been."

The captain gingerly peered at the skin of the girl's neck, and then lower, where it showed through her shredded dress. His eyes narrowed as he looked back at Magia. "You seem to know a lot about what has happened to her, don't you?" he said.

Magia felt Jan quietly take her hand. She knew what he was telling her: *Be careful*.

Suddenly, the crowd about them roiled with a wave of pitched voices as a man and a woman pushed their way to the gates. Both were as plainly dressed as the girl, and even paler than she was.

"Oh! Oh! My poor *dziewczynka*!" the woman cried, rushing forward. She pressed her daughter to her chest.

The girl began to blither again, almost sobbing. "*Wilk! Wilk! Wilk!*" were the only words Magia could make out.

"See?" said Pani Gomolka, thumping her stick so the crowd would look at her. "I told you! Mad as a monkey. And why? Because she didn't stay home where she belongs. And now listen to her! She's obviously given a *wilk* a taste of her blood! If we're not careful, it will bring a whole pack of them out of the Puszcza—on us!"

Magia took a step toward the Panie. "But there were no wolf tracks," she began. "Not—"

Pani Wolburska interrupted. "I told you I heard wolves," she said flatly. "I heard them again right after you delivered our wood."

"No—that was—" Magia felt a hot stab of guilt close up her throat. Then she flinched as the mad girl began to scream again.

"*WILK! WILK! WILK!*"

The crowd gasped in horrific satisfaction as the girl chewed at her lips till they bled. Pani Gomolka's stick clicked as she turned three times in a circle. Then she spat in the dirt—*pwchat!*—in case evil was looking for her, too.

"Hush, my dear, hush!" the girl's mother whispered. "There is no wolf here. You're safe with us now." She looked up at her husband as if to ask him to confirm this, but he'd stopped short of the two of them. To Magia, he looked afraid, and maybe a little ashamed. Was it because his daughter had disobeyed him? Gone where she shouldn't have?

The girl's mother glared at him and said, "I told you this would happen! I told you!" Then she turned her anger on the guards. "And YOU! You guard nothing! We gave you everything we had to move inside the gates. But it wasn't enough! Not with that wild music floating over the streets! They say *their* daughters need that music to keep them satisfied at home, but *our* daughters, who can't afford such things, are the ones who—"

Before she could finish, the man stepped in front of his wife and said quickly, "What my wife means to say is that we're grateful for your protection. We're taking our daughter home now."

The captain nodded, his mouth tight. "Glad to hear it," he said. "Still, I recommend you speak to your daughter. Girls shouldn't walk near the Puszcza. It makes their already weak minds go mad."

The mother's face darkened with fury, but her husband had cradled their daughter in his arms, and was slowly moving her through the choked streets. The woman, with an anguished cry, hurried after him.

Suddenly, Magia remembered the flutes' melody of aching beauty and pain. Was that the "wild music" the woman blamed for her daughter's unhappiness? If it was, Magia could see why it disturbed her. It was as if Miss Grand had caged a tantalizing piece of the Puszcza for those afraid to visit the real thing.

"Come on, Magia," said Jan, tugging at Magia's hand. "We should go home. Tata will be worried." He tried to move past the guards.

The captain held up a hand. "One minute," he said to Jan, his voice hard. "I've seen you before. Hanging about the gates, watching."

"Yes, sir," said Jan calmly. "I want to be a soldier one day."

"*You?*" said the captain. "Isn't your tata a woodcutter?"

He half laughed, and Jan winced before he drew back his shoulders. "Yes, sir," he said proudly. "Yes, he is."

The captain shook his head. "Then you of all people should know to keep your sister at home, where she belongs."

Magia felt fury building in her chest. If she'd been at home, they never would've rescued that poor girl! And as for Jan keeping her anywhere —

Then she looked around her. Now that the girl was gone, she'd thought the crowd would go, too. But not all of them had. Clumps of muttering people filled the nearby streets, and some of them were pointing at her and Jan. She remembered how they'd murmured when she'd shared what she knew of the Puszcza. Now they gathered near Pani Gomolka and Pani Wolburska, listening to their ridiculous stories.

Magia's heart twisted. The Panie had said mean things to her yesterday, but she'd always thought they valued the wood Magia and Tata brought them. If they'd seen her and Jan rescue the girl, then followed them back to the guardhouse, why hadn't they told the guards and the crowd the plain truth?

Magia squeezed Jan's hand and walked away from the gates. The Panie would talk themselves into a frenzy, and then they would go home and hide behind their spider-webbed doors as they always did. Magia and Jan, though, had been delayed so long that Dorota might be headed back along the path to fuss at them.

Sure enough, when their house came into view at last, Dorota was standing outside. Her arms jumped into the air at the sight of them, waving as if to hurry them along—but her mouth, even though it moved, made no sound. Since when had Dorota ever lost her voice?

Then Magia saw that the front of her sister's dress was red. Blood red.

Littlest Pig bolted straight for Middlest Pig's house. His brother lived near a stream, and had made his home from mud gathered from its banks. Whenever it rained, the house dissolved into a fabulous puddle for wallowing. But as it hadn't stormed lately, the walls only oozed dangerously.

"Wolf!" cried Littlest as he barreled through the sloping archway of his brother's hut.

Middlest caught him before he slid through the back wall. "Again?" he said. "I don't want to do this!"

"W-w-w-we have to," said Littlest. "W-w-w-w-wolf! He blew my house down!"

"He always does," said Middlest. He ran to the riverbank with a bucket, filled it with cold mud, and tossed the contents into the doorway of his hut. Three times he did this, until a thick, sticky pile formed. Then the two pigs began to desperately heap the archway with the mud, trying to seal themselves inside.

"Faster!" said Littlest. "Thicker! Higher! He's coming!"

But mud cannot be rushed. It's as slow as all the tales say it is. In the end, the pig brothers had to gather sticks from the forest. Together, they pushed the broken pieces of wood into the mud, trying to construct a door.

"Dry!" commanded Littlest to the mud. "Dry, dry, dry!"

"Be quiet," said his brother. "You're making the mud warmer with your hot air."

"I want my mama!" said Littlest.

"Me, too," said Middlest. "That's why we're doing this, remember?"

Then they both huddled behind the wall of soft mud and small sticks, and shivered. The witch's book had been terrible, but this was real. A wolf was coming. And only Biggest, in his brick house, was safe.

They didn't have long to wait.

"Little pigs, little pigs!" cried a voice. "Let me come in!" The wolf pawed a stick loose from their makeshift door.

"Not by the hairs on our skinny-skin skins!" cried Littlest and Middlest. But of course, they knew it was only a matter of time before the wolf made himself a way in. Before he could, they burrowed out the back, and scampered toward their brother's house, many hoof-prints away.

"Wolf! Wolf! Wolf!" cried Littlest and Middlest as they arrived at the house their brother had built. It stood like a squat dwarf in the middle of a clearing, a massive pile of bricks cemented together, with only one door to go in and out of. The door was banded with metal and locked with a brass dead bolt. Biggest had also made certain that the glass in the lone window was of such thickness that no one could see in.

The difficulty, of course, in building such a fortress was that no one could tell if Biggest was at home, which was why his brothers feared his absence as they pounded at his door.

"Wolf! Wolf! Wolf!" they cried. "Let us in!"

"Calm down," Biggest said as he ushered them inside. He slammed the door behind them and threw the dead bolt. "We've done this before, remember?"

"Yeah," said Littlest, "but you don't have your house blown down around you every time!"

"Yeah," said Middlest. "You get to sit here by the fire, dumb, fat, and happy. We have to *run*."

Biggest rolled his eyes. He wasn't dumb. He wasn't fat. He certainly wasn't happy. Not with the damper in the brick chimney propped open, offering a clear way in.

But that was the way it had to be. They had to crouch as far away from the heavy locked door as they could. They had to wait for the wolf's approach, each one trembling, each one feeling how little they were, each one counting on their Story to work. For it *had* worked, a thousand, thousand times before.

Then, outside the locked door, a she-wolf howled.

· ◆ · ·

She howled and howled and howled.

Her mate, atop the roof, didn't listen to her. He kept inching toward the chimney, intoxicated by the oily scent of Piglets with No Way Out.

"Ah-wwwoooo!" the she-wolf howled. "No! Come back! Think of our pups! You must be here when they are born!"

The wolf atop the house didn't stop or come back. Instead, he twisted himself into the chimney.

The she-wolf keened softly. Their pack had once had the roam of the Puszcza, but it had dwindled through forces she did not understand. All she knew was that human Stories were everywhere in the forest. If her mate fell into one of them, she would be well and truly alone. "Come back! Come back!" she howled.

But from the chimney, only smoke billowed into the sky. It reeked of Death So Close You Should Run.

Many achingly slow minutes later, the she-wolf heard footsteps in the distance. Crouched low and trembling, she watched as a pair of boots tripped up to the brick house. A human! That was a *human*! And it was knocking at the front door.

The she-wolf, concealed by a tangle of branches, hoped against hope that the door would open and reveal her mate. Her magnificent mate, with his mottled gray fur, his stately ears and bold, jaunty muzzle. Her love. Instead, she heard the squealing cadence of a piglet's voice.

"Tell Mama," he said. "Tell her we're still her little pigs."

"Of course you are," said the human. "That was our bargain, was it not? I always keep my bargains. Do you?"

The she-wolf lifted her nose toward the open door, hoping to catch her mate's scent.

"Tell her we're doing as she asked," continued the pig, his vowels squeaking. "Until she can come home."

"Enough snuffling!" said the human, harsher now. "Give me what I've come for. Or do you wish your poor, long-suffering mother to think you're lazy and won't pay your debts?"

"No," said the pig. "We will pay." He turned and went into the house, leaving the door ajar.

From her hiding place, the she-wolf gave one last, desperate sniff of the air leaking from the house. Alas! How desolate the Last Log of a Fire Collapsing into Ashes! How bleakly empty A Pot Left to Boil Dry! And how achingly bitter the smell of Gone Forever.

When the pig returned to the door, he handed the human a package wrapped in cloth. By that time, the she-wolf had fled.

Weeks later, Magia sat in front of the fire, picking worms from cabbage leaves.

"Be careful," Dorota said as she picked up her basket of mending and headed toward the door. "If you drop a leaf on the hearth, you'll have to use it, ashes and all." Then she slid her eyes toward Mama's room, and her voice lowered. "I've tended to Jan's eye. And Tata will be home soon. Don't worry about Mama. She needs time."

Magia ignored her sister until Dorota, bundled in three scarves, had closed the front door with a quiet thud. If she had to stay home and make cabbage soup, at least she could drink in the heady smell of the *dąb* log as it released its slow heat.

She stuffed great handfuls of cabbage leaves into the pot. Then she put the pot on the hook over the fire and stared at the limp, worm-riddled leaves. If only she had a bit of meat to throw in, too. But Tata wasn't hunting. He left the house only to chop wood to sell. And that was less and less time each day, it seemed.

Magia grabbed the kettle they used to make tea and headed to the door to scoop up snow to melt. As she opened it, the hinges squeaked in protest. She would have to guess how much water the cabbage needed to—

"Is that the baby?" a thin voice said.

Mama.

Magia hurriedly shut the door and went to her mother's room. "Do you need something, Mama?" she said.

Mama didn't look at her. Her eyes were focused beyond Magia, at the wall where her few dresses hung from a hook. None of them would fit her now; she was thinner than winter sunlight. This Mama didn't give directions for making and baking. This Mama didn't help Dorota braid her hair, or Magia comb the brambles from hers. This Mama didn't even exclaim over the bruise that Jan had brought home from the village this morning. This Mama only lay still in the dark.

"I must feed the baby, Magia," she said. "Bring her to me."

"I can't," Magia said. She took her mother's bony hand. "The baby's in the churchyard, Mama. Remember?"

"The churchyard?" said Mama, her fingernails digging into Magia's hand. "Why?"

That's what Magia wished she knew, too. Even now, she had a precise memory of the tiny rippled curve of the baby's spine. The baby had curled, naked and unmoving, on Mama's chest all of one day and night before Tata gently folded its body into a blanket.

But the baby was gone now. Weeks gone.

Magia wanted to run to the door and call for Dorota to come back. Instead, she took a flat-handled spoon and poured in some of her sister's syrupy medicine, brewed from bark. As far as Magia could tell, the bitter stuff only made Mama's limbs jerk while she slept—and the bedpan smell even worse than it already did. Still, Magia put the spoon to Mama's lips. A dollop of the medicine dripped onto the covers. Mama didn't notice.

"The baby isn't at the church," Mama said. Now she was looking directly at Magia. "She can't be. It isn't made of brick. It isn't safe. She's not prepared. Someone could take the magic from her bones."

Magia didn't move, even as her mind raced. Words were better than Mama's submerged silence. Still—

"This isn't a story, Mama," said Magia. "We're here. Safe. At home."

Mama's intent gaze on Magia's face didn't change. Magia felt trapped by that stare, even more than her mother's painful grip on her hand.

"Mama, please, let's get up. Help me make the soup. I'm . . . I'm hungry." As she said this, an ache swelled her belly. That was true, wasn't it? "Oh, Mama! Aren't you hungry, too?"

"If you're hungry, you should eat, Magia," Mama said in a whisper. "Eat. Or you'll starve the magic from your bones." Then her fingernails retreated. Her hand relaxed a little, slipping out of Magia's as her eyes closed again.

Dorota had said: "Mama needs time."

How much time? thought Magia. Seconds, unused and unnoticed, had already turned to long minutes, which had turned into empty hours, which had turned to silent days, until now, weeks had been eaten up as Mama lay in shadow-eyed grief.

When Mama's breathing finally deepened, Magia left the darkened room to see if the cabbage was cooked yet.

Psiakrew! She'd never added the water! The leaves were burned, blackened to the bottom of the pot. Magia grabbed for the braid of onions she'd made weeks ago. How many would it take to blunt the taste of burnt cabbage? Two? Five? Eight?

Magia used her axe to split the semi-dried things into raggedly shaped pieces. Why? Why wasn't Mama any better?

And why had someone thrown a rock at Jan today? Dorota had put a poultice of knit-bone and flour on the puffy purple stain on his cheek. To Magia, the bruise looked like one of those mushrooms that huddled in clumps under fallen branches. "What happened?" she'd asked her brother.

"Someone thought a rock was answer to my asking for work," said Jan. He lifted his chin. "Someone told him I wasn't to be trusted."

"Why?" said Magia. She couldn't imagine her cheerful brother being dishonest. But Jan didn't respond. After Dorota finished fussing over him, he went to stand in the yard. He was there now, with a stick in his hands.

Magia smashed the last onion. She dumped the whole mess into the cooking pot, and gave it a violent stir with the ladle. Then she opened the front door again to get the snow she'd forgotten.

As she stooped to fill the kettle, she took a long breath of air, hoping to catch a hint of the heady richness of the forest. She could smell nothing. She brought her hands to her face, and tried to scent the sap that always used to cling stubbornly to her skin. Nothing.

When she came back inside, Magia sighed as she dumped the snow into the pot. How long would the onion and cabbage take to make soup? An hour? Two? It didn't matter how long it was; Magia had more work to do than could be done in that time. On the table was another basket of mending—their household items, which Dorota had not taken, because there was no pay for them. Piles of socks with holes. Jan's coat to be let out at the seams. Tata's shirt, which had lost three buttons. And none of those things could be fixed with an axe.

Magia left the pot to boil, and took up a needle.

· ◆ ·

That night, as they ate Magia's soup, no one said a word as they picked onion from their teeth. Instead, Tata kept frowning at the bruise under Jan's eye. It had already changed color, from purple to a yellowish tinge at the edges. Then he quizzed Dorota about her visit to Tysiak. Did she feel safe going there?

Yes, Dorota said. But it was not worth going more than once a week. People didn't need her to watch their children because they were all at home. And there was less coin for her mending. Two more girls had gone missing, so people were scrimping and saving to buy those strange flutes instead.

"People say they draw the wildness from girls," said Dorota. Her face was skeptical, but her voice was flat and tired. "Make them less likely to seek the danger of the Puszcza. I don't know why. That woman who sells them, Miss Grand—she's hardly wild! And when I hear the music, I think of last year, when Mama told us about the shower of stars that comes late every summer, and we made apple-peel tea and sat looking up at the sky. Mama told me I would see those same stars when I was at school in Białowieża." Dorota stopped and bit her lip. "But— how would I know? I don't have a flute. Those are for other girls."

Tata's face seemed paler than Mama's. He looked from Dorota to Magia to Jan and his black eye. "What aren't you telling me, my little ones? What else are they saying?"

Dorota turned to Tata, her eyes wet, but her words fiercely angry. "I went to see the man who threw the rock at Jan. Demanded to know why he did it. You wouldn't believe it, Tata!" she cried. "He said that—that he'd heard the baby had one wolf eye where her nose should've been! That we should've burned her body instead of burying her in the churchyard! That more girls have gone missing because we didn't burn her. That we brought a curse to Tysiak."

Tata flinched. Magia didn't understand. "How can anyone believe that?" she said.

There was a dull silence, and then Jan answered slowly, "It all happened the same day, Magia. That's enough for some people. I touched the mad girl, and then I touched Mama, and so, after the baby died, the villagers thought—"

"Nonsense," said Dorota. "Utter nonsense. You weren't even home before Mama—" Abruptly, she rose and vanished into Mama's room.

Jan looked after her. Then he said to Tata, "I'll look for work in the next village, Tata. Maybe no one will have heard of us or mad girls there."

Suddenly, Magia remembered Pani Gomolka's stick clicking as she turned three times in a circle. Heard her mouth spit—*pwchat!*—in case evil was looking for her, too. She stood up. "I know who's behind this gossip. Pani Gomolka! Pani Wolburska! I'm going to take my axe and pound down their doors until they wish a wolf would come for them," she said. "I'm going to howl and pound until—"

She stopped. Tata's head was bent to his chest, as if her words were blows. Magia felt even worse when Jan shook his head at her disapprovingly and then went to sit outside with his carving knife, to hone yet another stick.

"Oh, my little robin," Tata finally said. "The Panie can wound with words, but even they wouldn't tell such bitter tales. Besides, I've lost too many customers as it is. If you go yelling and pounding on doors, I'll lose more."

"I'm sorry," Magia said. "I didn't mean it." When she hugged him, she could smell the delicious scent of the forest and the comforting, woolly smell of his sweater mixing together as he held her tightly.

As Tata released her, he looked in her eyes. "Still, you are right. We must do something. Would you do a bold deed for me tomorrow, my *siekierka*?" he said.

Despite herself, Magia smiled. "Of course, Tata," she said. "Anything."

Tata reached into his pocket and pulled out three coins. He placed them in Magia's palm. "Go into Tysiak tomorrow," he said. "Go to that fancy music teacher and ask if you can have another chance."

Magia couldn't keep her disbelief off her face. After everything that had happened, how could Tata ask her to go back there? Didn't he know how Miss Grand had slammed the piano lid on—

No. No, he didn't. Magia hadn't told him. And with Mama . . . not being Mama . . . she couldn't tell him now.

"Tata," she began as calmly as she could manage, "I'm not sure Miss Grand would let me come back. She's . . . she's . . . important in the city."

"Yes," said Tata. "It seems she is. Everyone seems to think her flutes are all that stand between Tysiak and a true plague of madness." He shifted his feet. "But, still—you sing beautifully, Magia. As if the magic and wildness of the Puszcza are in your voice. People should hear that instead of those flutes. Maybe then they'll know the stories they're telling about us are untrue."

"I don't know, Tata," Magia said. The coins felt hot and heavy in her hand. "You should've seen the way the gate guards looked at me and Jan when we brought the mad girl to them. Like we had fleas. Besides . . ." She held out Tata's coins to him. "I don't even *want* to sing in concert halls. Please don't waste your money on me. We need it to eat."

Tata didn't take back the coins. Instead, he curled her fingers around them. When he spoke, his voice was soft. "I know it seems foolish. Maybe we can't change people's minds. But your singing makes your mama happy. It always has. And right now, Mama needs to know that there is still music and light in the world. That her dreams for her children are still alive. If you go to your music lessons, you can bring her back hope of that. Can't you?"

From the bedroom, Magia could hear Dorota humming tunelessly as she rubbed Mama's arms and legs so they wouldn't get sores. She could almost feel the slow *scrape, scrape, scrape* of Jan's knife just outside the door as he drew it along his stick. And Tata — why, his shirt, which used to pop buttons after he ate, now hung loosely on his tired shoulders. Magia nearly choked as a deep sadness gripped her heart.

Of course she would do as Tata asked. But how could she bring back hope for Mama? Magia had sung to Mama to keep the baby still and safe. She'd sung of rivers that couldn't keep lovers apart. Of summer days so long that the sun never went down. Even of bears, who fell in love with mice, and tripped over their own lumbering feet trying to kiss the noses of their tiny husbands. That last was Magia's own story, to make her mama laugh.

What good had it done? What good would it do now? No matter what Mama said, Magia didn't have magic in her bones.

· ◆ · ·

The next morning, Magia's heart beat louder as she and Dorota stepped through the streets of the city. There were fewer people this time, but those who were out and about hurried with their faces to the cobbled street, and flinched at shadows. Magia hadn't liked Tysiak before, and now —

Was that man staring at her? Or that woman, who turned the other way at Magia's approach? Did they recognize her? How could they? The last time she'd been in Tysiak, Magia had been in a dress, with her hair braided. This time she was shrouded in Jan's old coat, and she'd stuffed her hair in his cap.

"Why don't they throw rocks at you?" Magia said to her sister. "How can you still work in the city?"

"I didn't touch the mad girl, I suppose," said Dorota in a low voice. Then she snorted. "But truly — I think it's because I work for less coin than anyone else!"

Magia grimaced as the wind took a wild curl from under her cap. She stuffed it back in. She hoped most people saw her as a boy, as the guards had. They'd hardly noticed as she'd walked by.

Dorota halted where two streets butted together. She tugged Jan's coat closer about Magia's shoulders. "Why didn't you tell Tata what Miss Grand did to you? Why did you agree to come back here?"

Magia brushed off her sister's words. Dorota had risen before dawn to brew Mama more medicine. Jan was looking for odd jobs a full day's walk away. And Tata had built the fire with extra logs before he'd sat to hold Mama's thin hand all morning. "You do your work," Magia said. "I'll do mine. Isn't that what Mama always says?"

Dorota shook her head, too tired to argue. "I don't know how long I'll be," she said. "I'll meet you at the gates. Don't walk home without me, do you hear?"

Magia nodded briskly, but as soon as her sister melted into the narrow streets of the city, she felt small and alone. She felt even more minuscule when she found herself, again, looking up at Miss Grand's stern house with its fancy sign. It looked the same, except that the words BY APPOINTMENT ONLY had been made even bigger.

Magia flexed her knuckles; her bruises had faded, but the memory of the searing pain hadn't. *Music lessons, my eye!* she thought.

"You might as well go home," said a voice near her.

When Magia turned, she saw a woman in the shadows. Her dress had been let out in the sleeves, and the fabric was faded to gray in several spots. She was surveying Miss Grand's house just as Magia was.

"You're never going to be able to afford a flute," she said. "The price keeps going up."

The woman nodded at the stream of customers mounting Miss Grand's steps. Every few minutes, one would enter through the door, and then, moments later, exit. Sometimes, that customer would be clutching a shrouded birdcage. More often than not, the customer would leave with nothing but a worried, sick look.

"I hear they're spectacular," said Magia cautiously. "Is that true?"

The woman eyed her with suspicion. "Where have you been that you don't know?"

"My . . . mother's been sick," stumbled Magia. "I've been helping her."

"It's true," said the woman heavily. "The music can cheer the sick and soothe the mad. But it's also true that the more one hears the flute's wild music, the more one needs it." When Magia said nothing, the woman shook her head. "We should've listened to that first girl. She was a canary."

"A what?" said Magia.

"A warning," said the woman slowly, "a funeral bell, a crack of lightning before the storm! If only we'd listened to her. She was simply mad. My daughter—she never came back at all."

Then she jerked loose a hunk of her hair, spat into it, and hurled it to the ground. "Curses on her," she said bitterly.

Magia didn't know if the woman was cursing her own daughter or Miss Grand.

Moments later, the woman left, and Magia, her legs trembling, mounted Miss Grand's steps. She didn't have an appointment. Or much of a plan.

To her surprise, however, Miss Grand opened the door at her first knock. She was no longer soberly dressed but was arrayed in a shimmering pink gown, with boots to match. Her eyes narrowed as she recognized Magia, even in her boy's clothes. "I'm surprised you've gotten this far," she said.

A stab of fear twisted Magia's chest, and without thinking, her hand dropped into her pocket. She ran her finger against the ragged edge of broken china nestled there.

"Most mamas and tatas would've forbidden their dear *dziewczynka* from walking alone," Miss Grand said, too sweetly.

Was Miss Grand saying that Mama and Tata didn't care about her? "I can find my own way," she said.

"Well, then . . . ," said Miss Grand, "what do you want? You can't think I'd be foolish enough to grant you another lesson."

"I thought you'd say that," said Magia. Her fingers left the piece of chipped china and found Tata's coins. She fished them out and held them up to Miss Grand. "I don't want a lesson. I'd like to pay for the metronome. And take the whole thing home."

Miss Grand cackled. "Three coins! That's not enough to—"

"It's only part of what I can pay," said Magia. "I'll pay you more as soon as I can. Perhaps you don't know," she said proudly, "but my tata is a woodcutter. We chop and deliver the longest-burning logs anywhere. They come from the depths of the Puszcza itself! Surely you need wood, even with your fine things?"

Miss Grand's laughter mellowed into an amused smile. "Oh, my dear, how delightful to offer to chop wood for me! But—aren't you afraid of the Puszcza? Afraid you'll go mad if you walk near it?"

"No," said Magia, thinking of the last day she and Tata had worked together near the forest. "I'm not afraid."

"Oh, me, such bravery," chortled Miss Grand, but her mocking tone didn't match her newly intense gaze. "But . . . tell me . . . for I'm not from around here—don't you have to wear red to dare the Puszcza's deepest depths? I don't see a stitch of it on you."

"Well, my tata could go," Magia said. "I know if I asked him, he would work for as many days as it took to pay for the magic."

"What magic?" said Miss Grand.

Magia didn't allow herself to think too long about her words. "The magic that makes your metronome come alive," she said. "I saw it."

Suddenly, Miss Grand threw her door wide open. She grabbed Magia and pulled her, heavy-footed, into the hallway. Before the woman's slight figure blocked her view, Magia caught a glimpse of the pink parlor and all of Miss Grand's twinkling things, piled alongside many more twinkling things. Somewhere, a dog yapped and yapped.

The old lady leaned closer to Magia and lowered her voice. "And why would you need such magic?"

Magia twisted her arm out of Miss Grand's grip. She wasn't sure how the woman's metronome worked, but at least she was admitting that what Magia had seen was real. "My mama," she said. "She's ill. She won't get out of bed. I thought maybe, if you had a china pig that could open its eyes and dance, you might—"

Miss Grand's renewed laughter was so abrupt it felt like a slap in the face. "Oh, my dear, you told me you didn't like stories—but what a tragic one you weave! Sadly for you, I don't care how much wood your tata can chop for me or how long your mama lies in bed. The only story I care about is my own, and perhaps when you hear it, you will know why I shed no tears for you—or your family."

Magia said nothing. If she wanted to help Mama, she had to be patient.

"Once there was a rich girl," began Miss Grand slowly. "A girl who had *everything*! Buttery-smooth ribbons in her hair! The most translucent jam in her *pączek*! The sweetest mama and tata, there to satisfy every wish! Even a promise to visit Białowieża on her name day!" Miss Grand plucked at her lace cuffs as she spoke wistfully. "Imagine such a girl!"

Then bitterness began to taint her smooth words. "Now . . . imagine that same girl waking up one day to find her fine things gone. Her tata owes the wrong men money. They take him away. The little girl cries. She cries so much that her mama cries, too. Until one morning—at the edge between dark and dawn—the girl's mama cries herself to death. The little girl is left all alone."

Magia winced. The stories the Panie told were awful, but this—

"They said I would never get anything back," Miss Grand went on, her voice choking on the harsh words. "They said without a mama and a tata, I would be forced to do as they told me. That was the tale they told everyone.

But they were wrong. Now I have everything I lost—and more." At this, she shifted to the side so Magia could see servants ferrying even more newly purchased items into the parlor. A pink quilt so plump the woman carrying it was hidden except for her slim legs. A rose-bordered mirror so large three burly men had to tote it. Even a square crate with a white dog inside it. The dog yapped and yapped because its ears were tied up with pink silk ribbons.

The only fancy thing of Miss Grand's Magia cared about was the metronome. "So," she said quickly, "you've obviously done well for yourself. Why not help me, too? I know I can find a way to pay for your magic, if it would help Mama."

Miss Grand smiled. "Of course it would. But you will never have such magic." She opened the door and shoved Magia out, back onto the front steps. "Because that's the moral of my story: Life is unfair, and takes things from you. The only way to make people pay is to take the stories back and make them your own."

Miss Grand eyed Magia with a modicum of sympathy.

"At least you still have a mama," she said as her door swung shut. "The Wolf Hour wasn't so kind to mine."

· · ◆ · ·

When she got home, Magia returned the coins to Tata. "It's no use," she said to him. "Miss Grand has no reason to help us. And even if I could get another lesson, I can't go back to Tysiak. The guards have forbidden it."

Dorota, with a furious shake of her head, confirmed this. "I waited at the gate for Magia. I told them she was coming soon! But the guards didn't listen. They said we should've stayed together in the first place. And that girls who didn't follow the rules weren't welcome in the city."

Magia's fists curled into tight knots. There was even more than Dorota was telling. When Magia had protested to the captain that the rules were unfair, he'd taken Jan's cap from her hair, and said, "You know that people now say you and your brother lured that poor girl into the woods? They think you pretended to rescue her to curry favor. Go home. I can't protect you here. It's for your own good."

Magia had felt heavy and sick.

Now she felt even worse, for weariness clouded Tata's eyes. "I'm sorry, my little robin," he said to her tenderly. "You did your best, but now — you'll just have to keep your heart open for spring. Maybe things will be better then."

• • ◆ • •

A week later, Magia stood in the doorway of the cottage. It was past the longest night of the year. Snow that drifted downward didn't melt but froze, layer upon layer, until it came up to their one window. Magia's hands were stiff from helping Dorota and Jan clear a path to their door. And her eyes were weary from the slow work of weaving snares, so they might catch any small animal that snuck into their home for warmth. Rodents were better than no meat at all. Nor could Tata chop much wood in this cold. As for Mama . . . she barely knew any of them were there.

Magia glanced in the direction of the village. She wanted to be angry at the Panie. But after her visit to Tysiak, she wasn't sure they were the ones to blame for how quickly Magia and her family had become targets of rumor. For somehow, no matter how they tried to chop up the tales into pieces they could haul away, the stories grew larger and larger. As if someone were fanning the flames. Someone with power. Someone like Miss Grand. Maybe that's how Magia had "paid" for breaking her metronome.

Magia didn't know. Still—the visit to Miss Grand's hadn't been a waste. She'd given Magia these words, which rankled her to her core:

"Don't you have to wear red to dare the Puszcza's deepest depths? I don't see a stitch of it on you."

And so now, when Magia stumbled through the snow to bring in kindling for the morning fire, she took a few extra steps. She dug with the blade of her axe into the rotting wood that framed their garden plot. She found still-fibrous bloodroot tubers—and a few lingering beetles—and crunched them between her molars. Then she spat the red-stained juice into a glass jar that she kept buried under the snow.

Back inside, as she sang in the dark to Mama, she carefully unraveled the lining of her winter coat at the inside seam. She might have nothing to wear in the deepest cold of the months ahead . . . but who cared? Soon, she would outgrow this old thing of Jan's and . . . well . . . be wearing another old thing of Jan's. Later, in secret, she would place the scrap of yarn in the jar of dye. When she'd gathered enough yarn, she could begin to knit.

Magia's voice rose on the last notes of her song for Mama. When spring came, when the darkness lifted, when Tata needed her again, Magia would be prepared. She would have her own red hat.

The she-wolf knew it was too early for her pups to be born. But, as labor pains wracked her belly, she stumbled into the first den she could find. The place was deep in the Puszcza, and abandoned, which should make it safe; but this strange dwelling had been made by humans, she knew. Lying, murdering humans. Why, their books lined every curved shelf inside.

At least the spiderwebs covering the books told her that humans hadn't been here in a long while. At least the place had but one door to guard, and one arched window to lock, and the latter was sensibly inset at the top of the tower's thirty-foot-high walls. At least the chilly gray stones would contain her labor cries . . .

Hours later, the she-wolf was exhausted. She'd borne four beautiful pups, but only one had survived the premature birth. She licked that one's face to help him breathe. She would not lose him, too. What fine ears he had! What fine white paws! And what a fine nose! She allowed herself a mother's pride. A wolf's nose is his glory, for when he is born, he is blind and deaf, and must find his first taste of milk by smell. This pup would have no trouble with that.

After she fed him, and her pup slept, dewy-furred, on the stones of this strange tower, the she-wolf rose to her feet. She had to make this human place a better one for her only son to shelter inside. She began by opening book after book on its shelves.

The she-wolf couldn't believe what she found. Not one of the stories featured brave and wily wolves who dismantled the cruel traps of human hunters; not one of them exposed lambs—those no-good, wobbly-legged bleaters—for their prejudice against wolfkind. Nor were there any stories about scheming pigs, who always cried "Wolf!" when things went ill for them. Worst of all, book after book was filled with dangerous portrayals of humans as chubby-cheeked innocents.

The she-wolf's fur bristled, and blood rushed into her ears, making them stand up. Even though pigs had taken her mate from her, she knew their behavior was unnatural. Pigs didn't kill wolves. Humans did. With their Stories.

Now she could purge such things from her son's life forever. She growled and began to remove certain books, one by one, with her teeth. Soon, working by day and by moonlight, the she-wolf had removed every lying book from the tower. All that remained were practical tracts.

Her pup had to learn to read, she reasoned, as every well-born wolf did. But her son would do so in a den filled with the savory smell of Facts.

No Stories. No Humans. No Lies.

You see, my little lambs? As promised, a Wolf's tale, and a Girl's. Both laid upon the table, juicy and fresh. Dinner is served!

Alas. There is a troubling smell in the air. If you don't scent it, ask yourself this question: Is a Story truly like a meal? Can we eat it in any order we please?

Of course not. A Story, no matter who makes it, isn't a series of events plopped hodgepodge on the dinner table. No, those events must be arranged in the right order. Served in courses, if you will.

Don't believe me? Try on this telling: What if the Wolf goes to the brick house first, instead of the straw and the mud ones? He can't huff and puff his way through brick. He gives up and runs home.

If, on the other hand, he blows down the straw house and scares out a Piglet, he's rewarded. He feels good! He goes to the next house, built of mud, and destroys it, too. Another terrified Piggy! He feels even better!

And then he gets to the brick house. At that moment, he's so sure he can get into any place that Pigs build that he refuses to believe that the Story could be different. He is so confident that he does something stupid. Like climb down a chimney.

Of course, if you're a Pig, this is what you want. A most excellent ending. But what if something goes awry? What if the Wolf never gets to the brick house that day at all?

Stories can be changed, my little lambs, so take care. For what if the Wolf comes to see you instead?

· PART TWO ·

"**W**hat are the rules?" Martin's mother said as they stepped outside their tower one early spring morning.

Martin looked at the expanse of heavy-limbed trees, which spread out in all directions. "We do not go into the forest alone," he answered dutifully. He shook his fur, delighting in the feel of sunlight and the fresh air filling his muzzle. It was still not as nice as the crisp smell of the book his mother had just read to him. That had smelled of Binding Glue and Voluminous Paper.

"And *why* don't we go into the forest?" said his mother. They began to circle the tangle of abandoned bushes outside the tower's walls, looking for the faint signs of animal tracks.

"The forest is filled with Stories," Martin said. He watched as his mother nosed the ground, which was partially covered with dead grass. It smelled of an Interesting Place.

"And?" Martin's mother said. She pawed methodically at the grass. A few mice pellets rolled out, and Martin heard squeaking. The developing ruff of fur at his neck stood up, and a rush of saliva sluiced into his mouth. The smell had now deepened; it was definitely not just an Interesting Place, but a Place Likely to Fill His Belly.

"AND?" his mother repeated. She put her paw between Martin and the twitching nest until he answered.

"Stories can kill you," said Martin obediently.

"Good," said his mother. She swiped the nest, flinging grass into the air. Rodents—juicy and plump—scurried in the sunlight. Martin leapt and pounced and twirled until he was dizzy.

The mice, however, didn't leap or twirl. They bolted straight for the unkempt rosebushes, whose branches twisted in all directions. Before Martin knew it, all of them were safe behind a tangle of thorns. All except the one mouse his mother had deftly pinned under her paw. That one smelled of Fear and Fate and Fast-Flowing Blood.

"Really, Martin," his mother scolded him. "You should be better at hunting by now. Perhaps if you took your nose out of those books more, *grrrhmmmm?*"

As Martin watched, she bent to take the rodent in her muzzle. With a few sharp shakes of her head, it was over. The mouse, its ears pink with freshness, hung limply from her jaws. Martin panted, expectant, but his mother turned and motioned for him to follow her back inside the tower's walls.

Not yet, she was telling him with her alert walk. *Not here.*

Martin trailed along. He knew he had to wait for her to partially chew his breakfast before she would deposit it into his gaping muzzle. But the more he thought about his mother's warnings about Stories, the less he felt satisfied with them. None of his books talked about Stories. Or danger in the woods. What kind of mice lived out there? And wouldn't they be easier to catch without thorns to hide behind?

As the tower's door closed behind them, he said, "I think we should be able to hunt wherever we want. Why, if a Story tried to kill us, we could—KILL IT BACK!" He pounced on the imaginary Story and shook it violently, as his mother had the mouse.

His mother stopped chewing and spat out their partially crushed breakfast. "A Story can swallow you whole," she said sternly. "It can suck you in for days at a time. It can make you change who you think you are. One took your father away from us."

Martin stared at the bloody mouse on the floor. He didn't remember his father, but still, he wished he had one.

"Do you see that spiderweb?" his mother said, lifting a paw to the shelf nearest them.

Of course Martin saw it. The tower was filled with cobwebs. They sagged in gauzy strips from the spines of the books his mother was using to teach Martin to read. Together, they had worked their way through the intriguing pages of *One Hundred Methods of Binding Foot Wounds, Illustrated*. After that, it had been *Standards and Practices of Crop Rotation and Irrigation*. At the moment, it was *The Scryer's Guide to Entrails*.

Still, no matter how many books they took off the shelves and read, freshly woven webs, their sticky strands taut and poised, appeared each morning to cover them back up. In the web his mother was referring to, a bristly-legged brown spider was wrapping a limp-winged housefly.

"A Story is like a spider," his mother said. "It throws out one gauzy strand, and then another. You're intrigued. You watch as a pattern develops. Ooh! So pretty!" She nudged her son sharply. "Then you're stuck. You struggle, but you cannot get out. It's a trap!"

Martin shuddered, looking at the half-wrapped fly. He ate bugs sometimes, if his belly growled before his mother brought breakfast—but unlike the spider, he didn't torture them first.

"So . . ." He tried to reason his way through his mother's warnings. "Spiders make Stories?"

"No," said his mother. "Humans do." She carefully dipped a fang toward the mouse, slicing its half-digested tail from its body. As Martin opened his muzzle in anticipation, she fixed him with her hazel-flecked eyes.

"Stay out of the forest," she said, "and we'll never have to worry." She deposited breakfast into Martin's mouth.

Oh! Mousemousemousemouse!

Martin sucked at the sinuous tail. Sooooo much better than spiders. But afterward, he still felt hungry. Hungry for everything the forest might hold. Hungry for everything he didn't know. Hungry for everything he couldn't have.

At least he had books to fill his emptiness. Martin pulled down a large tome entitled, simply, *Anatomy*.

"Aren't these creatures beautiful?" he said to his mother as he showed her the labeled drawings of human bones and ligaments and blood vessels. "I wish I could meet one!"

His mother, inexplicably, wept.

• • ◆ • •

The next day, Martin's mother told him as soon as he woke: "I'm going out."

"Again?" said Martin, thinking it was another hunting lesson. "Can't I finish my book first?"

"We're not hunting today," said his mother. "I must go alone."

"But . . . ," protested Martin, "you said not to go anywhere alone! You said the rule was—"

"I won't be alone long," said his mother. She nuzzled Martin to comfort him. "I'm going to find a new pack for us to belong to."

A new pack? That sounded interesting. Maybe.

Martin eyed a shelf of the thickest books, the ones he was most hungry to explore. He didn't want his mother to go, but if she did, he would have the day to digest all those words. Except—

"What if I'm reading and I find a word I don't know?" said Martin. "You won't be here to tell me what it means."

His mother nosed him toward the well-pawed dictionary. "Wolves are resourceful," she said firmly. "What they do not know, they learn. What they do not have, they find. If you don't understand something on your first sniff, then smell again."

"What about the spiders?" said Martin. The dictionary had a fresh web dangling from its left top corner.

A spider, its eight legs twitching, hovered nearby, watching him.

"They won't eat you," said his mother. "At least, not if you stay inside, and listen to your mother." She loped to the door, then turned back. "When I return, I'll have a new family for us . . . lots of pack mates for you to learn to hunt with." The door closed behind her before he could protest.

Martin opened his anatomy book. What did he need pack mates for? He had lots of words to keep him company, and lots of pictures to look at. But to his surprise, when he flipped to the page he'd been studying the previous day, he found a scrap of cloth pasted squarely over the drawing of the human heart. Underneath were the words:

Learn Well
This Smell

Martin knew his mother had left this warning for him. He even knew where the cloth had come from—a locked chest in the highest room of the tower. His mother said it contained "human things," and she never let him look at them. Martin had, of course, put his nose to the lid. He'd smelled Long Days Alone.

Now Martin put his paws on the down-filled cushion that supported the heavy anatomy book. He adjusted his magnifying glass to illuminate the tiniest details of the silky cloth. Sunlight from the tower's lone window formed a warm pool of light around him. Then he closed his eyes and inhaled a long draft of the smell, which was clearer than when he'd poked about the old chest.

Oh! It was like the wide sky! Or possibly like the clean, calm expanse of water he could glimpse from the tower window, for there was a solitary quality to the scent, as contained as that lake, and as deep, and as lonely.

Why had his mother left this gift of smell for him? And why in this book? It must be important. When Martin opened his eyes, he stared at the glorious riverlike map of human veins and arteries. He tried to read the words on the page, too. One of them, when he sounded it out, had a wonderful crunchy sound, even if he didn't know what it meant. Martin pulled out the dictionary.

" 'Capacious,' " he read. " 'Having the ability to contain a large volume; spacious; roomy.' "

Martin wasn't sure how a human's veins could contain a large amount of anything. Still, he reasoned, his mother wouldn't be gone long; he could ask her about the good smell and the book and the words in it when she returned.

In the meantime, he found a web-free spot on the thick windowsill that ran the length of the lone window. His tower was certainly capacious. As was his head. It had room for many more books. Before long, however, he fell asleep, for his belly was full of mice, and his books were tucked tightly about him.

◆ ◆ ◆ ◆ ◆

When Martin awoke, shadows had crept like a spiderweb over his book's pages. He nudged open the window, and stuck his muzzle out into the dimming sky. He could smell nothing but trees, and beyond them, more trees.

A wobbly, repeating thrum began inside his chest. His muzzle lifted and his stubby black ears pressed flat against his head. The thrum rose from his chest into his throat, making it ache.

Where was his mother?

Whoooere was his mother?

Whooooo! Ah-whooooo!

The sound rattled the dust-streaked glass in the raised windowpane, and startled a spider, who had been building a web there. It poised in midair on a thin wisp of silk, floating back and forth, back and forth, staring at Martin.

Martin stared back, feeling his chest expand with a wild, fur-ruffling wave of power. He had howled. HOWLED. And for a moment, even the rapidly graying branches of the forest had trembled at the sound.

If only his mother had been there to hear it.

Martin bravely crept past the dangling spider to the still-open anatomy book. From it wafted the silky smell his mother had commanded him to "learn well." Why wasn't she home, as she'd promised? Where was her musky, comforting odor? Martin didn't know.

Resting his nose on the square of cloth, he kept one eye on the spider and one eye on the darkening window. All night, he waited for the return of his mother and the day.

· · ◆ · ·

The next morning, Martin cautiously tiptoed through the untidy meadow surrounding his tower. He didn't like the army of fresh grass forcing its way through the dead husks of last year's growth. Its spiked blades pricked his paws.

Each step released a peppery odor, which stung his nose. Overhead, a raucous bird laughed at him. Martin felt exposed and small.

Should he go back to his books and his tower?

No. His mother said a wolf was resourceful. He'd waited all night. What he didn't know about the Puszcza, he would learn. What he didn't have — namely, food — he would find. He would smell and smell again until he found the path that ended in his mother.

He left the too-bright meadow and stepped onto the quiet, damp floor of the Puszcza. He felt safer under its deep, overhanging branches, and was delighted to recognize several trees from *The Arborist's Almanac*. It all would've been as perfectly interesting as opening a new book, except for the spiderwebs.

Martin had thought his tower was infested with the swarming things, but the forest was worse. Here, they had a thousand surfaces to cling to. The deeper he crept into the Puszcza, the more their grasping strands coated his fur, their wispy tendrils becoming thicker and thicker, until they clogged every gap. Gritting his teeth, Martin rose on his haunches and used his front paws, over and over, to swat a clear path.

It was with great relief that he spotted another dwelling through the trees. Finally! He would ask whoever lived there if they had scented his mother. Martin spat out a clump of balled-up spiderwebbing that had lodged in his throat and quickened his trot.

When he got closer, however, he had a moment of doubt. Was this a dwelling? His den was tall, and straight, and made of stones. This house was lopsided, and constructed of heaps of straw. The roof was barely attached, nothing more than one lump of straw piled upon four wall-shaped lumps. Still, inside the precarious structure, something rustled.

"Greetings!" called Martin.

There was no answer. Martin could see movement through one of the gaps in the straw. He shivered, for the sunshine that had filled the meadow around his tower had long since disappeared. The sky was a leaden color.

"I'm sorry to bother you," he called, his voice louder. "I was wondering if you could help me scent my mother."

Silence reigned. Martin looked at the sky again. A snowflake fell on his large nose, sticking there like a jagged flower. It was going to storm.

"You know," he said helpfully, recalling *Elementary Principles of Shelter and Safety for the New Builder*, "straw isn't a suitable building material. You should consider a substance that retains heat and is moisture-proof. Besides, your straw smells of Rot and Ruin."

There was no response.

How puzzling! He knew someone was in there! And he'd offered his assistance in a nonthreatening manner, as *Social Pleasantries and Other Underused Graces* suggested for awkward situations. Reluctantly, Martin stuck his snout into a gap in one of the walls. Hesitantly, he sniffed. What was that slippery, delicious smell? Even with all this straw dust clogging his nose, he should be able to identify —

But he could not, for Martin suddenly sneezed. To his shock, a hole appeared in the side of the straw house. He sneezed again. This time, the walls wavered and fell in; the lopsided bundle that comprised the roof followed. Loose straw wafted into the air around Martin's head as a small animal darted into the open.

"You see?" he said to it. "Not suitable."

With one hoof, the animal slashed him across his left ear. Martin yelped. Was that a . . . *pig*? Or . . . more precisely . . . a pig*let*? In the woods? Pigs were domestic animals, categorized with cows and chickens, neither of which Martin had seen, but the *Domesticated Animals Almanac* had—

The piglet slashed again, this time striping Martin's ear with two more wide, scraping blows. "Wolf!" the piglet cried. "Wolf, wolf, wolf, WOLF!"

Pigs could speak? None of his books had mentioned that. Then the piglet bolted, streaking by Martin as fast as his hooves could carry him. In two breaths, he was gone.

Martin shivered beside the flattened house, a paw pressed to his injured ear. It was bloody and bent in two. What could he do about it now, however? Clearly, the piglet knew what a wolf was. Martin had to find out if the animal had scented his mother. He turned and trudged after the trail of flying straw and crushed undergrowth.

By the time Martin discovered another dwelling and decided that the pig he'd been following was inside it, he was exhausted. He limped to the slapdash wall of mud and sticks that served as the front door. Oddly, it didn't have a knob or hinges. How did one go in and out? In any case, he remembered his *Social Pleasantries* and raised a tired paw to the door and knocked.

Ow, ow, ow. The jagged sticks stung his paw. He popped it into his mouth and sucked on it. The motion made loud slurping noises.

"He's practicing eating us!" he heard a voice inside the dwelling say.

Us? Now there was more than one pig?

"I'm not!" said Martin. "If you'll let me in, I'll show you!" He pounded again. With a sound like a puddle belching, the whole door detached an inch from the side of the muddy wall.

Another building with inadequate structural integrity, Martin thought. *What were the odds?*

Then the door collapsed, not backward, but forward, as if someone had *pushed* it. As mud and sticks flew at Martin, he fell, and one of the sharpest sticks pierced his right forepaw, pinning him to the ground. An excruciating pain shot up through his shoulder. Then, two piglets rushed out of the hut. Martin yelped as they pelted him with more sticks.

"Wolf! Wolf! Wolf!" the pigs chorused.

Behind Martin's ears, his fur, all on its own, bristled. He wrenched his twisted foreleg from under the stick and, half rising, bared his teeth. Then, to his shock, a low, menacing growl rumbled from his throat. The pigs and their oily smell fled.

Martin collapsed back to the cold ground. Several places on his body were now hairless from the assault, and his right paw ached with a stabbing, rhythmic pain. Worst of all, the piglets' cries rang in his torn and battered ears like a thudding bell.

WOLF! WOLF! WOLF!

Why had the pigs hit him? Was it something he'd said? Something he'd done? Nothing in the *Domesticated Animals Almanac* had prepared him for this.

Martin's eyes filled with tears, and he gulped. NO. He didn't have time to cry. He had to get up. He had to keep trotting. If he didn't find his mother soon, he—

Martin's tormented ears pricked up. He scrabbled to his feet, leaving bloody streaks on the ground. He lifted his head and listened. From the deepest depths of the Puszcza came an unmistakable, rising wail. The sound crested to a piercing high before descending to a pulsating, mournful finish. Then it began again.

A howl.

Magia pulled her creation from her pocket. No matter how carefully she'd handled the strands of dyed yarn, the stringy stuff had broken over and over again on her stick needles. Whole rows of stitches slid sideways, like the bricks of a falling-down house. In some places, the thing was no more than a net of lumpy knots. But it was a red hat, and it should let her enter the Puszcza.

She looked over her shoulder to make sure no one was watching. She'd sung to Mama until she slept. Dorota and Jan were in the garden hacking at the still-frozen dirt. And Tata had gone to deliver wood in the next village over. As for the prying eyes of the guards, she doubted any of them were brave enough to be this near the forest.

Simply looking at the Puszcza, Magia felt her heart leap. Even with fits of snow peppering them every few days, the forest was starting to wake up from winter. Paperwhites, tightly budded, stretched like veins from the heart of the woods, and the air was rich with the tang of fresh needles. Inside, Magia felt more awake, too.

She would make this a real test. She would prove to herself, and anyone who would listen, that there was no reason that a girl—a girl who was prepared, she reminded herself—shouldn't go as deep in the Puszcza as she pleased.

Magia trembled as she stretched the hat open with cautious fingers. Was the dye the right red? Would it buzz and tingle on her head as Tata's had? What if all her work had resulted in something as dead and lifeless as that bird Dorota had boiled for soup?

With her heart jolting raggedly in her throat, Magia tugged her hat over her hair. She'd hoped the hole-pocked thing would be large enough to cover her ears, but for all her efforts, it was the size of a *dąb* leaf. Still—

Ech. Ech. Ech. Ants. Bees. Maybe even . . .

Magia shuddered as the hat bit into her scalp.

Maybe even . . . wasps.

Her hat was as uncomfortable as Tata's . . . perhaps more! A smile lit her face. Magia took three deep breaths and entered the Puszcza.

Soon she was past the edge where Tata allowed her to chop wood with him, and into the real forest, where sharp bristles from the shaggy-armed trees tore at the ends of her hair. Where roots overwhelmed the path as her feet struggled to follow it, even as it twisted and turned like a snake. Where shadows sucked light from day as if it were cream before a starving cat. And where her hat, with every step, relished more deeply its grip on her tender skin. Then, at the edge of her vision, a hazy dot moved in the trees.

Magia stopped as the figure drew closer and closer. Her hat stung so fiercely that her eyes teared up, and she stomped her feet to clear them. That looked like one of the Panie! Magia had avoided them all winter, but she'd heard that Pani Wolburska had abruptly left the village, and Pani Golmolka had fallen ill soon after. So what would either one of them be doing out here, if—

Suddenly, the stabbing pain left Magia's head and flowed straight to her stomach. Yes, those were Pani Wolburska's piles of tattered shawls. But tucked inside them, cozy as a tree worm, was Miss Grand.

"You!" Magia said. "You. You."

She flushed. If only she had Dorota's quick tongue, or Jan's calm courage. Instead, she could only order her feet to stay still and not run from this horrid woman. Miss Grand was wearing well-worn half-gloves. Unpolished, dirty boots. And yes, that was Pani Wolburska's threadbare, faded black *chustka* wrapped about her head.

Miss Grand, for her part, seemed momentarily startled, but she recovered quickly. "Of course it's me. How are you? And how is your mother?" she said pleasantly.

How is Mama? She's not Mama! Magia wanted to yell. *And you refused to help her when I asked months ago!* But Magia didn't want to give this woman any more reason to taunt her.

"Those are Pani Wolburska's clothes," she said slowly, her mind trying to make sense of it. "What are you doing with them? What are you doing out here?"

"That woman talked too much," Miss Grand said dismissively. "And had too little to do. I suggested she might be happier elsewhere, and unburdened her of her belongings before she scurried away. So now . . . I can go into the woods without anyone knowing it's me!" She smiled thinly. "Except for you, of course. You seemed to have no trouble."

Magia didn't understand. "But why . . . ?" she said. "Why would you want to wander the Puszcza in old clothes?"

Miss Grand tilted her head, considering Magia's ratty sweater and patched-knee pants. "I could ask you the same, couldn't I?" Then her voice changed. "I'm terribly sorry about your mama, Magia," she said in a low, soothing tone. "And the baby. People tell awful stories, but you shouldn't believe them. They are ignorant of real magic and talk nothing but nonsense. You and I know better."

Magia felt heat rise to her cheeks. *You and I?* What business had this woman lumping the two of them together? Especially after Miss Grand had laughed at her pleas for help?

"You know what I think? I think *you* were behind those stories," Magia said, snapping out her words. "Everything started going wrong the day I came to your miserable house!"

"Now, now," said Miss Grand, seemingly unprovoked by Magia's accusations. "There are many who might start rumors. Perhaps someone hungry to pay your tata less than his wood is worth? Or someone hungry for your tragedy to ease their own?" She reached into her pocket and pulled out a tiny cake. "We're all hungry, aren't we, my dear? But as I told you the last time we met, I've done something about my hunger."

Miss Grand stepped closer, holding out the cake. Magia's lips sucked together. The cake was round and smooth. Covered with pink icing so sheer it gleamed. And it was dusted with sugar. Real sugar.

Miss Grand pressed the delicate bite into Magia's suddenly numb hand. "You should eat, my dear, to keep up your strength. How will you help your mama otherwise?"

Magia hardly heard the woman's words, for her belly was stiff from days and days of pretending that burnt soup was all she needed. She *was* hungry. Hungry for anything that didn't stink of death and darkness. Magia sniffed the petite cake. *Oh! Strawberries!* How could that be, when the ground was crunchy with frost? Where had Miss Grand gotten them?

"You're a strong, brave girl to be in the Puszcza alone," Miss Grand continued, her voice startlingly tender. "Still — there's much about the woods that I could teach you."

Magia felt a pain stronger than hunger twist upward, through her belly and into her heart. "I don't need *you* to teach me," she said, pushing the words past her lips. Oh! How sweet the cake smelled! She shouldn't take it, though. Not from this woman. "Tata is going to show me everything. He said . . ." Her voice trailed off. Something about the little cake in her warm palm was wrong. It was as if it were blurry about the edges. Or was that hunger, making her unsteady? Magia formed her words slowly. "He said . . . he would. When . . . it was time." She tried to hand back the cake.

Miss Grand only chuckled, a sound like branches rubbing together. "Did he now?" she said. "What a lucky girl, to have such a father. To have such a family. Such a home. What more could you want? With all that, why would you be out in the woods, alone, looking for something else?"

On Magia's head, her hat stirred. Reached its tendrils into her scalp. Wiggled thoughts back into her head: *What about Miss Grand? Why was* she *out here alone? What was* she *looking for?*

It didn't matter. Magia couldn't seem to form any words at all. Nor could she wrench her gaze from the perfectly formed cake. She'd made nothing but a hat. An ugly, twisted hat. Now, Magia thought, with a dull pang—now she could see how silly that was. Miss Grand was here in the Puszcza. Alone. *She* didn't need a red hat. She wasn't wearing red at all.

Magia swallowed hard, the cake almost at her lips. Could that be true? No red? Maybe she hadn't noticed. She knew she should be able to look at the woman and check, but how could she do that when the shimmering, sugar-laden cake was all she could see?

Psiakrew! This was worse than being pecked by a thousand starlings! Magia twisted the cake from her lips and forced her eyes to Miss Grand.

Yes. It was true. The strange woman wasn't wearing a stitch of red. Wasn't she afraid to be in the Puszcza without protection? Did the rules not apply to her?

Why did Miss Grand always make her feel so . . . so . . . irritated and unsatisfied?

Magia's hat, buzzing and wiggling, tore into her scalp, as if feeding off her sudden, angry clarity. "You wouldn't help me before," she said. "Why are you interested in me now?"

A smile creased Miss Grand's face. "Well done, my dear. Never let your hunger distract you from what you really want. And what you want is to be in the Puszcza, am I right?" She didn't wait for Magia to answer. "Well, I'm tired of being inside, too—of catering to my pompous customers and my timid students. Now that it's almost spring, I find myself restless." As if on cue, a pinch of rosiness colored her waxen cheeks. "Restless to be in the Puszcza! Even if I must conceal myself to be safe. That's an art, you know. A real art . . . and one I could teach you. How to make other people see you as you wish to be seen!" Now her face was fully alive; she gripped Magia with her eyes as if willing Magia to see her differently. "So you can be exactly who you want to be. Go where you want to go. Even if the world disagrees. Don't you want to know what that feels like?"

A cold shock nipped Magia's chest as she startled, unable to breathe for a moment. That *was* what she wanted. It was why she'd made her own red hat.

Her hat, which now began to nibble and claw her flesh again. Magia could hardly stand still.

She shook her head doggedly. "I don't know what you did to Pani Wolburska—or why you think I would listen to you—but I have to go home," she said, holding the cake out to Miss Grand. "Jan will come looking for me. Dorota will be angry. And Mama—Mama and Tata need me."

"Of course they do," murmured Miss Grand, her voice lower, but she didn't take the cake. She stepped toward Magia. "That's the problem, isn't it? They need you and you think you need them. But *I* survived without my mama and tata. In fact, you could say that I'm better off for it! Why don't you and your clever hat work with me in the Puszcza for a few days and see how doing exactly what you want feels?" She smiled as if the thought had flown down from the sky and landed on her lips. "Then everything will be right again."

Work with Miss Grand? The woman had no axe. No wood cart. What exactly did she do in the woods? Magia didn't know. Or was the woman offering more than that? Miss Grand had a house of riches.

It didn't matter. Miss Grand had shunned Magia's offer to cut wood months ago. She wasn't going to use her hat to help this woman now. Magia felt a shudder of sadness roll through her. If her strong and beautiful mama could be sucked dry of joy at the Wolf Hour, then so could anyone. As for cakes and songs and even a house of riches, they didn't always work against hunger and cold and darkness. She should go home.

"My hat's not clever," she said. "It's ugly. And I won't use it to help you, because you're wrong." She forced her numb, gloveless fingers open, and the cake fell from her hand. "Nothing will ever be right again."

Magia's hands trembled as she walked, slowly and carefully, out of the Puszcza. As the branches thinned, she looked up. Snow clouds were darkening the sky, even though it should be spring.

What she'd said to Miss Grand was true. Nothing was right. And yet — nothing seemed to have changed, either. And Magia hated it.

She raised her head to the leaden sky, and once more, she howled.

The nape of Martin's neck tightened, lifting each hair to alertness. He knew his mother's howl, and this wasn't it. These wild reverberations spoke of blood, and things breaking; an angry flaring of fire, and a sudden, desperate darkness. There was a fierce cry for something lost, and something yet to be found. Martin thought there might be words to it, but he couldn't tell. When the sound stopped, all he could be sure of was that whoever had made it was hungry, too.

Slowly, Martin sat back on his haunches. The sky had gathered itself into a crouching wall of black clouds. Soon, heavy snow would fall; he could smell it. He should run for the safety of his tower.

Instead, Martin drew in another extended whiff of air, searching each molecule for the source of the howl that had wavered and rolled through the woods. He was motionless so long that when he finally stood on all four legs, his damaged right paw burned with pain. But now he knew: Whoever had made the achingly hungry howl smelled—almost—like the scrap of cloth his mother had given him. The one she'd marked with the words:

Learn Well
This Smell

A human. A human had howled in the Puszcza.

His mother said humans made Stories, and Stories could kill you. He should return to his tower. Maybe she was waiting for him there.

Instead, Martin took another whiff of the silky human scent to ascertain its direction. If his mother had been able, she would have answered his howls by now. If she hadn't, well, it was because she *couldn't*. If he was ever to find her, he would have to go where he shouldn't.

．◆．

Where he shouldn't turned out to be far away.

For hours and hours, Martin loped slowly along on his three good paws. The scent of the human who had howled had been snuffed out by the enveloping snow. Soon, Martin picked up the scent of more humans. He followed those scents until they faded, too. In the end, he was so confused he wanted to cry. Where was he going? What was he doing out here, all alone?

．◆．

And then he scented it, finally: A Real, Live Human Being.

Martin should've fled. Instead, he concealed himself behind the ball-shaped form of a bitterbrush tree. He peered through the lower tree limbs.

Like all wolves, Martin didn't see many colors, but he could tell that the human's hair was as thin and pale as his own was dark and thick. He could also see that it wore a dress. Martin stealthily inched his nostrils higher. Didn't a dress mark this one as female? And she was young. Was that—was that—a girl?

If it was, her eyes didn't seem to be working correctly, for, as he watched in astonishment, she ran into a tree. Was this the human who had howled? Was she as filled with facts as his books? What was she doing out here?

"WILK!"

Martin startled at the now-familiar cry. A throat-closing wave of terror gripped him. The human had half risen from her collapsed heap and was shrieking blindly to the sky.

"WILK! WILK! WILK!" the girl screeched. Then she clumsily rose, tottered about in a crooked circle, and then stumbled and fell again, right into the outer branches of the tree Martin was hiding behind.

Branches slapped him in the neck, ears, and jaws. Martin closed his eyes and trembled. He heard her jagged breath as she hovered, trapped by the needle-sharp boughs. For a moment, he caught a strong whiff of Sweaty Fear.

This was *not* the human who had howled. This human wasn't hungry; this human was . . .

. . . vomiting at Martin's feet. The acrid odor of Bile and Semi-Digested Grain-Based Food burned his nose. If there had been any food in his own stomach, he might have vomited, too.

Martin kept his eyes closed. He could hear the young female as she sat down near him. How disturbed she appeared! Her lips were swollen; her eyes, too. *Ill,* Martin thought again. *Definitely ill, in both mind and body.* Was there nothing he could do for her?

For minutes upon minutes, Martin huddled, eyes closed, behind the tree—until he realized that he could no longer hear her panting. Or smell Sweaty Fear. He cautiously opened his eyes. The moisture that he'd scented earlier was now wetly falling, in shapeless clumps, from the sky. It was utterly unlike the pristine, delicate flakes depicted in his weather book. Everything was quiet, save for the harsh cry of a bird, dipping and circling overhead. No girl.

Martin blinked. That couldn't be. His ears were large. And he hadn't heard her walk away.

Cautiously, he left his hiding place, searching with his nose and eyes. In the spot where the girl had been, there was nothing but a spider scrambling from branch to branch. It smelled of Nothing to See Here. At his approach, it dived into a damp heap of blight-riddled leaves, now coated with snow. Next to the leaves was a round, bug-covered object, half submerged.

Martin sniffed the round object, and was shocked to realize it was food. Not a tender-boned, soft-eared mouse, or even a crunchy bug. This was sticky and soft. It crumbled when he licked it.

He gagged, trying to get the taste off his tongue. It was soddenly sugary, and laced with the odor of something he had no name for. Something harshly medicinal, like the bark his mother had once made him chew for his upset stomach. Upon closer examination, Martin realized it was a tea cake. He'd seen illustrations of them in *A Baker's Compendium of Sweets, Trifles, and Other Delights*. His mother had refused to read the accompanying recipes, of course; wolves ate everything raw. No wonder. This thing smelled horrible.

Martin shivered, and shook the accumulated snow from his fur. Was he still on the right track? He thought again of the twitchy, drooling state of the girl. Could wolves get human illnesses? Was his mother close, but ill and unable to call to him? He hated to think of her stumbling into trees, as vacant-eyed as the girl had been.

Then he saw them: a purposeful line of rounded impressions embedded in the dirt. The imprints were rapidly filling with snow. In another moment, they would've been completely covered. Wolf tracks!

Cautiously, his heart beating fiercely, Martin dipped his nose to the trail of prints. Then he began to limp alongside the tracks. He couldn't be certain, because the taste of the cake had clogged his sense of smell, but the prints were the same size as his mother's.

Soon, Martin spotted another dwelling. The piece of land surrounding it was crisscrossed with oddly shaped marks. Studying them, Martin thought they must've been made by those pieces of leather that humans called shoes. The girl had been wearing some. Was this where she lived? If it was, then why did the wolf tracks lead straight to the door?

Martin regarded the structure, which, unlike that of the pigs, was well made. It had a solidly shingled, pitched roof, similar to the one on his taller den. Four sturdy wood sides. Two square, dim windows. It was a cottage, decided Martin — that is, if he was remembering *Popular Architectural Styles of the Countryside* accurately. The door stood ajar.

Martin pushed his head inside. It was like a page from one of his books. A human bed. With human sleeping cloths on it. A human candle for light beside the bed. And on the floor . . .

Blood poured from a four-legged body.

The gland at the base of Martin's tail contracted. In wolves, this released the message DANGER, DANGER, DANGER into the air. But Martin couldn't even scent his own fear, for the world, once filled with a multitude of smells, had gone dark.

Later, when he studied *The Layman's Guide to the Brain's Natural Defenses*, Martin would realize his smell blindness was his mind's way of protecting him. In the moment, though, it felt as if he'd simply crossed a threshold, and the world smelled of . . . nothing. Not the emptiness of Where a Mouse Had Once Crouched but Did Not Any Longer. This was a numbness, a cessation of feeling, an absence of everything. The room was as blank to his nose as a wordless page.

Martin, unable to stop himself, stumbled closer and closer until he crouched next to the inert form. Slowly, he sank down beside it. Blood soaked into the underbelly of his coat. Then he heard footsteps.

In the space of two breaths, he scuttled underneath the unkempt bed. Saw a human approach. Watched as two boots, buttoned with hooks of bone, clicked rapidly against the floor.

And then he closed his eyes in despair as the body of his mother was dragged away.

That night, as Magia choked down Dorota's dreadfully sour beet pie, she wished she'd eaten Miss Grand's tiny cake. Or at least licked off the frosting.

Tata still wasn't back from his visit to the next village. He'd taken his canteen of water—no *kwas* now—and a hunk of Dorota's brittle bread with him. With the snow coming, he would probably have to spend the night . . . somewhere.

Magia left the table as soon as she could, thinking she would stand outside and stare at the distant forest before Dorota could task her with scrubbing beet juice from the cooking pot. But as she put a hand on the door, her brother stopped her quietly.

"You shouldn't go out alone, Magia," Jan said in a low voice. "I saw you coming back on the path today. You didn't go near the Puszcza, did you?"

Magia lifted her chin. "I can take care of myself," she said.

Jan shook his head. "Tata wouldn't like it. Besides, they still haven't found those missing girls. It's not safe!"

Magia wanted to pull her red hat from her pocket and show it to Jan. She *was* safe in the woods. She was.

But she could still feel the way she'd wanted to devour the cake before she'd managed to force it from her hand, and how Miss Grand's words made doubt creep into her thoughts. Perhaps she should stay inside tonight.

Slowly, she closed the front door and went into her mother's room. She sat down on the chair, tucked up her knees to her chin, wrapped her arms about her legs, and looked at her mother. Magia had a dreadful feeling Mama was getting worse. She slept for hours and hours at a time, and when she woke, sometimes she didn't recognize Magia sitting beside her.

Magia's hand hesitantly reached for the straw pallet on which Mama lay. It was clean, and turned regularly, because Dorota kept it so, but had her sister —

She fumbled among the ropes that supported the mattress on the wooden frame. Her fingers met the familiar smooth sheen of the cloth Mama had taken from an old apron. She slowly pulled it out, unfolded the thin fabric, and looked at the inked lines, carefully fitted to the width of Magia's own fingers.

Then she played the notes Mama usually played, and sang softly, pretending that her mother could hear. There was no metronome, only the gentle wavering sound of breath leaving and entering her mother's body. There were no fancy rugs or proud sofas or grand curtains. And yet, here, Mama had listened while Magia sang—even though her poor piano hadn't made any noise at all.

Magia wanted to tell Mama all the things she had missed. The dancing pig . . . the red hat . . . and especially, today's disturbing encounter with Miss Grand. It was strange, but Magia thought no one else in her family would understand how frightened she'd felt as she'd let go of the round, perfect cake.

If only Mama would wake from her sadness.

But Mama didn't wake. She remained submerged, like that frozen deer Magia had seen once in a lake, its eyes open but seeing nothing.

· ◆ · ·

The next morning, snow had piled itself around their house and stopped—at least for now. Tata still wasn't home. And Magia couldn't stand being inside any longer. She needed to hear the thud of her blade against the thick bark of a *dąb*. She put a hand to the red hat, which seemed to burn in her pocket.

"Tata's not home," she told Dorota and Jan, "and there's barely any wood if the fire gets low. I'm going to get more."

Dorota pursed her lips. Jan protested, too. But Magia didn't plan to go far—only to the edge of the forest. She gathered her axe, opened the door, and marched into the snow.

By the time Magia reached the Puszcza, however, she saw that the storm had scattered snapped branches along the edge of the woods. She didn't need her axe at all, not to bundle loose sticks. With a sigh, Magia put down her axe and knelt to gather branches. As she did so, the snow-hushed air was pricked by an odd, squeaky crying.

What was that? Magia peered into the woods. *Was it a bird?* Their songs often sounded like people hooting or chattering or fighting. But not crying. Or could it be—

Magia squinted at the wood's edge. There, tucked neatly at the root of a tree, was a dark basket.

Magia's gaze rose to the Puszcza, scanning for any sign of an owner. Now everything was quiet. The snow was a snug blanket, white and untouched in every direction. She was alone. A shiver stole up her back. Why would anyone leave a basket, unattended, at the edge of the forest? Magia rose and went over to it. Slowly, she reached for the rough linen overcloth. Maybe the contents would tell her more about the basket's owner. And why they had left it.

But when she saw what was inside, Magia gasped. The basket overflowed with the soft folds of a fabric that glowed deeply, like embers pulsing in a banked fire.

Red. It was so . . . RED.

Transfixed, she gently tugged the crimson cloth from its dark nest. It flared out into a full circle. It wasn't raw cloth, but an exquisitely stitched cape! At the neck was a hood, from which cascaded two ribbons, as red as the sky the morning before a storm. And, Magia noted with a sharp-edged hunger, it was a cape that was neither too big nor too small, but perfectly sized for a girl such as she.

It was a river of crimson; it was ferociously beautiful;

and oh! how touching this much red made the restless tingling in Magia's feet rise to her chest. She wanted to know everything, everything that Tata could teach her about the Puszcza, and she wanted it *now*. Was that wrong?

Then Magia saw a fleck of pink caught in one of the fine stitches of the cape's hem. She brought it closer to her face. Sniffed it with her nose. And recoiled. The cape smelled like strawberries.

With a sick feeling in her stomach, Magia forced her hands to release the velvety soft cape. She straightened to standing and took one step back from the basket. As she did so, the same piteous noise she'd heard earlier came again from the Puszcza.

Something in there was definitely crying.

It wasn't another mad girl, was it? Her hand dipped into her pocket and fingered the lumpy stitches of her red hat. What would Tata do if he were here? Would he tell her to run home for help? If she did, would the girl be here when Magia returned? And wouldn't going home only drag her brother and sister into possible trouble?

Magia inched the hat from her pocket. She hadn't donned it because she hadn't planned to go beyond the edge of the forest, and it was too painful to wear for mere warmth. She didn't have to go far into the Puszcza, she reasoned. Whatever was making the anguished sobs was close. Briefly, she looked down at the cape, asleep in its basket. If such a thing were hers . . .

It wasn't. Magia firmly put the square of rough linen back over the cape. If that cape was Miss Grand's — and the strawberry scent made Magia sure that it was — the last thing Magia wanted was to be seen poking in her basket.

Turning her back on it, she stared deep into the Puszcza. The forest was more glorious than ever, for its branches, coated with white, waved soundlessly, like the tail of a silver fox she'd glimpsed once, darting from shadow to shadow on a brittle, cold morning. Magia took a deep breath and pulled her red hat over her hair.

A shock of pain gripped her scalp, shot down her spine, and bolted into her hands. Yesterday, her hat had hurt, but it hadn't seemed this *hungry*. Now it gnawed at her skin, with teeth as stealthy as a slender forest of splinters, sidling their jagged edges into her scalp.

Good. That meant her hat was working. Besides, whatever was crying in the forest was in worse shape than she was. She could do this. She could. Magia bent to retrieve her axe, and then, with deliberate steps, she entered the Puszcza.

Slowly, she picked her way through the trees. Above her, the grasping, tangled overhang of branches had been softened by snow into full, lacy boughs. Below her, the spreading roots of the thickly needled *świerki* were also submerged. On her head, her red hat buzzed and itched and burned like mad, of course, but everything between was silent. Eerily still. What had happened to the sound of crying?

Had the mad girl — or whatever it was — sensed her coming? Or had the Puszcza smothered the poor thing's cries with a deep quiet of its own? Magia felt the silence like a heavy cloak; a refreshing change from the too-closeness of sitting inside all day with Mama.

It made her feel . . .

Magical.

Magia laughed at herself. What a silly thing to think! Dorota could heal people with herbs, of course, and Tata and Magia provided wood for Tysiak that burned longer than any other logs—but that was the Puszcza's magic, not theirs.

Still. The feeling was a good one. It gave her courage. She was going to be a woodcutter one day. She *belonged* here.

Soon, Magia had walked past the point where she'd stopped yesterday. Before long, in the dim light, the *świerki* branches seemed not white-edged with snow, but inky gray. The trunks of the *sosna* were not mottled brown; they were pitch-black. Even the snow-drifted ground under her feet was obscured in the dusky light. It was as if the day was going in reverse.

And yet . . . Magia hadn't found the source of the crying. Walking without a plan wasn't helping. She should think. Do as Tata told her. Picture exactly where she wanted to end up. So . . . So . . .

If she were hurt and alone in the Puszcza, where would she hide?

Why, somewhere dark. Somewhere close to the ground. Slowly, Magia began to retrace her steps, and this time, she turned her head from side to side until she spotted a disturbance in the snow. Then she squatted, her loose pants dragging in the wet drifts, and gently pushed aside one of the branches brushing the forest floor, expecting to see a terrified, wild-eyed girl.

Instead, engulfed by the tree's twisting roots, half hidden in the dim light, there was an animal no bigger than a young dog. Magia stared at the beast. Stubby, ebony-edged ears lay flat against its square head, and a snuffling whimper came from its deep brown wet button of a nose. Its eyes were pressed shut, no more than black slits in its bristly gray fur. It was desperately thin, and shivering so violently that Magia was afraid it was ill.

Carefully, she leaned her axe against a tree and dropped to her knees. As she did, she could see that the creature's right forepaw was nearly flayed of skin, and maimed by a jagged hole. Its left ear was nastily torn in three places. Dried blood edged these wounds. Magia crept toward the animal. How long had it been here? Had it gotten lost in the storm? And who had hurt it so badly?

All these questions flew from her head as its eyes opened. They were yellow-gold, and suddenly, Magia knew what it was:

Wilk!

Magia suppressed the urge to say the word out loud for fear of spooking the poor thing, but—yes! She was sure it wasn't a fox or a stoat or any other creature Tata had taught her to recognize. Trembling, she stared at the brownish fluid coating its fur. Pani Gomolka had said that even a drop of *wilk* blood would spoil you—make you leap from your clothes and howl in desperate hunger for human flesh until you wanted no other food. In the end, you either ate up your own family, or, if you resisted, died a slow death as your tongue dried up in your throat. Was *that* how the girls had gone mad?

No. Those stories were only stories, as silly as the ones the Panie had told to get her to sweep their footprints. Besides, this creature needed help. Its rough fur looked knotted and sticky. If it was hurt, she should help it. "Hello, little nut," she said softly, reaching out a hand.

The pup bolted from its hiding spot.

"NO! Don't go! I won't hurt you!" cried Magia. She threw out her arms and caught hold of the pup's flailing limbs. With a thud, they both landed on the ground. Wet blobs of snow rained down on them as they struggled.

"Please!" Magia cried. "Be still!"

It was no use. The pup, though wounded, was strong, and nearly as heavy as she. The harder she held it, the more fiercely it fought to be free. Worse, her hat had suddenly come alive again, and was jabbing its fibers into her scalp as viciously as fish hooks.

Rapidly, everything began to spin—the hat clawing her hair, and the pup clawing her chest—and Magia clawed the fear that between the two of them, she would be shredded like cabbage. Quickly she flopped over, belly-first, into the snow, and pinned the wolfling and his scratching nails beneath her. Then she slowly wiggled one of her hands free and ripped her hat off her head.

Her eyes widened. The hat was a brilliant, juicy red. It oozed with warm . . . was that . . . ?

Magia's hand found her scalp; there was a raw patch where her hair had been torn away. Her breath came in jagged gasps. The hat had drawn *blood*!

And so would the pup, if she didn't get it under control, too. "You're hurting me!" she said to it, still struggling beneath her. "Stop it! Stop it right now!" She used Dorota's best ordering-about voice.

The pup, to her surprise, stopped moving. All she could feel was its trembling chest heaving shakily under hers.

Carefully, Magia rolled over, cradling the pup's body. Her smile faded as she sat up. The pup lay limply in her lap, its eyes closed. Its entire underbelly and paws were soaked with caked blood.

Could all of that have come from the wounds on its ear and paw? Or had she somehow hurt it further? She should take this pup home. Everyone would be shocked to see her with a wolf, of course, but Dorota . . . yes, Dorota would nurse this pup back to wholeness, if Magia could only get it home. But . . .

Which way was that? With a start, she saw that the Puszcza around her was nothing but a wall of black branches. How could that be? She'd gone only a few feet off the path. She looked at her hat, which lay where she'd thrown it. She thought of what Tata had told her:

A red hat isn't enough. You must learn the paths of the forest, and how to find the direction of the sun when there is no light overhead.

How was she supposed to do that now? Magia gingerly poked at her hat. She could don it again . . . but *ech*. It might take more blood! And even if she wanted to put it back on, that was impossible without putting down the pup. Leaving the Puszcza was only a matter of walking in an ever-widening circle, until one edge of that circle touched the path she knew, or until she saw daylight leaking through the edge of the woods.

See? she told herself. She hadn't gone mad. Not yet, at least. She grasped her hat with two fingers and hastily wiggled it into her pocket. Then, firmly tucking the pup under her loose sweater, she stood and shook off the fresh snow settling into her hair. She would find her way home herself.

• • ◆ • •

Endless, plodding steps later, Magia's clothes were soaked, torn, and pricked with tree needles, for holding the pup under her sweater meant she'd had no way to defend herself from slapping branches, nor from the increasing wind. Worse, her plan to walk in larger and larger circles had managed to bring them both not out of the woods, but deeper in.

Magia peered through the enveloping snow. She should've known that this morning's calm was only a break in the storm. Her arms ached, for the pup was limp, unwieldy, and heavier with every step. She was going to have to turn around and trudge back the way she'd come. But which way was that, exactly? And could she first, for a moment, sit down and rest?

As she stumbled on weak legs, trying to get her bearings, Magia saw a blocky shape nestled among the trees. Was that a house? She fought against the wind to get closer, and found herself in front of a small brick structure. She shivered and shifted from one icy foot to the other. The house had one window, but no light was coming from it. The door was banded with metal, and it was firmly closed against the storm. Who lived out here, in the middle of the Puszcza?

None of the possibilities comforted her.

Magia raised one stiff, swollen hand and pounded quickly at the door.

Nothing. No flare of light. No sound of footfall.

Still, no one called out she wasn't welcome, either. Taking a deep breath, Magia pushed at the door. To her relief, it opened, and she cautiously stepped in, a layer of straw crunching under her feet.

Inside, the house was blacker than the crows that descended on their *buk* trees every autumn. And as loud, for some *gapa* had left the damper to the fireplace open. A steady stream of wintry air wailed down the chimney.

"There, little twig!" she said to the pup, too loudly. "I don't know where we are, but it's better than being out there!" Quickly, she slammed the door on the howling wind and snow.

Listen to her; she was as bad as Tata, calling the pup everything but what it was: a wolf.

Even as miserable and stiff with cold as she felt, Magia was jolted by a twinge of excitement. A *wolf*. She'd carried a wolf pup through the Puszcza and found it shelter! If her face hadn't been frozen, she would've smiled.

The pup still hadn't moved, though, not in response to her words, nor the sudden relief from the wind, nor even the slam of the door. She wanted to examine him again, but the storm had choked off the light outside, and here in the empty house, it was practically night. And far, far too cold.

Magia inched her way to the fireplace. Snow was piled in lopsided drifts on the fire grate. A long hook protruded wickedly from one side of a stone arch, and on it hung an enormous cooking pot, empty except for a slushy puddle of icy water. The logs under the pot had long ago burned to ashes. It was as if someone had thought about making a meal—and then left.

Magia looked around for more firewood. If she could rebuild the fire . . . But there was nothing to rebuild it with. She could chop more wood, of course, but . . .

Psiakrew! Magia's stomach twisted with shame. In the excitement of finding the pup, she'd left her axe against that tree! She wasn't much of a woodswoman if she left her tools behind. What if she'd rescued the pup only to let him die of the cold?

Still holding the pup close, Magia reached around the cooking pot and groped one-handed inside the chimney for the squat metal handle of the damper. If she could at least close its soot-covered metal plates, she could seal the bitter bite of the wind outside.

To her frustration, though, no matter how hard she wiggled the handle, or put her shoulder into the effort, or swore with any of Tata's outside words, the damper resisted her. After minutes of battling its protesting, rasping, creaking, and moaning with her horribly stiff fingers, all Magia managed to do was narrow the opening until the metal sides formed a perfect, iron-lipped mouth for the wind. The whole chimney now emitted a shrill sound.

Ay-yiiiiiih! Ay-yiiiiih! Ay-yihhhhhhh!

Magia wanted to clap her hands over her ears, but she couldn't even do that, not with the pup in her arms. She should put the creature down, but it might not let her pick it back up again. Instead, she reached into her pocket and cautiously pinched her hat by an edge before drawing it out. Keeping it away from the pup, she quickly leaned into the fireplace again, and with awkward, one-handed jabs, stuffed her ill-shaped creation into the wailing mouth of the chimney.

The wailing choked. Sputtered. And was silent.

Magia sagged against the side of the fireplace. Slowly, she drew the wolf from under her sweater. Tenderly, she rubbed the ear that wasn't torn, massaging it with her fingers. The wolfling's fur was matted and rough, but it felt pleasant to touch something warm.

"Don't worry, little one," she said to the pup. "I'm going to make us somewhere to be safe."

In the darkness, the pup's eyes opened. They shone like two river stones. It was as if it were responding to her voice. Magia felt a lump in her throat. It was counting on her. She carefully tucked the wolf pup into a bumpy nest of straw away from the fireplace.

"Wait there," she said to it as she returned to the hearth. She grabbed the ash-blackened grate by one of its iron legs. It squealed alarmingly as it bumped against the brick hearth, catching at every uneven joint and throwing her off-balance as it bucked and heaved against her strength. She was sweating by the time the beastly thing rested on the straw-covered dirt of the floor.

She eyed the cooking pot on its hook. That had to go, too.

She wrapped her arms around it, struggling to get a firm grip. It was heavy and round, like a tree stump. She could feel the pup watching her, its eyes glowing. With all her strength, she wrestled the pot from its hook. The weight of it took her to her knees with a bone-grinding thud.

She couldn't lift it again. She had to put her shoulder to its thick rim, and shove it, inch by inch, until it squatted against a wall. The last bit of frozen sludge in it sloshed dully in the dim light. The thing was big enough to hold a person.

Magia shivered. Why did she think such chilling thoughts? She had work to do. Moving rapidly, she threw handful after handful of straw into the now-empty fireplace. She didn't stop until it was knee-deep. Then she crawled inside and put her back against one rough wall. There. Tata had told her that pack animals often burrowed underground to escape storms, and piled one furry body on top of another. This wasn't as good as an underground burrow, but it would do. When she looked back into the room, the pup was staring at her with the largest eyes she'd ever seen. She laughed.

"My, what big eyes you have," she whispered. "Come here."

Obediently, it limped to her, and she took it in her arms again. Slowly, she drew up her legs inside her baggy sweater until she was nothing more than a brown lump of cloth wrapped around the wolfling. She bent her head against her upright knees and sheltered the pup underneath her trembling arms.

Ka-thump. Ka-thump. Her pulse thrummed in her ears. As the excitement of the rescue drained away, she shivered uncontrollably in the darkness. How long could she keep the fire of her heart beating inside her? She was tired. Too tired to push down the thought that now raged worse than the storm:

Jan and Dorota and Mama and Tata . . . they had no idea where she was. She should be home.

When Magia opened her eyes, she found a layer of frost had coated the straw inside the house. The wolf pup was awake, and wandering slowly, muzzle down, around the perimeter of the room. It was starkly quiet, and Magia felt as if she and the pup were the only living things within miles. She raised her head from her knees. Immediately, the cold's teeth sank into the exposed skin of her forehead. Her breath puffed into the air, making faint clouds.

Huff. Puff. Magia sat still, watching the shimmer of air as she slowly breathed, each lungful so cold it burned her nose, each exhale warmed and filled with moisture.

She'd been dreaming she was a wolf with thick fur, sleeping deep underground. Into the dream had crept a repeated melody that howled and swirled about the cozy feeling, forcing her to scrabble with her paws into the earth, burrowing deeper and deeper to escape the whine of the song that wouldn't die. That must have been the storm, she thought. Was it over? How long had she slept?

At the far side of the room, the pup lifted its leg.

"Hey!" said Magia. She sat upright. Not much light came through the one thick window, although she was sure it must be morning. "What are you doing?"

The pup pricked its ears and looked at her with a comical expression on its face, as if it wanted to say: *Can't you see?*

Then it peed. No, *he* peed.

Magia wished she were a wolf, too. It was bound to be even colder outside the house than in here. Slowly, she uncurled herself from the fireplace, pulling straw out of her sweater. She walked to the door, keeping one eye on the pup. He seemed to be moving well despite the state of his smashed paw and the hideous amount of dried blood in his fur. She would examine him again outside in the morning light. In a minute. After she did what a human girl had to do. Wrapping her fingers in the sleeve of the woolen sweater to protect them from the bitter cold, she turned the doorknob and tugged the door toward her.

A cascade of snow flowed through the open door with a hushed hiss. By the time it ceased, a line of white reached to the back wall. Try as she might to swing the door back to its closed position, Magia could not. And in the doorway, a barrier of snow glittered, as if a thousand spiders had woven a web of silver mesh. They were snowed in.

Magia turned back to the pup. Snow covered him, from his black-tipped ears to his white paws. The incoming drift had backed him into the cooking pot.

"It's okay," she said to him. "It's only snow." She shuffled through the powdery drift toward him. "It will melt. I promise." She might have to use that cooking pot for a privy in the meantime. Magia grinned, thinking how shocked Dorota would be if she were here.

Before she reached him, the pup began whimpering.

"What's wrong?" she said, although she knew he couldn't understand her. She knelt to comfort him, and he dived into her lap. As he buried his nose in her clothes, she looked into the maw of the cooking pot, which loomed behind his tail. Was that . . . ?

Magia tried to look closer without leaning on the pup. Last night, she'd thought the pot had contained only icy water, but this morning, even though the light was still dim, she could see that its sides had clumps of fur stuck to it.

Nausea wormed its way into her belly. She knew people ate animals; her family ate animals; even animals ate other animals. Still—*ech*. What kind of idiot didn't skin their meat before cooking it?

In her arms, the pup whimpered louder. "Shhh, now," she said to him, stroking his head, but as she did, she noticed that his wiry gray fur was the same color as the fur stuck to the pot. She remembered thinking that it was large enough to hold a human body. It was, but that wasn't what had been in it. A thatch of wolf hair floated in the dregs of water.

With deliberate calm, Magia crawled as far away from the pot as she could, carrying the poor pup along with her. From his trembling, she suspected he'd already smelled the death of his own kind, but she wasn't absolutely certain.

She needed to distract him while she thought of a way around that snow.

Did wolflings like music?

Ah-la-la, she sang.

Ah-la-lo
ah-la-la
ah-la-lo

The same song she'd sung for Mama once.

The pup shifted in her arms, and pricked its ears. Was it listening to her, or was it bracing itself for danger? Magia's eyes slid from the blocked door to the pot and back again. What if the owners of the house came back? If they ate wolves, they were not going to help her care for this wounded one. Perhaps they would even kill it.

No. She wouldn't think about that. She would think of those first steps she'd taken into the woods yesterday, when she'd felt magical and as if she'd belonged. Before they'd gotten lost.

Ah-la-la
ah-la-lo,
she sang again.

This time, as her voice floated into the air, she felt the pup's limbs relax under her fingers. His body, even blood-coated and half hidden by the smudgy darkness of the snow-blocked house, was magnificent. His muzzle was as wet and dusky as the *kwas chlebowy* Magia loved, his fur as finely bristled as the *sosna* needles that clung, fragrant, to her hair. His white paws were as puffy as the clouds she'd once howled at. Magia's voice trailed off in wonder. Tata had said that in the Puszcza, the trees, the animals, even the dirt—

"It's as if we're made of the same stuff . . . ," she whispered to the pup to comfort him. "In the Puszcza, we are close to the wildest magic there is."

The pup, as if understanding this, stretched in her arms and looked at her with wide eyes. Even wounded and half grown, she could see what a predator he would become, his teeth staggeringly sharp and his haunches sinewy with muscle. But for now, he needed her.

"Now. Let me look at this blood on you, little twig," she said calmly, turning him on his back in her arms. "Where did all that come from?" Keeping her body between the pup and his view of the pot, she explored the crusty maze of matted fur and blood on his underbelly, delicately fingering every inch of his tender skin. As far as she could see, there was no further wound there. If he was fit to travel, they should leave this place as soon as possible. She wouldn't let him down. They were of the same stuff. They both belonged here. They were not lost, but together.

When she was finished with her examination, she gazed at the pup's face. "I think you're going to live," she said. "But I wish I knew how you were hurt. I wish you could tell me everything."

The pup stared back from her lap; his expression had turned bleak. He opened his muzzle a few inches, and then closed it. Slowly, his eyes dimmed with tears. He shook his head from side to side. Magia was too astounded to move.

"Can you—" She struggled to keep talking. "Can you understand what I'm saying?"

Again, the wolfing's muzzle moved, this time dipping up and down.

Magia's heart thumped. Was that a yes? She swallowed hard, searching for more words.

"Why were you alone in the woods?" she whispered. "What happened to you?"

The pup shivered in her arms. Magia's stomach lurched. Had she said the wrong thing? If he could understand her, could he answer? The wolfling's eyes were desperately sad. He looked so . . . so . . . *lost*.

Suddenly, Magia remembered how Dorota had stood in their doorway on that day last November, her dress stained with blood. How her sister had been unable to make a sound, either. She touched the dried ocean of matted blood on the pup's belly again.

"This blood isn't yours, is it?" she said.

With a jerk, the pup twisted away from her. He fell with a thud to the hard floor. Magia jumped to her feet, but it was too late. The pup was tearing about the room like a rabid dog. Straw and snow flew everywhere as he leapt and snapped at the brick walls. The cooking pot rocked unsteadily on the uneven floor, making a harsh, clattering cry.

"Stop!" she cried. "Stop! You'll hurt yourself!" She stumbled after the pup, hoping to grab him on the next pass. Why had she said that about the blood? Her words had been no better than a blow to his wound. And now . . . now it was as if the pup had lost his ability to communicate, and his sight and hearing, too. Round and round he raced with no direction, until he burrowed back into the nest she'd built for them in the fireplace.

For an instant, Magia thought that she would be able to grab him, calm him, apologize for her hasty words. Then, as she crept toward him, her arms reaching for his trembling body, her feet tangled with the blunt-edged iron of the fire grate she'd wrestled with last night. She fell, face-first, and landed awkwardly, cutting her knees on the uneven brick of the hearth.

At the noise, the pup stirred. Hobbled to his feet.

"Mama!" he cried, his muzzle quivering. "I want my mama! Mama! Mama!" The last word was a howl, and it echoed through the hushed room.

Magia's heart nearly stopped. The wolfling had talked. TALKED. As plainly as if it were human.

She'd been right about the blood. She'd been right about the pup understanding her. She'd been right that he needed help. Her eyes flooded with tears of pain and amazement.

But the pup, as he cried these words, wasn't looking at her. He was looking up. Eyeing the blocked chimney.

Magia struggled to rise, but she was too slow. The pup ripped her hat from the opening and fell back to the ground with it. Then he was biting and tearing at the hat, or was it biting and tearing at him? Magia could hardly tell. Bits of yarn spat from the fireplace like sparks.

"No!" she yelled at him. Flopping on her belly, she elbowed her way into the fray. "No! I need that to get home! To take you home, too!" Frantically, she tore the hat away from the pup, and then tried to grab him by the scruff of his young neck, but he leapt up and away from her, his one good front paw extended, and caught the slanted edge of the partially open damper. He dangled there, barely holding on, his belly swaying. A piteous wailing poured from his throat.

Magia half rose and placed one bruised and bleeding knee over her hat. As she extended an arm to the pup, the damper creaked open under his weight.

Whoof! The pup dropped several inches lower, still hanging from the damper. His wailing suddenly stopped. He pricked up his ears, as if listening for something. Then his nose twitched, and his eyes filled with terror.

Magia was on both knees now. Slowly, she stretched out her other arm, waiting for the right moment. The pup was swinging his hind legs back and forth, back and forth. The only noise was the faint rising and falling of the wind through the chimney.

Stay calm, she told herself. *He's going to let go. He's going to fall. Catch him.*

Then, with one mighty swing, the pup launched his whole body past Magia and landed behind her. Magia twisted on her aching knees and saw him gather his legs beneath him, and smash into the wall of snow blocking the door. As he tunneled into it, his tail whipped once . . . twice . . .

And then he disappeared.

Breathing hard, Magia slumped to her seat. Bits of red yarn were stuck to her pants, snagged in the corners of the brick, and strewn over snow and straw. She picked up her hat. The outside edge was intact, but in the middle was a large hole. She put her fist through it.

Hades! She'd found a talking wolf pup . . . cared for him . . . somehow upset him . . . and now he was gone.

Magia thought about following the pup out the door. She couldn't make herself do it. The snow—it was deep! What if it caved in on her? Despite her pity for the pup, she felt a surge of anger. Why had she rescued him if he was going to run off at the first opportunity? That ungrateful *szczur!*

Magia swallowed hard and turned back to the fireplace. At least he'd shown her another way out. She wedged the red hat into her pocket, and found that if she dragged the grate back inside the fireplace, and if she balanced on its iron bars, and if she grasped the edges of the open damper with both hands, she could hoist herself up until her head was inside the chimney. She looked upward at the square of sky.

It was a steep climb. And her head was reeling from her encounter with the pup. No matter how often she raced through what had happened, it was the same. She *thought* he'd spoken to her. No, she was *sure* he had.

That was impossible, though. She must be ill.

Or . . . mad.

That was impossible, too, because she felt fine.

Fire and sticks! Magia couldn't take the endless churning anymore. She had to get into the sunlight. Carefully, she wiggled her body farther up into the chimney, until her elbows rested against the sharp edges of the damper. Bracing her legs against the walls of the fireplace, she shifted side to side and managed to crab her way upward, until the rest of her squeezed through the opening. Her scraped knees stung as she brushed through the tight space. Not as smoothly as the pup had tunneled through the snow, but then, she wasn't a wolf.

This chimney didn't smell of sweet-burning wood. It smelled more like the time Dorota, tired of her braids, had tried out a "city" style by smoothing her hair with a hot coal and set half her head to smoking. Looking up, Magia could see that the shaft to the roof was large, but it was roughly made, with bricks that jutted at every angle. Caught in every crevice were clumps of hair.

No, not hair. Fur. Half-burnt fur. Like the pot.

If the poor pup had smelled this . . . Magia ached at the thought of how terrified he must have been.

Slowly she began to shimmy up, handhold by handhold. It was rough going for a girl with dreadfully flat fingernails instead of claws. Worse was the grimy soot that smeared her palms, and the spiderwebs that latched on to her face, and the clumps of fur, which broke free at her passing and lodged in her throat. Magia spat out a coarse hunk. *Whoever lives here*, she thought grimly, *is a brute.* With relief, she emerged into the daylight and flopped on the roof.

The view wasn't what she expected. She'd thought she would see row after row of snow-covered trees jumbled against one another, the branches of the *dąb* bumping into the full, prickly *świerk* limbs. And if she followed them out to the horizon, there would be the end of the Puszcza, and there would be Tysiak, and there would be home.

What she saw instead was an expanse of shimmering white snow around the brick house, and beyond that, a blur. As if, out there, it were still the gray hour before dawn. Magia rubbed her eyes. No matter how she looked at the Puszcza—sideways, or through a circled fist, or with wide-open eyes—everything beyond the snow-covered house was shrouded. Nor did she see any other dwellings—although, swamped by drifts, it was hard to tell. Was she lost, then, with no hope of finding her way out?

Magia stared down the steep slide of the roof. She could picture herself flying off the edge and into a drift higher than her head. She could picture herself floundering there, trying to swim in the snow, until she sank to the bottom and froze. Maybe she should wait. Wait for the snow to melt.

Even now, the snow from the roof was starting to drip into the drifts below, spattering the surface with ragged blotches, like tree blight. The drips had nearly erased where the pup had emerged from his tunnel. She could see a set of four shallow prints, leading away into the Puszcza. He must've been light enough to scamper over the top of the drifts. Was she? Magia didn't know. Besides, if she slid down, which direction should she go? She had no idea where home lay.

From her pocket, Magia pulled out her damaged hat. The pup made such a hole in the hat that if she put it on, it would slide down around her neck. And she wasn't even sure she wanted to put it back on. Magia reached into her other pocket. She'd scraped the yarn bits she'd salvaged into a tight packet before she climbed, but in the sunlight, the blob looked like nothing more than one of those clumps of hair from the chimney. Putting the skeleton of her hat in her lap, Magia took one wisp of yarn from the wad, spat on it, and threaded it through a gap at the edge of the hole. No matter how carefully she coaxed it, though, she couldn't get it to knot in place. It kept slipping out, or blowing out, or . . . this was a silly thought . . . crawling away from her fingers.

Before, when she'd knitted the yarn on her homemade stick needles, she'd quickly learned that the bloodroot softened it, swelled the fibers, and helped them cling and catch. Her spit seemed to do no good. She needed blood-root. Or . . .

Her scraped knees hadn't scabbed over. If she rubbed at them . . .

Was she really thinking of feeding blood to the yarn as if it were a *kania*? Well, it was no crazier than sweeping away footprints to avoid curses.

Magia took a scrap of yarn, and this time, she popped the whole thing in her mouth, wetting it with saliva. While it was soaking, she picked at the thin slashes in her pant leg until there was a single gaping hole. Then she looked at her stubby fingernails — it was ridiculous how often she could use some claws! — and scraped them over the tat-tered skin of her knee. The flesh tore and droplets of blood popped to the surface. She plopped a bit of yarn, fattened by her spit, into the blood and waited. The yarn wiggled and turned bright red.

Magia quickly took the strand and offered it to the hat. The hat gobbled it up.

Well, not exactly up. More like *in*. If Magia squinted, she could see that the rip in the hat was a teeny bit smaller.

Spit. Plop. Wiggle. Red.

Strand by strand, Magia reknit her red hat. And as she did, she felt as if her head were trying to knit together thoughts, too.

The hat had taken blood from her. It was taking more now. Was it *alive*? That hardly seemed likely. She'd made it herself, out of bloodroot and unraveled coat strings. But it no longer seemed under her control. Was it because she was deep in the Puszcza? Tata had said a red hat could keep you from losing your way. But how did you know which way was the right way? Should she have left the wolfling in the woods, alone and injured? She couldn't believe that was what a good woodswoman would do.

Or . . . she shivered . . . had touching the wolf blood made her go mad? Was that what had happened to those other poor girls?

Gah. She wasn't good at following her thoughts on such a twisty path. She'd been gone all night. When she returned, Tata would be back from his trip. He would be white-faced with worry and anger. Dorota's lectures would be never-ending. Even Jan would scold her.

Still . . . she'd rescued a wolf pup. She'd made her own hat twice over. And she'd survived a night in the woods.

She'd proven herself. Tata had to teach her everything he knew about the Puszcza now. She deserved that much.

Magia tugged the repaired hat over her sleep-tangled hair. The knots hummed with delight as they cozied up to her scalp and crawled, leechlike, down to the tips of her ears. Slowly, she swiveled her head around the horizon. Just as slowly, the haze cleared.

Beyond the endless lines of trees, she spotted the thinner underbrush that marked the unraveling edge of the Puszcza. There. Where her hat burned so she could hardly see. That way was home.

Home where the fire stayed lit and the chimney didn't stink of burnt fur.

Home where there were fresh socks, and dry underthings, and a soft bedroll.

Home where there was food to eat.

Magia's stomach growled. She'd had nothing since yesterday. Even Dorota's cracked and dry bread would taste good. She wondered if the pup would be able to find anything to eat on his own. If he truly had been alone. Looking over the expanse of forest she had to traverse, Magia shivered. Maybe full-grown wolves were patrolling the Puszcza even now. Those wolves wouldn't have wide baby eyes but hungry, adult ones.

Magia curled one remaining strand of red yarn about her finger. As much as the thought of full-grown wolves made her uneasy, she'd been sure, looking in the pup's eyes, that the blood on him was from someone he loved. That he'd cried *Mama, Mama, Mama!* Maybe she'd lost her wits. Maybe the pup hadn't talked to her. But, if he had . . .

Magia soaked her last bit of yarn in the blood that oozed from her leg. Again, the fibers seemed to become sticky, and strong. Then, returning to the chimney, she threaded herself, inch by horrid-smelling inch, down the jagged shaft once more. When she reached the damper, she wedged her feet against the chimney's walls and yanked its iron lips closed with both hands. Then, firmly, with the blood-soaked yarn, she tied the Hades-made, howling mouth shut.

There. The chimney was unusable.

No one was going to eat any animal who could talk in this house again.

·· ◆ ··

Later, as she made her way through the Puszcza, Magia refused to look over her shoulder at every cracking branch. She refused to wince as the hat clawed her blood to the surface. She refused to worry that it would dig so deeply into her scalp that she would never get it off. Instead, she began to sing:

> *My wood feeds the fire*
> *The fire feeds the pot*
> *The pot feeds my family*
> *And my family's all I've got.*

Her hat, content on her head, cozied up to her flesh and pierced her scalp in one thousand places. *Heh.* Magia paused in her singing and smiled darkly. It was the Tysiak of hats: One thousand mouths; one thousand biting, nasty voices. If she navigated by its burning fibers, she would be out of the woods before night fell again. She would be home.

It had begun with the snow. When Martin had seen it, flowing into the house, his legs had told him to run. Which was silly. It was snow.

The human girl had told him exactly that: "It's only snow."

He'd believed her. Snow was snow was snow. All through the night, she'd sheltered him from that snow and worse. She'd even sung to him, and whispered mysterious words he couldn't forget: "It's as if we're made of the same stuff . . ."

He'd been as warm and numb as a tree root.

And then she'd said, "Let me look at this blood on you. Where did all that come from?" Words so gentle, so tender, that he hadn't felt them slice him open, until seconds later when she'd guessed the blood wasn't his. By then, he was an open door. Everything he'd fled from had come rushing in:

The sound of his mother's fur ripping against the nails in the floor as she was dragged away. The warm liquid that poured from her body. How it had seeped darkly into his downy underbelly as he cowered under the bed. He could smell it on him still.

He'd run from the memory. But there had been walls. Hard walls. He'd leapt for the only exit he sensed—the sliver of air coming from the chimney. He'd torn through the barrier she'd left there to block the storm—how it had fought him, as if it wanted him to stay with her! He almost had. For when the girl's eyes filled with tears, he knew. He knew she was the one who had howled—the howl that had led him deeper into the woods. She'd been lost and desperate and hungry, too.

If the damper hadn't banged open—if his nose hadn't filled with that disgusting smell—if death hadn't seeped from the chimney, like blood, into his nostrils—

But it had. And Martin had plunged, dew claws extended, into the frigid shock of the snow blocking the door. When he'd emerged from the drifts, he'd seen the silhouette of his tower. And he could've sworn he'd heard his mother, howling for him. *Come home. Come home.*

So he'd run and run and run.

Faster and faster and faster.

Until the slam of the tower's door had bounced to the peak of the high walls. Until even that echo had been stifled by the motionless audience of row after row of books, and the swaying silence of the spiders.

The howl saying "Come home, come home" had been nothing but the wind, blowing through the chimney's empty mouth. His mother wasn't here.

· ◆ ·

Back inside the walls of his tower, he'd thought . . .

he'd hoped . . .

he'd desperately, desperately wanted . . .

to find it had all been a horrible dream.

Martin crawled, inch by aching inch, to the top of the tower stairs. In the scant warmth of the square of sunlight there, he curled his nose into his bloodstained belly and tried to become a blank page again.

As Magia neared the edge of the Puszcza, she took off her hideously buzzing hat, stuffed it in her pocket, and began to skip. She knew she should be walking slowly, her head hung in shame, words of apology ready. She hadn't meant to be gone a whole day and a whole night.

But, oh! The wolf pup! A real wolf! She would tell her family about how she'd cradled him inside her sweater. How alone they'd been; how scared; how lost. And how brave together. And then, in the morning, how he'd talked to her—*talked*! It was a real story, even better than Mama's!

As she emerged from the forest and put her feet on the path home, Magia shook her hair out, feeling light and free after all those steps with her hat chewing at her scalp. The only thing worrying her was her axe. She'd looked for it as she went, but she hadn't been able to find it. Each time she'd thought she'd been close, she'd found nothing but spiderwebs. Hundreds and hundreds of spiderwebs. She would have to look later. Later, after she told everyone —

Magia stopped. There was Tata, on the path from the village, also headed toward home. Had he been out looking for her? Was he angry? Or —

"Tata!" she cried. "Tata! I'm over here!"

Tata turned, but he didn't burst into a run. Didn't hurry to enfold her. Instead, he shifted the plain, long, wooden box in his arms.

"My little lapwing!" he said as she ran to him. "What are you doing here alone? Do you want someone to see you close to the forest and —"

Magia interrupted him. "Tata! I'm safe! I'm here! Were you worried?"

Tata gave her an odd look. "Worried? Why? Has something happened?"

Magia was dumbfounded. He hadn't been worried about her?

Tata smiled. "Wait until you see what I've brought for Mama. I had to sell my cart to get it, but . . ."

Magia felt even more confused. "You sold your cart?" she burst out. "How will you deliver wood, Tata? I mean — I know you don't have many customers anymore, but we can get them back!"

"Maybe, my twig," said Tata. He scooped her hand to his lips and briskly kissed it. Then he drew her by the hand toward home. "But you shouldn't fret about that. I've something much more important to show everyone. I've bought Mama a present!" He nodded toward the box under his other arm.

A present? It wasn't Mama's birthday. Not even close.

They were in sight of home now. Jan bounded from the house and called to Dorota, who came outside, her face flushed from the heat of the fire.

Hades! She'd gone to get her brother and sister wood and she'd brought back nothing. And yet—the fire was lit. It hadn't burned out. Even more strangely, neither her sister nor her brother exclaimed at her absence. Did no one care that she'd been away a whole day and a whole night? Magia slowly released Tata's hand as Dorota and Jan crowded near him.

"Tata!" exclaimed Dorota. "What's in the box?"

Tata put a finger to his lips and swept through the door of the house, all three of them trailing him. Then he set the rectangular box on the broad table where they took their meals.

Magia thought the box resembled a miniature coffin, like the one they'd put in the ground not five months ago. She shivered. But when Tata raised the lid, it was lined, like a nest, with packed straw, and in that nest was the shiny face of—

A *clock*?

"Oooh!" said Dorota. She helped Tata clear the straw from the rest of the box, giving it by the handful to Jan, who carefully bundled it together to save for the fire. "It will keep time just for us!"

Magia pressed in closer to the table. Her head, which had felt odd before, had now begun to hurt. Beneath the clock's oval glass face was an ivory-white surface marked with black numbers, to which pointed two hands, one large and one small. And hanging from the whole thing was a piece of metal, one that looked like an upside-down brass spoon.

Magia didn't understand. Why did they need a thing of wood and glass and metal to "keep" time for them? Time wasn't something you could hold; the sun rose and set; the moon and the stars, too. The day ran from dark to light to dark again—there was no stopping or trapping it. And, more important, how would a clock help Mama?

She kept quiet, though, and watched as Tata fished an odd little key from the remnants of the straw, and stuck the key into a hole in the thing's back. Then he began to wind the clock.

As he did, Magia stared at the key. Her temples throbbed. It was pale. Not metal, like the few keys she'd seen. Instead, it was as white as the splinters Tata cleaned from his traps.

Was that key . . . made of . . . *bone*?

Magia tried to peer at it more closely, but Tata had finished, and slipped the key into his pocket. Then, since they didn't have a mantel—their fireplace was a simple rectangle of rough stone—Tata told Jan to use the poker to pound a small peg into the wall. After that was done, Tata hung the clock on the peg. Set the hands to twelve and six. Pushed the upside-down brass spoon to one side, and let it go.

CHOC! the thing said. *CHOC! CHOC! CHOC!*

Magia recoiled from the harsh sound. "Where did you get that, Tata?" she asked. "It's . . . LOUD."

Tata smiled. "Only the best place to buy Mama's clock." At her blank look, he said, "You've been there, my twig. For your music lesson."

Magia's knees buckled. Miss Grand's house? Tata had gone *there*? As she stared at the fancy clock, the metal spoon inside the clock's case moved back and forth, back and forth, back and forth . . .

Like Miss Grand's metronome. What had Tata—

"Mama!" said Dorota.

"Mama!" cried Jan.

"Mama!" whispered Magia.

The three children's voices, as disorderly as the clock was orderly, squawked in amazement. For Mama had appeared at the entrance of her bedroom, smiling. Her face was flooded with color, and her hair fell about her shoulders.

As Magia stared, Mama stepped forward and ran a finger over the face of the clock. "Oh! It's like the ones in Białowieża!" she said. "Such a city! Such a real city! All the families there have clocks in their houses, sometimes two or three!" Her thin arms wrapped around herself, and she swayed, as if hearing grand city music, her eyes far away.

Magia's heart thudded as Mama's feet shuffled. How could a clock do what Magia's singing and Dorota's nursing and Jan's watching had not? And whatever had Tata paid Miss Grand for it? The thing looked more expensive than a simple wood cart would bring in trade.

Mama stopped twirling and smiled. "Why are you standing there like four fat pigeons?" she said brightly.

"It's six o'clock! Time for dinner! Get the bread and the cheese."

Tata beamed. He went to Mama and lifted her into his arms. She let him hold her. Magia could only gape at her mother, who seemed as if she had changed into a new skin. Was it that easy to return from darkness?

Maybe it was. A few minutes later, Mama was wrapping a cloth around her hand before lifting a warmed stone with cheese on it from the hearth. Jan was reaching for his bread even as the stone hit the table.

"Sit, Piotrek," Mama said, as Tata hovered near her, smiling as if his face would crack. "Or Jan will eat your share, too."

As they said grace, Magia's head ached worse than ever. All she could hear was the too-quick clicking of the clock, which fought with the rhythm of the words they said together.

"Bless us, O Lord—" *CHOC.*

"And these—" *CHOC* "—thy gifts."

"Which we are about to—" *CHOC* "—receive."

Magia wanted to put her hands over her ears. How could everyone ignore that sound?

But they did, and soon everyone was dipping pupes of bread into the gooey cheese, which Mama had sprinkled with bits of diced onion. Oh! How Magia had missed this! Still, as she ate, she felt light-headed. She hadn't had a chance to hug Mama as Tata had. Maybe the miraculous cure would seem real when she did.

And what about the rest of the day? Didn't anyone want to hear about her adventures? She'd rescued a wolf pup! Held his trembling body and examined his wounds. She'd guessed the secret of the blood on him. And he'd talked to her. Talked!

Hadn't he?

Soon, Jan was reaching for the last of the warm, sweaty cheese. Dorota was going round with the kettle, pouring out tea into five cups, and Tata was stuffing more logs on the fire so they could linger at the table. Mama, though, was frowning at the empty dishes.

"I wish I could've made more for you, my loves," she said, her finger swirling the tiny crumbs of bread that remained. "Why, in Białowieża, the great families have fatted pork for dinner every night."

"Tell us, Mama," Dorota said. "Tell us about Białowieża! Before you came to Tysiak with Tata!"

Instead of answering, Mama left her tea and stood behind Dorota. She grasped Dorota's braids with her delicate hands and began to deftly unbraid her hair and twist it into a high bun. "Well, my lovely," said Mama, "for one thing, you would put your hair up; no city girl goes to school with braids."

Dorota closed her eyes, smiling, as Mama worked with her hair. Magia thought it looked as if her sister was going to melt, like the cheese, off her chair. Then Mama went to Jan and pulled him to standing.

"Janusz!" she said, laughing. "Your pants!" Jan looked down. Even on a diet of Dorota's food, Jan had grown three inches over the winter. His skinny ankles looked like exposed tree roots. "How will you march in the mayor's parade with trousers like these?" she scolded him lightly.

Jan's shoulders straightened and he saluted smartly, as if the mayor were there. "Oh, Mama," he said. "When I'm a soldier, I'm going to march through Tysiak, on to Białowieża, and then round the world and back again! I'll bring you a fatted pig, and . . ." He paused. "And a piano! I'll carry them home, one under each arm!"

Dorota actually giggled. "Jan! That's ridiculous! You've no idea what a pig weighs!" She flicked a bread crumb at him, and the two of them burst out in laughter.

Magia glanced at her father. He was standing near his axe, lifting it and putting it back down, in a fitful sort of unease. The giddiness that had filled him earlier seemed to have vanished. She wanted to go to him, but Mama had come to her at last.

"And you, my quiet one?" she said. "What would you do in Białowieża if we lived there?" She put an arm around Magia, and Magia buried her nose in her mother's dress. Mama smelled musty, from lying in bed, but also of the fresher scent of tea, and the tangy onion she'd sprinkled on the cheese.

Magia wanted to pull her red hat from her pocket. She wanted to tell Mama that she'd changed while Mama lay in darkness. That she'd had adventures of her own. But the clock's unrelenting tick filled the room, and Magia couldn't find any place to put her words.

"I don't want to talk about the city, Mama," she said. "But I'm glad you feel better."

The next morning, Magia hurriedly crawled over Dorota, who was sprawled beside her. She stepped around Jan, whose body blocked the door. She was already dressed in three layers, because it was still too cold to sleep otherwise. Not that she'd slept, with the chocking noise of the clock filling the house.

Magia reached for her boots by the fire. She'd lain awake for hours trying to figure out how she could've been gone in the Puszcza all night and yet no one had missed her. Maybe time ran crookedly in the forest, like the paths. She would have to ask Tata.

Magia was sure Tata would want to leave the house to chop wood as soon as first light hit the trees, for they didn't have a cart to haul wood now. They would have to carry the logs on their backs, she supposed, and it would take a long, long time. She didn't care. She needed to talk to him. Alone.

Rawk! Rawk! Rawk! Rawk! Rawk! Rawk!

Magia startled, dropping one of her boots. She glared at the clock. Was it going to call out the hour every morning? Jan grunted in his sleep and Dorota flopped to her other side, but neither woke. How could they sleep through that noise?

As she put on her boot, Mama slowly stepped from her bedroom. Magia tucked her hat behind her back. No need for Mama to be upset by it. But Mama didn't look at her. She dazedly walked to the clock, and stood staring at it, as if asking its shiny face what she should do next. Quietly, she swayed back and forth, back and forth, as she had when she'd first seen it. Magia suddenly had the strange thought that her mama was being wound up somehow, just as Tata had used the key on the clock.

"Mama?" Magia said quietly. "What are you doing? Is Tata up yet?"

Mama jerked as she turned, and for a second, Magia saw emptiness in her eyes. Then her mother righted herself and said almost mechanically, "He will return when the clock reads six o'clock again."

What? Magia scanned the fireplace. Tata's red hat was missing from the peg beside it. He'd left without her!

Magia ran to the door and threw it open. In the distance, a sliver of reflected light bobbed as it moved toward the Puszcza. Tata's axe! Magia burst from the house, red hat in hand.

"Tata!" she called as she slipped on the icy remnants of the late snowstorm. "Tata! Wait! Wait!"

She was out of breath and her clothes had turned damp and cold by the time he heard her. He halted, his eyes widening as he turned to see her. "Magia! What is it?" A shadow passed over his face. "Is it Mama? Does she need me?"

Magia slowed beside him, her legs tingling and her face flushed. She shook her head, unable to speak. Mama was acting strangely, but she didn't know how to talk to Tata about that now. This was her chance to talk to Tata about joining him in the forest. Finally. She gulped air and held out her hat.

Tata, his own hat pulled deep over his ears, leaned his axe against his leg and took Magia's roughly stitched effort from her. He fingered every snarled stitch, his face unreadable. In the dim light, Magia worried the thing didn't even look red.

"I made it this winter," she croaked finally, her words barely audible. "From my old coat, and bloodroot."

Tata's eyes rose from the hat. "This is yours?"

"Yes!" Magia cried. "And I've tested it! It works! Of course, I'll have to find my axe—" She struggled to get out the most important words. "But don't you see, Tata? Mama is awake! It's spring! I can come with you now!"

"No, my *podrost*." His voice was tight. "You cannot."

Magia felt as if the last snow under their feet had turned into a river, and was washing away the solid ground beneath her. She was NOT a little sapling. She had grown a lot since last year. "But, Tata . . . why not? Surely you can't think we have to obey the city's rules forever. They aren't the rules of the forest!"

"No," Tata said firmly. "Remember? We talked about this. You promised to listen to Mama. Mama has big dreams for you. So do I. Miss Grand said we could arrange for you to start singing lessons again."

"What?" Magia said incredulously. She was going to have to tell Tata about the broken metronome and her odd encounter with Miss Grand in the woods. Even though she wasn't supposed to be in the woods at all—and—

None of that would make Tata believe she was ready to work with him.

Magia fixed her eyes on her hat in Tata's hands. He was squeezing it between both palms, as if to make it disappear. She felt the weight of all the days she'd sat knitting in the darkness with Mama. A taste as bitter as the bloodroot she'd chewed flooded her mouth.

"You promised, Tata," she whispered. "You said I could be a woodswoman. I don't want to sing for Miss Grand. Or for anyone but you and Mama. Please let me help you. I'm not so little, not anymore."

"Magia!" Tata said. "Enough. If I say you cannot go with me, you cannot go. And if your mama says you will take singing lessons, you will." As the sun topped the trees and illuminated Tata's face, Magia could see a net of angry lines tightening around his mouth and eyes, pinching them to a forced stiffness. She hardly recognized her gentle father.

Magia's own face set into hard lines. "I won't go back to Miss Grand's house, Tata," she said. "Do you know what she did to me? When I didn't sing to her liking, she slammed my fingers in the piano lid!" She lifted her knuckles, but of course, the bruises had long healed. "You didn't ask about my lesson. Not once! You only cared about the baby and Mama and—"

Magia choked back her words, horrified. That wasn't what she'd meant to say. She started again. "Something's not right with that woman, Tata. And something's not right with the clock you bought from her, either. It makes Mama act strangely, and I hate it!"

Abruptly, Tata set down his axe and bent his knees so his face was near to hers. He said fiercely, "Don't you think I know what I've bought and at what cost? Did I not tell you that a woodcutter's life is an ugly one? At least Mama is awake! And with each passing day, she will be more and more of the Mama we love!"

Magia willed herself not to shiver in the blast of chill air that swirled around them. She suddenly felt small and stupid. What was Tata talking about?

Then Tata, still holding her hat, cupped her face in both hands. The rough, knobby stitches pressed into her cheek. "Magia. Magia," he said. "This hat you've made—it's not enough. Not enough to keep you safe. I've lost so much. I can't lose you, too. I'll talk to Mama about choosing another singing teacher. Be patient with her, and with me. But you must listen. The Puszcza is no place for a little girl. Now go home. Your mother is waiting." He released her face and retrieved his axe, but her red hat—that he swallowed deep into his coat pocket.

Magia could do nothing but watch him walk into the woods without her.

·◆·

When she trudged back to the house, Mama was in the same spot, near the clock, but she seemed more animated.

"You're the first one awake, Magia," she said brightly, as if Magia hadn't gone anywhere. "Please get water for the tea." She nodded at the battered black kettle. "I'll rouse the other lazybones. In Białowieża, the school bell would be ringing already."

"School?" Magia said weakly. Her whole body ached from Tata's rejection. He hadn't even let her tell him how she'd tested her red hat. How she rescued a wolf pup. She'd been brave—and so prepared!

"Of course," Mama said. "Lessons will begin promptly at eight." She looked at the clock, as if it would confirm this.

Magia tried to steady herself. Mama had always taught them things: how to play chess, how to read, how to track the stars in the sky, and of course, how to sing. But she'd never needed a clock to tell her when or how to do it. Tata had said to be patient, that Mama would get better; but Magia felt confused and alone *now*. She couldn't wait.

"Mama?" she ventured. "So much happened while you were sick. I want to tell you everything but—I don't know where to start."

Mama smiled. "Begin, Magia," she said tenderly. "I'm your mama. I love you. Just begin."

The clock seemed to tick louder as silence fell in the room. Magia struggled to find words. Where was the beginning? When she'd broken the metronome? When the baby had been lost? When she and Jan had helped the mad girl?

Magia said finally: "Mama, I think I met a *wiedźma*."

Mama's face whitened. Fear returned to her eyes. She looked as if she might sink to the floor. Magia reached for her, horrified at her sudden weakness. Then, with a shake of her shoulders, Mama looked at the clock. Stared at it while she swayed.

CHOC! it said. *CHOC! CHOC!*

Then Mama's face cleared, and the mechanical tone returned to her voice. "My goodness, Magia!" she said crisply, stepping back from Magia's embrace. "You've started to believe the foolish talk in the village. Go and get water for tea, and then we must start lessons right after breakfast!" She reached for the kettle, pressed it into Magia's hands, and scooted her out of the house.

Numbly, Magia began to scoop a patch of snow into the pot. The icy slush burned her fingers. She wasn't foolish. Something had been wrong at the house where Mama had sent her to get singing lessons. Something was wrong at their own house now. She knew it. Didn't anyone care what she knew, what she'd made, where she'd been?

When Magia reentered her house, her mother was lovingly using the edge of her dress to wipe a smudge from the clock's face. Dorota was awake, and stuffing her arms into her coat.

"*Ech,*" she said. "I wish we had indoor plumbing." She banged her feet into her boots and grumpily stepped over Jan before stomping out the door.

Magia hung the kettle on the hook over the fire and watched the flames dance. Their fireplace was small compared with the one she'd slept in yesterday.

"What's wrong, Magia?" said Jan, who had risen and come up beside her to steal warmth from the fire. "You look like you've swallowed a worm." He elbowed her. "Don't worry, we have Mama back now. No more of Dorota's cooking!"

Magia stole a glance at Mama, who was again transfixed before the clock. She was humming a tune Magia recognized, a song from Mama's childhood in Białowieża.

Magia inched closer to Jan. "Yesterday, I went into the Puszcza," she whispered.

Jan's grin left his face. "What?" he said loudly.

Magia squeezed his arm. "Shhhh! I found a wolf pup!"

Worry and excitement crisscrossed Jan's face. "A wolf?" he said with awe. "Where?"

"He was hurt, so I carried him through a storm," Magia said. "We spent the night in a brick house with a huge chimney! I found a big pot with water and wolf fur in it, and the pup was afraid he might be cooked, so he ran away."

Jan took a step back from her, and then laughed out loud. "And then you saw three little pigs, too, right? Like in Mama's story?"

Magia felt as if she were back in the snowstorm, everything fuzzy and swirling. She hadn't realized . . . the brick house, the chimney, the pot big enough to boil a wolf in . . . all the details *were* like Mama's story. The one she'd said her mother's mother's mother had told. How could that be?

Jan put his arm around her. "I had a dream, too," he said in a normal voice. "I dreamed I grew taller." He pulled her close and measured her head against his chest.

"Nope." His grin was wide and unforced. "It was only a dream. Or else you're getting taller, too . . ."

The teakettle began to puff out curls of steam. Magia tried to smile back at him. A dream? Was that what it had been? Or—she had a chilling thought—was this what it was like to go mad? She was already blathering about a *wilk* she'd seen. How long before her eyes turned into giant bloodshot blisters? How long before she—

CHOC! said the clock. *CHOC! CHOC!*

·◆··

Days later, Magia still felt fuzzy. Meanwhile, Mama rose in the mornings to the clock's awful screeches:

RAWK! RAWK! RAWK! RAWK! RAWK! RAWK!

And then Mama, after staring and swaying in front of the clock for a few moments, seemed to come to life, at least enough to order their days around its equally awful ticking—

CHOC! Time for breakfast.

CHOC! Time for lessons!

CHOC! Time for chores!

CHOC! Time for prayers, and bed! And then . . .

RAWK! RAWK! RAWK! RAWK! RAWK! RAWK!
Time to start all over again.

When Magia tried to complain to Dorota about the strangeness of all this, her sister only said she liked having their days so precisely planned. As for Jan, he was so happy to be eating Mama's food that he didn't mind doing it at the exact same time every day—or listening to Mama talk about how fine the meals in Białowieża were. As for Tata, he was hardly ever home anymore.

Today, under Mama's direction, Magia sat at one end of their table, and Dorota dutifully sat at the other. Both girls had just haltingly recited a poem Mama said was written by a great poet from the city. Between them, Jan had set up the chess set. Nearby, Mama dug her thumbs into the bread dough, which had already risen once in its thick brown pot.

"Come on, Mama," said Jan. "Let Magia play a game with me. Then we can do more lessons."

Magia stared at the board with the double line of carved wooden men on each side. She didn't feel like chess or lessons. All she wanted to think about was the memory of the pup's eyes as they opened, or when she'd first seen him, a trembling, hurt ball under that tree. How he rained down wet snow upon her as he'd tried to run. How her hat had bitten her as she'd held tight to him instead.

"Try moving a pawn," said Jan helpfully. He reached over and moved one for her. "Look! That puts my knight in danger."

"Put the board away. Chess is for after lunch," said Mama. "The morning is for lessons."

"But, Mama, we can—"

"No," said Mama, covering the dough again and leaving it to rise once more. She looked at the clock. "We only have so much time, and there is much to learn. You want to be an intelligent *and* brave soldier, don't you?" She untied her apron and put it over the chessboard, hiding the pieces.

CHOC! said the clock. *CHOC! CHOC!*

Magia, as always, winced at the sound. She wished Tata wouldn't wind the clock every day before he left for the Puszcza.

"Now," Mama said firmly. "Ask Magia her multiplication tables. When she misses an answer, she can drill you. It will be a battle. A battle of wits."

Jan winked at Magia. "Yes," he said. "We'll see which little pig is the most prepared."

Magia said nothing.

"Six times six, Magia," he said, giving her an easy one to start with.

Magia couldn't concentrate. What had happened to her wolfling after he had run from her? Was he wondering what had happened to her, too?

"Magia," prompted Mama. "You know this!"

"Thirty-six," Magia said dully.

"Nine times five," Jan said. Another easy one.

"Forty-five," Magia said, but her eyes slid to the empty peg beside the fireplace where Tata kept his red hat. If only she could convince Tata to return hers!

But Tata hadn't spoken of her hat again. It stayed in his pocket. Worse than that, he'd never scolded Magia about her missing axe. The one that had been Tata's when he was a boy. The one she had used so many times to help him. Instead, Tata came back from the Puszcza with precious little firewood, and a haggard look on his face.

"How are the orders for wood, Tata?" she'd asked him last night.

"The same."

"No one wants more?"

"I haven't asked."

"Tata, you look tired. Let me clean your axe."

"No, my robin. I must do it."

And now, looking at the empty peg where Tata's red hat usually hung, Magia raised her hand to her scalp. Yes. There was a bare spot where her own hat had taken blood from her. It hadn't been a dream. And she wasn't mad. She'd made a red hat; she'd been into the deepest reaches of the Puszcza; she'd rescued a wolf pup. So why couldn't she help Tata now?

Littlest and Middlest and Biggest moaned. They'd built their three houses, one of straw, one of mud, and one of bricks, as their mama had said they must. They'd lured many wolves from one to the next. Fooled each one into thinking he was stronger and cleverer than piglets were. Until each one had wiggled into Biggest's chimney. So many wolves. So many twinkling white wolf bones to deliver to the witch.

But now, something had gone wrong.

They'd gotten a wolf—a small one, but very wolfish!—to chase them. But he hadn't gone to the brick house. He'd left their Story altogether! The fire in Biggest's hearth had burned to ashes. No wolf.

Biggest had come out of the house, finally, to see what his brothers had messed up. They'd all gone looking for the wolf together. And then it had snowed. They'd had to take shelter where they could, and they'd nearly frozen their tails off. Worst of all, when they'd returned to the brick house to figure out what had gone wrong, they'd scented a girl.

A *girl* had been in Biggest's house.

There was NEVER a girl in their Story.

"And now, Mama. Oh, Mama!" Biggest and Middlest and Littlest moaned, although their mama was far away and couldn't hear them. "It's worse than we feared. Our Story is broken. It's been weeks since the storm, and yet—wolves no longer come to huff and puff. They don't fall down our chimney. We can't pay the *wiedźma*, Mama—so—oh, Mama! We're not three little pigs anymore. We're growing *big*."

Every day for the next two weeks, Magia woke with the hope that Tata would change his mind, and take her with him to chop wood. But he did not. He had little to say, except to ask how Mama had fared while he was away.

How could Magia answer that? The mama she remembered had sung hymns to rouse them from bed; now she relied on a clock. The mama she remembered had laughed while her children acted out her tellings of old tales; now she stiffly nodded her approval at what they learned each day. At least Mama still baked bread with globs of sweet raisins, which they gobbled at dinner with her tea made from soaked apple peels. But even as her belly warmed with the food, Magia would often catch Mama swaying in front of the clock after supper, as if waiting for it to tell her she could lie down in the darkness again. And over and over, Mama would talk of how lovely the clock was, and how everything in Białowieża was as fine as it.

"She's about the same," Magia told Tata. "About the same."

Then Tata, while the clock ticked, would slump by the fire all evening, scraping his axe clean. *Scrape, scrape, scrape.*

After that, music. After that, prayers. After that, bed.

The same every day—

CHOC! CHOC! CHOC!

—until this morning, when Magia couldn't bear to sit at the table when the clock said it was time for lessons. Instead, she stubbornly pressed her palms too long and too close to the fire, nearly burning them, just to relish the stinging snap of the logs against her bare skin. Behind her, she could hear Mama sigh. Dorota was already mumbling her list of the names of the bones in the human body. Jan was reading about battles in Mama's one battered book of history.

Magia didn't care that Mama wanted her to turn from the fire to her lessons. She'd been in the Puszcza, and now it sang to her, calling to something deep in her chest. If she didn't answer that song soon, her heart was going to gnaw its way out from the inside.

Then Mama came up softly behind her. "Would you like to go out with me this morning, Magia?" she said. "I need to visit the baby's grave, and I don't want to go alone."

· ◆ ·

As they walked toward the village, Mama plucked blooms from the meadow: Violets and saxifrages. Laserwort and striped comfrey flowers. Chrysanthemums, with golden centers and white petals. When she couldn't hold any more in her hands, she gave them to Magia. By the time they reached the church, their hands were overflowing with flowers.

Mama gently put them all, one by one, on the baby's grave. Then they lit a candle next to the headstone, and prayed.

"I feel like I've been away in a strange land," she said softly to Magia when they were finished.

Magia didn't know what to say. The graves in this part of the churchyard were all freshly dug. Candles were everywhere, for many people had lost loved ones over the winter. Had they all mourned as deeply as Mama had?

"But I'm back now," said Mama. "And we can—"

She stopped because Pani Gomolka had sidled up beside them.

"Good day," she said. "And my sympathies." She tipped her walking stick toward the tiny gravestone. "It was a long, hard winter, wasn't it?"

Magia was startled to see that the Pani's curved back was stooped even lower. The woman's fingers shook as she gripped her walking stick.

Mama nodded. "Yes, it was. But it's spring now. Time for new things." She took Magia's hand as if to leave.

Pani Gomolka cleared her throat. Didn't move out of the way.

"What is it?" said Mama, but her fingers gripped Magia's tightly. Tata had certainly told her about how the Panie had gossiped.

Pani Gomolka inched closer, and then winced as if her one good leg were going bad, too. Her walking stick, Magia saw, was splitting near the bottom. Probably from thumping it at everyone.

"I need to walk into the city today," she said. "And since your healthy, strong-legged daughter has nothing to do, she may accompany me to the shops. It might do Magia good to be seen helping someone as frail as I am."

Magia nearly bit off her tongue. Beside her, she could feel Mama twitch, as if words were building.

When Mama didn't say anything, Pani Gomolka slowly added, "Your other one might do, I suppose, if this one doesn't want the chance." Magia supposed that "other one" was Dorota.

"I'm sorry," said Mama briskly. "Neither of my daughters has time. My children and I have much to catch up on."

Then, pulling Magia down beside her, Mama knelt and prayed again at the baby's grave. She prayed and prayed until they could no longer hear Pani Gomolka's walking stick anywhere near them.

"Heavens," said Mama, as they rose. "I'm so tired of people poking their noses where they don't belong." She took Magia's hand and drew her through the churchyard. "Oh, my dear, if only you could see somewhere else. Somewhere where there are concerts, and dancing, and so many books you wouldn't believe it!"

Magia tried not to sigh. Mama had always missed Białowieża. But the fine clock had made her miss it more.

Still—what good did it do to talk about a faraway place so much?

"But what about guards?" she said. "And rules? And gossiping, bossy old Panie? Doesn't Białowieża have them, too?"

Mama slowed her steps, and her voice slowed, also. "I know you've struggled, Magia, living here," she said. Hand in hand, they turned onto the path out of the village and toward home. "And I'm proud of you. But—you must choose to do something with your life, my dear one. Before someone who thinks 'you have nothing to do' chooses for you." At this, she mimicked Pani Gomolka's grim face.

Magia didn't smile. She knew why Pani Gomolka had to walk alone. Miss Grand had somehow scared away her only friend. And suddenly, Magia felt guilty for not telling anyone she'd seen the music teacher in Pani Wolburska's clothes.

"Don't worry, my love," Mama said, at Magia's solemn face. "You don't ever have to work for Pani Gomolka. There will be other choices soon."

Yes, other choices. For one thing, Magia hoped more people might ask for Tata's wood now that Mama was up and about; stories that she and the baby had been cursed might look silly in the light of spring. Why, clearly, even Pani Gomolka seemed ready to put all that behind them. Mama and Magia walked in silence until they crested the path toward home. In the distance, Magia could see the *buk* trees circling their house; they were full and lush now, with spring here in all its greening glory. She should speak now, while Mama was away from the clock. Maybe her mother would hear her clearly at last.

"Mama," she said, stopping at the top of the path. "I did choose. Before you were ill, I told Tata I wanted to be a woodcutter. He said he would teach me."

Her heart pounded as she said these simple words, but to her surprise, Mama didn't argue. She only squeezed Magia's hand and said, "You think I don't know how you feel, Magia? That you want more than our small lessons every day? I see your restless feet. I see your sad face, thinking of things far away."

Then she swung Magia's hand, to pull her down the path. "Tata once told me you were the strongest in the family," Mama said. "And I believe it. Everything's going to be fine, my love. Things will change soon, I promise."

· · ◆ · ·

That night, when Tata came home, Mama insisted he put away his axe. Dinner began promptly as the clock crowed six.

Rawk! Rawk! Rawk! Rawk! Rawk! Rawk!

Magia sat in front of her bowl of *bigos*. Jan had managed to spear a rabbit, so there was meat, but Magia wasn't hungry. Not with so many unspoken words inside her. But no one seemed to notice.

Finally, when the bowls of stew were cleared, Tata rose and stood near his seat. His face was solemn.

"I am a woodcutter," he said. "As my father was before me, and his father, and his father before that. But . . ."

He looked at Mama. "There is always a time for change. Many of my customers no longer appreciate the wood I cut for them. Many of them never will. My eldest darns holes in socks for too little coin. My son was hit with rocks when he asked for work. As for my youngest . . ."

Here, his eyes slid toward Magia, and her heart turned over with a loud thump. Was he going to say something about her red hat?

"My youngest has been doing her best to help me," Tata finished, "but she does not know how deep the dangers of the Puszcza are." He went to stand behind Mama's chair and put both hands on her slim shoulders. "Most of all, my wife—my dearest, my only love—wasn't given care when she needed it most. Everyone was too afraid to come near us. So, although I fit this life . . ." His voice wavered. "It no longer matters what I want. What matters is that my family is safe. I'll remain here to work because I must; but all of you, my precious ones, must go to a new home." He leaned down to kiss the top of Mama's bright head. "A new home in Białowieża."

A giant lump rose into Magia's throat. "Białowieża?" she managed to squeak out. "We're going to live in a city days and days away? *Without you?*"

Jan looked hurt and bewildered, too. "Why would we do that, Tata?"

"I don't like it," Dorota said flatly. "We should all move together. Mama! Tell Tata he can't do this!"

But Mama's slender face was alight with more emotion than Magia had seen in months. "Whatever is the matter with all of you? Can't you see how hard it was for Tata to say this? Already he's gone from us for hours every day, to chop wood that people hardly pay for! Shouldn't we have bigger dreams than that?" she said earnestly. "In Białowieża, Dorota will be able to study healing at the university. Jan will be able to train as a true soldier. And Magia can charm everyone with her gorgeous voice—or she can choose anything else she likes, for in Białowieża, there are many ways to be happy." Here, Mama beamed at Magia, as if this would be enough to make her smile. "As for Tata staying here, why—it's only temporary! He will find new work in Białowieża, and then of course he will join us. Won't you, my love?"

Tata shifted from foot to foot behind Mama's chair, his face twisting with a tortured expression that Mama couldn't see. Magia couldn't stop herself; she jumped up and grasped Tata's wide hand. He didn't want new work in a city! He belonged here! *She* belonged here!

But before she could form those words, Jan rose and went to stand next to Tata. "I'm sorry, Tata," he said. "I didn't mean to speak against you. I can look for work in the city, too."

Dorota jumped up and stood on Tata's other side, behind Magia. "Promise, Tata," Dorota said. "Promise you will come join us as soon as you can."

Tata nodded, but as the clock ticked louder and louder in the room—

CHOC! CHOC! CHOC!

—only Magia felt Tata's hand slacken in hers, as if he'd let go of something bigger than her fingers.

The next morning, Magia woke early. She kept her eyes shut as Tata entered the main room. There—there was the thunk of his axe as he set it aside briefly while he shuffled into his boots. There—there was the rustle of him putting his prepared lunch of brown bread and cheese into his pocket. There—there was the final, hard clunk of the door closing. And there—*CHOC!* There was the awful sound of the clock's hands moving one notch closer to six.

Magia could sense her mother, in the other room, poised to answer its impending call.

Carefully, so as not to disturb Dorota and Jan, Magia crawled out of her blankets. She stood before the cold face of Miss Grand's clock.

What was the clock's power over Mama? It was a mechanical thing. A way of measuring time, nothing more. And yet ever since it came into the house, Mama had been ruled by the clock, judging every action by it, staring into it for hours a day.

Magia preferred the timekeepers that lived in the sky. The sun that told her what hour it was. The birds that tattled on Tata's return. The breeze that brought the scent of dinner. If you paid attention, you could always know what hour it was. How to keep your own time.

That's what Magia wanted—to be in charge of her own life. But she couldn't have that. Her red hat went into the Puszcza with Tata, but she couldn't. Her axe was lost somewhere in the forest. She would never get to see if her talking pup had been real. And soon, Magia would even lose Tata, when they moved to Białowieża.

It wasn't fair. Miss Grand seemed to control everything— and have everything. Freedom to walk about the Puszcza. Power to wake Mama. And more red than Magia had ever seen.

Magia shivered as she remembered how the cape in Miss Grand's basket had draped lushly against her skin. How deep its crimson color! How alive she'd felt, touching it, as if the whole world belonged to her. How unfair that a worthless, lying person such as Miss Grand had that cape and not her. If Magia had it, she could go into the Puszcza and retrieve her axe, and try one more time to talk sense into Tata. He couldn't stay here to work alone. He couldn't!

But she didn't have the cape. And it had been weeks since she'd seen it. Surely, if Miss Grand had left her basket near the woods, she would've come back for it by now. Unless . . .

Unless she *wanted* Magia to have the exquisite thing.

What a fool Magia had been! The cape was too valuable to leave behind accidentally. Miss Grand *knew* Magia came to that part of the woods. She was offering the perfectly sized cloak to *her*.

Miss Grand had asked Magia to work with her. Magia would never do that. Nor would she take such a gift and be forever in debt to that woman. Still—Magia couldn't see why she shouldn't borrow the cape for a few minutes. If it was still there. Just to find her axe.

Slowly, she unlatched the glass face of the clock. If she was going to sneak out, Mama shouldn't wake. Her fingers deftly grasped the longest of the arrow-shaped hands and pushed it backward in a sweeping circle so that the clock would no longer be on the verge of chiming six.

CHOC! said the thing. *CHOC! CHOC!*

Magia turned her back on it. Miss Grand's clock wasn't going to keep time for her this morning. She cracked open the front door as narrowly as possible before she slipped out.

Minutes later, Magia was lifting the cape from the basket, which was exactly where she remembered it. Had Miss Grand left it there each day, hoping Magia would find it? What did it matter? The beautiful creation was nearly weightless, but it exuded a deep warmth, and oh! It encircled her whole body with light and ease, as if it were sunlight itself. Magia had never loved dresses or any fancy thing—Jan's hand-me-down pants were good enough for her. But this cape—how beautifully it fit her! No lumps or bumps or bags anywhere. And then there was the strange, floating feeling the enveloping fabric gave her as she tied the crimson ribbons about her neck. As if she could be anything, anything in the world. Best of all, the cape's bright, unashamed red proclaimed her intention to walk where she wanted!

Magia picked up the basket and stepped toward the Puszcza's entwined branches. She would find her axe before Mama woke. After that, she would insist that Tata let her stay here near the village and help him pay whatever he owed Miss Grand for the clock. Otherwise, they might not see him for years and years, and she couldn't bear that. Bravely and boldly, with the red cape flowing from her shoulders, Magia plunged into the woods yet again.

The Puszcza greeted her with delight. And it began to spin the Story it had spun many times before . . .

Once upon a time, a Girl entered the forest. As she skipped along a path in the deepest, darkest, most dangerous part of the woods, she twirled; she jigged; she hummed. For she was wearing a marvelous red cape and carrying a basket that smelled of sugar and cream cake.

With calculated haste, the Wolf placed himself behind a tree along her path. When she reached his hiding spot, he slunk out with studied ease. His eyes fixed upon the square of flesh that gleamed between the two dangling ties of her hood. Her neck shone with the most delicate softness, and he could see how her breath passed through her throat before filling her lungs.

"Where are you going, little one?" he asked.

The Girl, not as startled as she should have been, answered, "Why, to my grandmamma's house. I'm bringing her sweets and she will tell me stories!" She showed the Wolf her basket of iced cakes.

The Wolf inwardly shuddered. The gooeyness of baked things! Why would one eat cooked, if one could have raw? On his wolfish visage, though, he kept an expression of bored interest. "You seem to be in no hurry to get there," he said.

"I am hurrying," said the Girl. The Wolf saw a smidgen of worry in her eyes, as if she felt the darkness of the woods around her for the first time. She looked at him closely and frowned. Then she looked down at her shoes, which were even now tapping against the dirt of the path in an aimless rhythm. "You see? My feet move."

"Of course," said the Wolf, careful not to wake her from the beat and sway of her dazed state. "Perhaps I might speed you along your way?" With a graceful sweep of his black paw, he indicated a faint track that wound outward away from her path. "The animals who have lived in these woods for thousands of years know its ways better than—forgive me—even a bright Girl such as you." The Wolf sniffed at the earth beneath her feet. "If you wish to be free, you must depart from the known ways and follow the older, wilder track."

The Girl eyed the barely visible path. "It will get me to Grandmamma's?"

The Wolf nodded.

"Faster?" she pressed him.

He bowed to her as if she'd already swept by him.

"You promise I'll be safe?" In her dull eyes, he saw a flame leap briefly.

He let a tear rise in his eye, to show how her doubt had wounded him.

Not wishing to insult him further, she took the Wolf's advice and left the marked path for *the fainter animal track. Once on it, her feet steadied and she plunged into the darkest trees, her pace quickening to an urgent beat. She only saw the trees, and more trees, and beyond them—*

Beyond them—Grandmamma! How spry she seemed! Not old at all! And how did she already have the basket—the basket that Magia had been taking—and what had happened to the path? The path she'd been following—the one, the—suddenly Magia couldn't remember who had said this path led to—where had she been going?—to Grandmamma's? She had no grandmamma! Both of hers were dead. Mama prayed for their souls every night. Was it nighttime?

Where *was* she?

· ◆ ·

Magia blinked rapidly. A woman, lopsidedly hobbling with her basket against her hip, was coming straight for her. As she approached, each branch she pushed aside rubbed against every other branch, and made a mad melody of wood upon wood.

Magia felt queasy at the barrage of noise. Light stabbed her eyes as if she'd emerged from a root cellar. Every inch of bare skin on her face stung. And her feet! They were stiff as stones!

"Oh, thank goodness!" Miss Grand said in a gratingly loud voice as she reached Magia's side. She put one hand over her heart, which was once again hidden behind Pani Wolburska's tattered clothes. "I thought you might be . . ." She peered at Magia. "You are safe, aren't you, my dear?" She reached out to stroke her hair.

Magia recoiled from the woman's touch; pain rushed into her feet and she nearly fell over. She looked down. She was ankle deep in a puddle of slushy snow. At her feet was her axe.

How long had she been standing here like a *gapa*? And what was Miss Grand talking about? Of course she was safe! To steady herself, Magia gripped her axe by its handle. Oh, how heavy it was! How rough, as if it were nothing but splinters! The sight of the well-oiled blade made her remember her purpose in coming to the woods. She'd set the clock back an hour, and left Mama and Jan and Dorota asleep while she went to find her axe. She'd taken the red cape to . . .

Suddenly Magia was aware that her shoulders were bare. Where was the cape? She felt a pang of loss as she remembered lifting the gloriously rich fabric from the basket. Oh! How it had caressed her shoulders! How cozy she'd been as she'd walked deeper and deeper and deeper into the Puszcza. And then . . .

Nothing. Magia could remember nothing. Not even how she'd come to find her axe. She felt like a baby bird pushed from its warm nest. Her heart flapped helplessly in her chest.

She stole a glance at the sky. Branches blocked the sun. How long had she been gone? How far had she walked? As feeling poured back into her toes, prickles of pain shot up her legs.

Magia finally looked at Miss Grand, who seemed content to wait while Magia stamped and struggled with her thoughts. Why was the woman standing there, staring at her like she was a strange tree root in her path?

"You don't have to worry about me," Magia said loudly. Her throat was dry and her lips numb, but she forced words out. "I'm on my way home."

"Of course you are," Miss Grand said. As Magia shook her aching feet out of the puddle, the woman reached into her basket. "But you wouldn't want to go without your clever hat."

Magia's throat closed up again as the woman pressed a brilliant red wad of yarn into her hands. Tata . . .

Miss Grand leaned closer. "Blood and wolf tracks," she whispered. "And your hat lying right in the midst of it all. I'm telling you, it shook the breath from me. I've seen woodcutters taken before!"

Magia squeezed the swollen fibers of her hat. Its startling crimson glowed against the dim depths of the Puszcza. Tata always had her hat with him, in his pocket. If he no longer had it, then . . .

Magia jammed the red hat over her ears. As it chewed into her scalp, she shoved past Miss Grand, her axe tight in her fist, and ran toward home.

No smoke came from their chimney. Footprints lay unswept on the front porch. Magia banged her elbow as she rushed through the door.

"Tata!" she cried. Surely he was home. No matter how deep he went into the Puszcza, he always came home. "Tata! Mama!" she cried again. "Tata! Mama!"

There was no answer. No fire burned in the hearth. No meal was waiting. The house was dark. Magia struggled to adjust to the dim light. Why had someone left bundles of oddly shaped, scattered logs on the floor? She should gather them up; she should —

A wretched shudder of recognition buckled her knees, sending her to the ground. The logs were not logs.

Jan!

Magia dropped her axe and crawled to his body, which was nearest the door. His arms were folded underneath him, as if he'd risen and then collapsed to his bedroll. His feet were warmed only by socks. He hadn't been up long enough to put on his boots.

"Jan!" Magia cried. "Get up! Get up!" Jan was breathing, but his head lolled to one side, eyes closed; his body didn't twitch, not even when she yelled in his ear.

Magia crawled to Dorota and lifted her sister's head from her pillow, braids dangling. "Dorrie!" she whispered. "Dorrie, it's Magia! I need you!"

Dorota also took a breath, but it was slower than Jan's, as if she slept even deeper than he did.

Magia stumbled into Mama and Tata's room. Mama stretched across the bed.

"Mama!" cried Magia. "Wake up! Wake up!" She searched her mama's dress for blood. There was none. Her mother breathed, too, even if Magia couldn't wake her.

How long had they lain here, alive but not seeing? How long had Magia been gone? She'd only meant to take an hour . . .

Suddenly, Magia heard a noise in the other room. Tata! She stumbled out of the bedroom.

"Whatever did you do to the clock?" said a voice.

Magia stopped dead in her tracks. Miss Grand leaned against the door frame, taking in the motionless bodies with casual ease. She nodded at the clock. "It was such a pretty thing, wasn't it? And your tata was desperate to have it. Now look at what's happened when no one was here to wind it!"

Magia turned to see the clock. It was no longer making noise, and the face of it was covered in spiders—coarsely haired dung-black ones and bulbous, pale white ones and swarming clusters of minuscule, delicate brown ones. Their thick webs coated the clock's hands, and Magia could hardly see the circle of numbers, but she realized with a jolt that it had stopped just after six. What had happened in the hour Magia had taken?

Miss Grand walked past her to stand in front of the clock. "I expect it might work again," she said. "If someone knew how to fix it." With her right hand, she tapped the frozen face with a white key. The spiders inside the case quivered at the vibrations.

Magia felt a pit of ice form in her stomach. That key had been in Tata's pocket, too.

"My father was in the woods, ahead of me," she said slowly, but her voice shook. "Didn't you see him?"

A frown creased Miss Grand's face. "Oh, dear, it's clear you don't understand. Perhaps I should begin with when your tata came to see me this spring in Tysiak, just as you did last fall. I knew your mama was ill, of course, but he said the winter had only made her worse. He begged me for one of my flutes to cure her. I couldn't do that; the flutes cost far more than he could ever afford." Her frown deepened, and she began to peel off Pani Wolburska's shawls. Underneath, her shoulders and hips were draped with pink silk. "Still. I'd seen you, poor little one, wandering alone in the woods with your ill-stitched hat, telling me everything was fine at home when I knew it wasn't. So, I helped him with the gift of a clock."

A cold chill of sweat formed on Magia's forehead. She felt her fists open and close, open and close, as she tried to understand what this horrid woman was telling her.

Miss Grand seemed not to notice Magia's distress. "Of course, my temporal treasure was also more expensive than he could afford, so we worked out an arrangement." She glanced at Magia. "But, my dear, are you saying that you don't know where your father is? How worrisome."

Magia's head ached. "Tata went to work in the woods," she managed to whisper. "As always. He had my hat. And that key."

"Oh, my dear, did he now?" said Miss Grand. She dumped all of Pani Wolburska's shawls on the floor. "I'm sorry. As I said, there were wolf tracks . . . and blood.

But, as you know . . . everything has a price. Everything must be paid for."

Magia stared at the key, which Miss Grand was casually twirling in her fingers. Maybe if Magia got the key, she could wind the clock and everyone would wake up and Tata would come home and everything would be as it was.

In her head, though, Magia saw the piano lid, like a stiff wooden lip, banging into her hands. If she wanted the key, she, too, was going to have to start from the beginning. Apologize for the metronome. Beg. Promise to pay whatever it took to undo every twisted stitch that had led to this moment.

"I didn't mean to break your pig," she whispered.

Miss Grand's lips pursed. "I doubt that, my dear," she said. "But it's easy to say it was an accident, isn't it? To believe that we don't have real power. When we do. We do, my dear girl! Don't let anyone tell you differently."

When Magia didn't say anything, Miss Grand continued, "In any case, I quickly got over your clumsy mistake. I repaired my metronome, and I had my nimble-legged . . . *associates* . . . look for you. I was curious to know who could interfere with my magic. Alas. They only brought back the tales the Panie had been telling. Such nonsense! Then I tried to help you the day we met in the woods," she went on. "Alas, again: You were too afraid to join me. But when you went into the Puszcza once more, and meddled where you shouldn't have, I knew it was time."

Time? Time for what?

"I don't understand," said Magia.

"Do you like stories, my dear? Did your mama and tata ever tell you any?"

Magia was silent.

"Of course they did," said Miss Grand. "All parents do. But which ones are real and which ones are not?"

Magia still didn't answer. She didn't want to talk about Mama or Tata with this woman.

Miss Grand laughed loudly. "It's a trick question, my dear. The answer is: It doesn't MATTER." She laughed again, even louder. "All Stories, true or not, have the same power: They help us see outside our own lives, outside what is happening to us in that moment. They help us see the future and the past."

She reached up, unhooked the clock from its peg on the wall, and held it out in front of her with stiff arms, regarding its face as if it were a strange wooden child. "In fact, in some ways, Stories are like clocks. They make time visible."

Miss Grand looked up from the clock. Her eyes gripped Magia's. "But it appears that *you* can stop clocks. Break metronomes. And change Stories."

"No," Magia mumbled. "No, I can't." *I'm not good at anything,* she thought. *Except helping Tata. That's all I want. I want to be in the woods with him. I want my tata!* She hardly knew which words she was saying out loud and which ones were only in her head.

Miss Grand began to dance with the clock. *One, two, three. One, two, three. One, two, three. One, two, three.* Round and round she waltzed, stepping over the discarded shawls, while Magia stared, stupefied.

Suddenly, Miss Grand whirled to a stop; she cradled the clock in her arms and spoke to it. "You see, though, I don't want the Stories changed. They bring me everything I need." She cooed at the clock face. "Riches. Respect. Revenge. Yes, they do. Yes, they do."

Was the woman crazy? "Please," Magia begged. "Whatever I've changed, I'll change back! I'll do whatever you ask!"

Miss Grand's eyes were suddenly alert and hard.

"I think," she said, making her words tick from her lips as precisely as her metronome had clicked, "in light of our past—disagreements—we should talk about payment first. Your tata still owes me for this clock."

"How much?" said Magia. "How much wood does he . . . do we owe?"

"Who said anything about wood?" said Miss Grand. She leaned forward. "Why do you think there were wolf tracks? And blood? And how do you think my flutes howl with such wild and magnificent music?"

Magia felt strength drain from her body. It was as if she were suddenly back in Miss Grand's kitchen, while cage upon cage of quivering bone-white flutes screamed at her. Tata hadn't been chopping wood; he'd been—

"Your tata promised me bones," Miss Grand cackled. "Fifty fresh wolf bones! Straight from the Puszcza itself."

Oh, little lambs. Things were going so well. And now look where we are—lost.

If only we could see through the dark forest! If only we hadn't left the marked path! If only we could start this Story over, knowing what we do now. If only time were not so determined to run out.

Perhaps, if we are lucky, time will creep. Perhaps it will crawl. Perhaps, day after day after day, time will be sticky and tangled and slow. That way, we will have plenty of time to find our way.

Or perhaps, if we are luckier still, time will fly. Perhaps it will rush. Perhaps it will be smooth and straightforward and quick. That way, we will have no time to fear what lies ahead.

So which should we hope for? Which kind of time do we need? Here in the Puszcza, it all depends upon the tale. And whether you are a Wolf or a Girl.

Nonsense, you say. You must think we will believe anything! We can count our minutes and hours and days.

Can you, my lambs? Then count on this: As you ate up these words, two years of such minutes and hours and days have disappeared in our Story, never to return. Perhaps those years crawled. Perhaps they flew. Or perhaps you did not feel them go by at all?

No matter, my dears. You can still look away if you wish. The fire is laid. The pot is coming to a boil.

But we still have time.

· PART THREE ·

Two years later . . .

Pigs are fast.

It was a fact Martin had known in principle but hadn't fully comprehended until he saw a streak of grayish pink barreling toward his legs. With his one good paw, he clutched *The Vintner's Almanac* to his furry chest and ran for his tower.

Only seconds before, he'd been safe inside its thirty-foot walls. He'd been surrounded by shelf after curved shelf of books. Why, oh, why had he come outside? Why had he thought to compare that fascinating diagram in the almanac to the real roses that—

OOF.

Before Martin could finish his thought, he was slapped flat to the ground. His book flew far from his reach. The enormous shadow of a pig loomed over him.

Martin had never seen a full-grown pig in the Puszcza—only those squalling piglets who had thrown sticks at him long ago. And slashed his ear. And injured his paw. But Martin was certain he hadn't destroyed any more dwellings. He hadn't been more than a few steps from his tower in—

OUCH.

Two more pigs sat on him. They were somewhat smaller than the first pig, but still, their muscled haunches squashed his belly into the loamy black dirt. Then the largest pig—the one who had bowled Martin over—wrenched his forepaws together and tied them with a length of sinewy vine. Something rancid and slippery coated the fibers, making them supple and easier to cinch.

Dazedly, Martin tried to recall the page in *The Vintner's Almanac* that illustrated how to tie vines to an arbor—which, granted, wasn't the same as binding them to his own sturdy limbs, but surely the principle was similar? Did it detail any weakness in knotting such vines? Could he—

No. No, he couldn't. For while he was thinking, his hind legs were bound the same way. The knots bit into his pelt, reeking as they twisted into his flesh. A sickening mix of anger and fear made Martin's fur stand on end. He should've spent more time with his *Animalia Prodigica*, which detailed the anatomy of the porcine torso. Then he'd know exactly where to aim a blow against these bullies, if only—

HOLY CLAWS AND TEETH!

A jolt of pain seared his neck as he was grabbed by the ears, his head hoisted off the dirt. Before he could snap his jaws, a leather hood was jammed over his muzzle and rolled over his eyes. Each of his tufted ears was yanked through a pair of narrow slits in the top. Then the hood was laced behind the broad ruff of his neck with hard, jerky pulls. Martin was plunged into darkness.

"Aa-ooooooh!" he moaned in confusion. Except because of the stifling confines of the mask, the sound came out as: "Oooooh. Aa-ggggg."

"Get him out of here," said a deep, booming voice.

The two pigs sitting on Martin rose, grunting and stomping. Martin bucked and wrenched his body from side to side, but it was no use. He was seized by each trussed end. He was raised into the air like a rolled carpet. And then, in that undignified manner, he was carried off.

Soon Martin was deep into the forest, far from his tower and all his beloved books, for . . .

Pigs were fast. Yes. Martin knew that now.

Why had the pigs taken him, and where were they going? What would happen when they got there? And why hadn't they bothered talking to him before snatching him up?

He wondered if they knew *he* could speak. After all, when they had pounced upon him, he'd only howled. Maybe if he . . .

No. Any conversation from inside the hood and in his upside-down position might make him choke. Still, the idea that the pigs would treat him differently once they discovered his linguistic equality helped him endure the nauseating journey—even if it did nothing to ease the bites of twisting pain in his old wounds.

Finally, as he was contemplating howling once again, no matter how pitiful it would sound, the pigs lurched to a stop. A door banged open. Martin was pushed into a chair and his bound feet were shoved under a table. His bruised belly bumped against its hard square edge.

Then: *Snip. Clip. Rip!* Metal flashed as the stitches were torn from the hood's left eyehole, then the right. His muzzle, however, remained in place.

Martin blinked rapidly, and saw a broad-shouldered pig. The pig's face was smooth, his eyes sharp, and his nose exactly the right proportion to the breadth of his face. The two somewhat smaller pigs huddled together by the door.

Martin stretched his jaw against the confines of the muzzle and tried to recall lines from *En Garde! A Guide to Verbal Self-Defense.* He should say something to put his captors back on their cloven heels.

"Hat oo you hant?" he said.

Aargh. That wasn't how a verbal virtuoso began a conversation. Still, the lead pig—Martin decided to call him Biggest, for *En Garde* said naming your attacker would give you power over him—didn't seem surprised that Martin could speak. In fact, he loosened the leather muzzle so that Martin's jaw could move more easily, and then calmly seated himself at the opposite side of the table.

"We know you can track anything. Anyone. It's what wolves do best," Biggest said.

Martin was puzzled. Could wolves, in general, track anything? Anyone? He only knew what was true for one wolf—himself.

Biggest seemed to be waiting for a response, even though technically he'd never asked a question.

"I oo—*do* not track anything," said Martin carefully. If he spoke slowly, he could almost talk normally. "Or anyone. I like to read. And write." With a twinge of happiness, he thought that indeed, sometimes, he did both at the same time. His tower held five thousand books, and he'd read and made notes in all of them.

"In that case," said Biggest. "You're familiar with Stories, yes?"

"Hwat?" Martin said, the muzzle tripping up his tongue. *Stories?* He didn't want to talk about those.

Biggest gestured curtly to one of the pigs by the door. The pig lumbered over and placed a book on the table.

Martin leaned as far forward as his bound limbs would allow. The leather cover was warped and swollen, as if it had been dropped in water over and over, and the rough-edged paper between the bindings was a dull, ashen black, as if it had been burned. Martin cringed at the book's ill treatment. Who would do such a thing?

"This is a Story," Biggest said. "Are you familiar with it?"

This day was growing worse by the minute. Now Martin was going to have to lie, too. He growled to work up his courage. "I don't know anything about . . . Stories," he said. "I like facts. And the fact is, I don't want to converse with you at all. I want to go home."

Biggest rose from his chair. He walked behind Martin and grasped the leather hood by its laces. With a swift downward motion, he wrenched Martin's face over the book. Then, with his other hoof, the pig opened the book, revealing a fiercely bright image of a young girl wearing a cape. In mid-leap over her body hung a drooling, fanged wolf.

Martin's limbs clawed uselessly against the vines that held him. The book was uglier on the inside than on the outside! Who would create such a terrible scene? Wolves did not attack humans. He began to cough and choke. To his horror, his spittle landed on the book's pages.

"I see that I've whet your appetite," Biggest whispered, his voice sliding into Martin's ears like a knife. "Shall we . . . *converse* . . . now?" He tightened the laces, so that Martin could no longer breathe.

Panic surged in Martin's chest. He desperately wanted to close his eyes, but *En Garde* counseled that if one was cornered, one should maintain control and stay engaged, no matter how vicious the provocation. If he couldn't move his head, at least he could shift his eyes away from the book and scan the room for something, anything, that might help him redirect this encounter.

Blessed Jawbone of the Mother Wolf.

Martin froze. He'd been masked when they brought him in, but still—how had his nose missed this? A fireplace covered most of the wall. It was made of stone, with an opening big enough for . . .

"I'm waiting," Biggest said.

Martin tried to speak, but his chest felt as if he were submerged in a barrel of hot, heavy tar. He'd been here before! But he'd run from this place. Run from all Stories. How could he be back?

Above him, Biggest murmured, "And they say pigs are

stubborn." Brusquely, the pig tapped his blunt hoof against the lurid picture. "It's simple. We need you to bring us this girl. You will be well rewarded, I promise. After that, we'll let you go back to your tower, and your life." As if to emphasize this last word, he loosened the laces slightly, gifting Martin a minuscule sip of air.

With great effort, Martin shifted his eyes back to the figure on the page, huddled fearfully inside her soft, hooded cape. What did the pigs want with her? She didn't look at all like the girl who had sheltered him. How many girls were there in the world? He'd known only one—once—and she was deep in his past.

Then Martin thought of his tower, and how safe he would feel if he were ensconced there with his books and not quivering, his old wounds stabbing him, under the massive shadow of a deranged pig. He thought of all the beautiful books he'd left behind, and all the words in them.

Slowly, with the strength he had left, he plucked out the only word he knew was right.

"No," he said.

Biggest wrenched the laces closed, and this time, darkness consumed Martin. He pitched into the unyielding, rough edge of the table.

· · ◆ · ·

When Martin awoke, but before he opened his eyes, he felt weak sunlight on his fur. He stirred, testing his limbs. They were unbound, but matted and itchy. He wiggled his ears. They moved freely—no hood pressed against them or against his throat. Perhaps he'd had another of his terrible nightmares. Perhaps all along, he'd been in his tower, his sleep disturbed by too much time with his *Encyclopedia of Common Tools*, which made him dream of seam rippers and sharp-toothed saws. With hope in his heart, he opened his eyes.

He lay in a nest of trampled straw. Four brick walls confined him. The only window, through which eked the faintest touch of sunlight, was sealed shut. There were no books.

Martin licked his paws. One claw on his rear leg was torn away, clear to the nub. He could see circles of raw flesh where the vines had stripped the hair from his limbs. At least the brutish pigs had left him water. Slowly, he crawled to the metal bowl, which had been rudely left on the floor, along with a chunk of bread. He retrieved both from the grimy straw and placed them on the table. Seating himself, he picked up the bowl and drank the water with dignity. When he swallowed, however, he could feel the ache where the bite of the cinched hood had choked the air from him.

Martin ignored the chunk of bread. He didn't need to eat; he needed to escape. Walking stiffly on his paws, he made his way to the door. When he pulled at the handle, however, the massive thing didn't even creak on its sturdy metal hinges. As for the lone window, when he pressed his eye directly to the surface, he could see nothing out of it. More important, it was as tough as deep winter ice. His repeated attempts to smash it were only rewarded with a goose-egg lump to his forehead. The place was airtight.

In the stillness, however, Martin became aware of a sound—a wavering hum in his ears.

No, that wasn't accurate. He struggled to categorize the sound. It wasn't a hum. Was it a diffuse mutter? A subdued gurgle? Perhaps . . . a muted murmuration?

One thing was clear: It came from the chimney.

Martin turned slowly to the fireplace. When the girl had brought him to this house, the chimney had wailed upon their arrival. He remembered the lonesome sound: *Ay-yiiiiiih! Ay-yiiiiih! Ay-yihhhhhhh!* Until she'd silenced it with that wad of yarn she'd pulled from her pocket.

He swallowed his unease. The chimney was no longer howling, but it was still making an odd noise. If he was going to figure out how to escape, he was going to have to investigate all the parts of this house. Even the ones that frightened him. Even the ones whose smell he'd tried to forget.

As Martin approached the fireplace, his heart was in his throat. He stopped near the hearth and pricked up his ears. He was sure he should know what the sound was, but he didn't.

Think, he told himself. If the chimney was large enough to let him wiggle up and out—

He had to try. Bravely, he leaned forward and cautiously inserted his head inside the fireplace. He would keep his nostrils pressed shut, so he could smell nothing. He was only going to reach a paw up to—

Auuuugh. A gigantic spiderweb sucked into his muzzle, and the cloying silk stuck in the back of his throat. Those blasted spiders! They were everywhere! Martin rolled away from the fireplace, wracked with a loud, uncontrollable cough, which sounded as if he were barking. He tried to swallow the humiliating sound, so any pigs lurking outside wouldn't hear, but that only made him retch more. Finally, Martin ejected the wad of spiderweb onto the floor. *Augh.* Then he lay still, his heart pounding.

No one had come to see what the commotion was about. Maybe he should eat something before tackling the chimney again. Martin went back to the table and poked at the bread the pigs had left him. It was as hard as a stone and speckled with dirt. If the pigs ever bothered to check on him, he could use it as a weapon. He licked the bread.

Blech. It tasted of spider legs.

Tiredly, Martin curled up on the floor again. If only he could block out the pain in his stomach, the ache in his head, the throbbing places on his throat and paws! If only he had one book, only one, mind you, to distract him from . . . all this.

But he didn't. Closing his eyes, Martin sighed and stuck his nose deep into the straw. Beneath its grassy odor, there was the ordinary scent of Long Packed Dirt—and hovering in the background, the boring smell of Fired Clay Bricks. And . . . yet . . . something else . . .

His nostrils twitched. Slowly, he got back to his feet and put his nose to the floor, searching. What *was* that smell? And where was it coming from?

Once, his mother had named every scent for him. But since then, he'd been alone. His nose had been tucked inside an encyclopedia or an almanac, where the only odors were of Parchment Paper and Binding Glue. He'd stepped into his garden for food, certainly, but on the whole, he stayed within his tower's walls. He'd wanted nothing at all to do with the surrounding Puszcza and its smells. But now, every scent fought with every other scent, mixing and crowding and blurring.

Martin stopped. There it was! The sharp tang of it filled his nose, and every hair on his ill-treated body stood up.

Human Blood. *Hers.*

Oh, no, no, no! thought Martin. He shouldn't be dredging up long-buried odors!

Still, using his paws in a methodical, digging motion, Martin scratched at the dirt floor. He was only looking for information, he told himself. The same as opening one of his books. He pressed his muzzle against the scumbled earth. The smell grew stronger.

To his surprise, the girl's blood, even crystallized and faded, stank of Hidden Fear. How had he not known that? He remembered her as all arms, reaching and holding and carrying. He remembered her as comfort against his first taste of pain and blood. And he remembered the fierceness with which he'd struggled when she'd first picked him up, how he'd been all claws and teeth, scratching and biting and mewling and, well . . . panicking. Martin knew he'd only been a pup, but he cringed at how he might've hurt her.

He inhaled deeply again and, for the first time in a long while, remembered his human anatomy book. How his mother had pasted a scrap of cloth over a picture of the human heart. After his return to the tower, how carefully he'd avoided that book! And every other book. They were made by humans, after all.

It had made no difference. He still dreamed of the Story that had taken his mother. Of human feet approaching. Of boots made of animal skins and buttoned with bone. Choking and shrieking, Martin would wake, knocking books from the shelves in his panic.

Now, Martin withdrew his nose from the floor, and crawled as far away from the girl's smell as he could. He had to be careful. He might have read five thousand human books — oh, yes, after he'd stopped avoiding them, he'd plunged his nose into all of them, hoping to understand what had happened to him in the Puszcza. But even now, with the girl's scent lingering in his trembling nose, he still didn't know why the last time he'd left his tower, he'd found nothing good in the forest but her.

In the hour between deepest night and dawn, the hour the old tales call the Wolf Hour, Magia woke. Under her thin blanket, she sucked her breath back into her throat and listened.

Was that . . . ?

No.

Maybe.

She couldn't hear properly in the silence. It was as if the quieter she lay, the more the darkness threaded itself around her, stopping her ears with black knots of steady, thudding sound.

Magia reached one foot out from under the covers. Cold air bit into her toes. She listened again.

Was that her heart beating . . . or was it . . . ?

Magia double-wrapped herself in the blanket and stood. The bitterly cold floor numbed her feet. For a moment, she stopped in front of the fireplace and looked into the hearth. Mama used to whisper to the embers each morning, coddling them to life. Now Magia's breath, which puffed out in soft clouds, was the only heat and sound in the room.

Except . . .

In Mama and Tata's room . . .

Was that the smallest of . . ?

Magia opened the door. She'd moved them in here together. It seemed kinder that way. And maybe, if one stirred, the others might, too.

But her family remained as unmoving as on the first day she found them. Whatever Magia had thought she'd heard, whatever small voice or rustle of covers or rush of pulse, it wasn't in this room. The bodies of Mama, Jan, and Dorota lay, alive but motionless, underneath a fresh canopy of spiderwebs.

The thin blanket fell from Magia's shoulders. She was already dressed in Jan's hand-me-down pants, which fit now in length, but still bagged about her waist, and two of Tata's old shirts. She leaned against the cold stone of the fireplace and put on her socks. Then she reached for the mud-caked, worn-heeled boots near the door. She shrugged into Jan's shabby sweater, which fit her better now. It no longer smelled of him, but of her toil and sweat.

She tugged her red hat from its peg by the vacant fire. She remembered how angry she'd been with Tata when he'd said she couldn't come with him. How he'd taken her snarled, knotted, ill-matched, broken-yarned mess of a hat from her hands. If she'd never made the ugly thing, Tata might still be here.

Magia felt a surge of rage at the wolves that had left nothing of him but blood and their tracks. For months, she hadn't wanted to believe that her father was gone forever, but night after night of waiting for his step on the path had driven all hope from her. If he'd been alive, he would've come home by now. Only her guilt and rage were left, and they fueled her for what she had to do.

She looked out the window. The first light of morning had touched the rutted path. Beyond it, the humped back of the inky forest crouched, no single tree visible yet. On the wall beside her, the clock, clogged with spiders, watched her silently.

For days after she'd found her family, she'd torn away the wisps of sticky silk from her mother's face. From her brother's nose. From her sister's eyes. She'd chased spiders to the corners of the room, and beat them with a broom until their legs shriveled underneath their plump bodies. Then she'd swept an army of their black, clotted forms out of the house.

And finally, Magia had wept, for no matter what she did, more spiders poured into the house overnight. In the darkness, their swift and silent bodies wove blankets for her family, while outside, the sun and birds, nature's timekeepers, circled a world that never touched those she loved.

Now the clock's thin brass hands, sharp as pointed arrows, served only to mark the moment, two years ago, that Magia had stopped it to slip out before dawn. For her, it was always the Wolf Hour.

Magia pulled her red hat to her ears. Fibers of twisted yarn dug themselves, like stingers, into her flesh. Then she picked up her axe and opened the door.

"Please stay alive," she whispered to her family. "Please don't leave me while I'm gone."

Over the next set of dreary days, the sound that Martin had heard in the chimney repeated itself. It was a pattern, he'd determined—one he could, upon several tries, mimic. It wasn't like howling; this was more subtle, and required him to modulate his vocal cords in unfamiliar ways. What was it? And why did Martin feel that he should *know* what it was?

He'd already tried, bravely, to push away the spiderwebs in the fireplace, and yank at the handle on the damper. It had opened once before, he reasoned. It should open now. But he'd tugged. He'd twisted. He'd contorted his body into every angle he could think of to gain more leverage. The damper didn't budge. It didn't even creak as it should have, even if hobbled by inactivity. Rather, it resisted his efforts with a quiet but firm force. And it had hummed.

Martin had also tried appealing to his captors.

"You must let me go," he'd told the pigs firmly when they brought him food and water. "Wolves do not track girls! They don't drool on them, either. Perhaps your book wasn't properly sourced?"

The two pigs who came wouldn't respond. They made him crouch in the back of the room while they slid in the same bowl of water along with the same hardened hunks of bread. If he didn't do as they said, the beasts simply didn't leave any food.

Did they think he was going to eat *them*? How? They weighed more than he did! Besides, the idea of munching on another talking being made him queasy. Still, how bothersome that his wolfishness scared them . . . and yet, how little good their fear seemed to do him! He couldn't even get them to bring him something—anything! Even a seed catalog!—to read.

Martin left the disappointing fireplace and curled up beside the girl. Or what was left of her: her smell. He knew he should ignore it, but it was impossible, for he had quickly discovered that this girl smelled of Red.

That was absurd, Martin knew. Humans didn't smell of colors, not in any encyclopedia or reference book, no matter how antiquated the source. Furthermore, he had no idea what the color red looked like, exactly, for wolves' noses discerned more than their eyes ever could.

What he did know was that there was a book in his tower called *Mastering the Color Wheel*. Inside were pictures. When Martin paged through them, there was a "color," used by human artists, that burned from the delicious paintings. That color—spilling from human hearts in battle, streaking in slices of cloud across a dying sky, leaping from a shattered tree ablaze from lightning, and touching the cheeks of humans as they embraced—that color, he knew, from the accompanying text, was red. As red as the smell of the girl who had rescued him had been.

Martin put his nose to the scent steeped into the ground. How could he have fled from this girl? Even now, he could almost hear the warm *bu-bump*, *bu-bump* of her heart beating close to his, reminding him:

Once, he had been held. Once, he had been warm. Once, he had been loved.

Would he ever be again?

By the time Magia reached the clearing deep in the woods, the screams had stopped. She scanned the ground. In front of the cottage door were footprints. The marks were shallower at the heels than at the toes, for, of course, the creature had skipped. She always skipped. And there was also, if you paused—and were not skipping, but thinking, watching, deliberately approaching!—another set of prints.

Magia raised her boot and jammed her toe into one of the five-clawed indentations. She twisted her foot back and forth in the dirt, scrubbing away the mark. Her father had left her with a hard debt to pay, but at least, in paying it, she made sure the woods were rid of his killers.

She set her lips into a tight line and approached the cottage. At the doorstep lay a cake, its icing squashed into the dirt. A stream of ants swarmed over the sticky mess. The door was ajar. She pushed it open with the heel of her axe and stepped in.

The wolf sprawled on his side, his slightly open muzzle turned to the ceiling. Congealed drool flecked the fringes of his lips. The bedcovers, half off the bed, twisted under his thickly furred body, emerging like another tail from his splayed haunches. Only a torn nightcap dangled from one ear.

So. He hadn't bothered donning the nightgown. Too many buttons, Magia supposed.

She stepped closer. The pink skin of the wolf's under-belly bulged tightly; the sparse hairs there stood upright, bristling whitely in the single stream of sunlight that came in through the cottage's window. The weight of what was inside him made his stomach loll against the packed dirt of the floor like a tongue.

Magia knelt beside his swollen body and slid her hand down the axe's handle until she grasped the blunt end of the blade. Then she took the blade and angled it precisely against the wolf's trembling belly.

This was the moment Magia dreaded most. The moment when all her rage and guilt failed her, and she was haunted by the image of the trembling, matted body of the pup she'd found. But — she told herself —

This animal didn't have white paws, one of them maimed.

This animal didn't have three slashing scars on its left ear.

This animal didn't have eyes that shone up at her like river stones.

This animal was not her wolf.

She put a hand against his twitching muzzle and pressed his head to the floor. She leaned in until her mouth hovered over his tufted ear.

"I'm sorry," she whispered, not kindly, "but this is the end." She sliced into flesh.

The wolf's last breath was a scream that died into air after three choking gasps. Then an old woman, her saggy skin loose, sat up from the wolf's belly.

"Stop gawking," Miss Grand barked as she reached for the cloth Magia handed her to clean herself. "And mind you don't stain my fresh clothes! Is the fire laid?"

Magia avoided stepping on the exposed entrails as she gave Miss Grand her pink silk dress and clean boots. The old woman took the gown and turned her back. The vertebrae of her spine spiked and twisted, corkscrewing as she bent her withered neck to put the billowing fine cloth over it. She tugged on the boots with little huffs. Then she swished out the door.

The other body lay, not moving, inside the wolf's belly, like a hairball. Magia briefly wondered, as she always did, what it was like to be eaten whole. It was better than being eaten piece by piece, she supposed. She poked a finger into the puffy pelt of the cape. "Get up!" she commanded.

The hairball curled into an even tighter lump.

"You're going to live," she said. "Get up! Look around!" For good measure, she firmly thumped the back of it with the handle of her axe.

The lump whimpered.

Magia reached under the creature's neck and felt for the ties that kept the hood in place. Yes. There. Knotted in a delicate bow. Her fingers deftly slipped the loops of thin silk one from the other. She grasped the cloth where it peaked into a point over the quivering head, and remembered, all over again, how dazzlingly inviting the cape had been when she'd first encountered it, coiled in Miss Grand's basket near the woods. What Magia hadn't known then was how Miss Grand, with the help of her poisoned cakes, made the cape speak of wildness and wonder to each person who encountered it. Even now, a fierce knot of desire flamed in her chest. If she were to don this cape, she would be free to walk anywhere she pleased, do as she pleased, and be as she—

Lies. Lies. Lies.

Angrily, Magia yanked the cape up and away. It came off, all of a piece. The creature squalled. How flat its teeth were! How pink its face! How—

OUCH! How hard the girl could kick!

For it was a girl, no matter how much Magia thought of it as a foreign creature. A girl like her. With two feet and two hands and two eyes, which now raged in her face as she leapt up and pummeled Magia, trying to get at the cape. Magia tasted blood in her mouth and breathed out slowly. Anger and pain would change nothing.

Deliberately, she shoved the girl backward, knocking her to the floor. Magia used that split second of time to put down her axe. Swiftly, she secured the cape beneath the blade as bait. She poised herself beside it.

What had the cape promised this girl? What longing, what desire, what hope was it offering, even now? What did it matter? The crimson cape was tinged with the Puszcza's wild magic, and like Miss Grand's flutes, left those seduced by it hungrier for it than before.

The girl climbed halfway to her feet. Her head low, she threw herself at the pinned cape on the floor.

Deftly, Magia grabbed the tail of the girl's hair. She twisted the thick strands into a tight coil until her fingers were against the scalp. She forced the girl's head under her forearm. In seconds, her swirling fists hit only air. Magia held the writhing, sobbing thing and spoke softly:

"Do you remember who you are?"

The girl shook and spat and gnashed her teeth.

Magia waited.

The girl thrashed and struck her own face. She began to bite her lips.

Magia felt a pang of pity, but she didn't let go. She herself had been numbed in Miss Grand's cape and lost everything. How hard it was to be woken to your own folly.

She kept the girl's head tucked safely downward and her eyes away from the door. Miss Grand was now dragging the wolf from the cottage, the red of its blood soaking into the floorboards. Its body would soon be boiled for its bones, and the blood—once Magia had cleaned it from the floor—would make the cape crimson with promise.

Finally, the girl shrieked out real words. "He ATE me!" she wailed. "He ate me. He ate me!"

"Yes," said Magia. "There are worse things."

As Biggest stepped into the house, Martin knew he should make a break for the door. Both of Biggest's forefeet were holding a tray, and under his arm was a large book. His captor was compromised, vulnerable, disadvantaged.

But Martin couldn't move. Everything in the room was blurry except for that tray. It held two heavy silver forks, two folded, creamy white napkins, two china plates, twin mugs sloshing with tea . . . and a whole chicken! The room filled with the intoxicating odor of meat as Biggest used his hind leg to jig the door closed behind him.

Biggest slid the tray onto the table, and then put the book on the floor. Martin recognized it as the one with the terrible wolf pictures, and he shuddered. "Perhaps . . . ," said Biggest, and then he stopped awkwardly. The pig shifted from hoof to hoof, regarding Martin. Martin stared back, keeping his nose alert. Why was Biggest acting deferential? Because it *was* an act. Obviously.

Finally, the pig cleared his throat. "Perhaps I was mistaken in treating you as the enemy," he said. He made a show of indicating the chicken on the tray. It glistened with fat. "Shall we eat together?" He pompously pulled out one of the chairs, and, with a grand gesture, indicated that Martin should sit in it. "And discuss our mutual interests?"

Martin felt a stab of fury. What did the pig mean by *discuss*? Or *mutual interests*? The brute had choked him! He thought briefly of using his unmuzzled teeth to nip the pig. And yet—when he gazed at the sweet-smelling chicken, his empty stomach contracted. Martin cautiously raised his tail and lowered his bottom into his seat.

Meanwhile, Biggest had settled himself in the other chair, and was tying a napkin about his corpulent neck. Then he began to tear chunks of meat from the chicken with his fork. Place them slowly into his mouth. And chew them with deliberate, delicate bites. Between each bite, the pig didn't put down his utensil. Instead, he deliberately held his fork upright, almost imperceptibly tilted in Martin's direction.

Martin wanted to laugh. Did the pig think a fork would be defense against a wolf's claws and teeth? At the same time, a flood of saliva filled his dry throat. The chicken was disappearing into the pig's mouth, quickly!

No. He wouldn't take this pig's offerings. Not after what Biggest had done to him. Martin lifted his ears as high as they would go. "I do not have any mutual interests with you," he said. "You snatched me from my home, and I want to go back there. Now."

Biggest paused in his eating. He wiped his mouth with the napkin, then delicately circled his snout to remove any meat there. Finally, he slowly released the fork, letting it rest on his plate. He took a breath and looked at Martin.

"Ah, but we do have mutual interests," he said. He paused, and leaned closer. "We are both animals."

Animals? Well, yes, technically, they were. However, one of these animals had kidnapped the other animal, so if Biggest meant that his actions were to be explained by the laws of nature, Martin would have volumes to say about that.

"Pigs," Biggest said, in a lecturing tone, "are communal beings. We're born in litters of three to nine. We live, always, in the company of other pigs. Even after we're adults."

Martin tried to look interested, but the smell of the remaining chicken was filling his nose.

"The other pigs you've seen are my brothers," Biggest continued. "Do they have their faults? Yes. Nevertheless, I care for them as if they were as wise as I am. Which they are not. Not by a long shot. I believe you met them before this recent unpleasantness?"

Martin opened his muzzle, and then shut it again. He'd met some pigs once before, at the straw and mud houses, but they had been juvenile specimens. Vicious, but definitely little.

As if he could read Martin's thoughts, Biggest chuckled. "Oh, I see you're confused. We're bigger now. As you are."

Martin was silent. Of course. He'd been safe in his tower for two years. The piglets had grown—bigger AND meaner.

"I, of course, never met you," said Biggest. "If I had seen you that morning, I would've . . . uh . . . greeted you properly. Perhaps we would have had a meal together." Here, he pushed the remaining chicken closer to Martin. Several slices of flesh were left on the thigh bone. Martin ignored it.

Biggest went on, "Instead, from what my brothers told me, and what we could tell by your paw prints, you chased them—but then headed off in a different direction entirely. Would you care to tell me why?"

"I heard a howl," said Martin slowly, trying to figure out how little he could say and yet still draw out information from this pig. "I . . . I thought it was . . . someone I knew."

"Ah," said Biggest. "I see. You left our Story for another one. We spent a long time trying to figure that one out."

Martin felt a stab of panic. He looked up from the chicken. *Our Story?* Did that mean—

"Am I in a Story now, too?" The words squeaked from his mouth in a higher pitch than he intended. "But . . . ," he started. "But . . . there are no humans here!"

"Quite correct," said Biggest quickly. "This place is ours." He took a lengthy sip of tea. He didn't look Martin in the eyes.

Martin decided the pig was nervous. How could he use that to his advantage? He had no idea.

"Anyway," Biggest said. "Let's get back to my point. Pigs live in groups. So should wolves. But—you're alone. That isn't normal."

Not normal? This from a pig who drank tea from a china cup? And yet, Martin felt an underlying, dangerous surge of self-pity. He was alone. That was a fact.

"Or am I wrong?" continued Biggest. He rested the tea-cup on the table. His voice rose. "Are there more of you? A mother and father, perhaps?"

Martin thought the hood had choked him; he was unprepared for how this question would take the air out of him again. He'd never known his father. And, ensconced in his tower of books, he'd tried to forget the day he'd lost his mother, too. Instead, he'd devoured his *Guide to Beetle Migration Patterns* and his *Atlas of Winter Constellations* and his trusty, well-pawed dictionary. Over and over. Plus countless other books. Those were his pack now.

Biggest didn't need to know all that. He did need to be reminded that he was only a pig. Martin recalled the words of *En Garde! A Guide to Verbal Self-Defense*: When backed into a corner, parry.

"Calling your brothers 'family' is imprecise," Martin said curtly. "I think you mean that since you were birthed by the same mother, they are your *littermates*."

Biggest slammed a hoof down sharply. Cups and plates clattered into one another and what was left of the chicken nearly jumped off the table. "Do you always hide behind words?" the pig cried. "Yes! They are my littermates! We have the same mama! But you're not worthy to say her name!" To Martin's shock, tears filled Biggest's eyes. "Mama was wise. Mama was strong. She taught us how to live so that everything ran like clockwork! If you don't help us, she will never be back!"

Martin was thoroughly confused. Why was their mother's absence his fault? "My parents are gone, too," he said harshly. "So — congratulations! You're right; I'm alone. That doesn't mean I can help you get *your* mother back."

"Perhaps that is true," said Biggest. "But the girl—she can."

Martin froze. "You still think I can track a girl for you?" he bluffed. "I've never even smelled one!"

Instead of answering, Biggest, with one gulp, finished the remainder of the chicken. Martin's stomach contracted in agony. Then the pig got up from the table and trotted to the matted spot on the floor where Martin had curled up, day after day. He put his snout to the ground and flipped the straw into the air.

The smell of Red bloomed, and Martin, unable to stop himself, closed his eyes and quivered.

"Oh, I think you know the scent well," Biggest said quietly.

Hours later, Magia stood tiredly in Miss Grand's garish pink parlor in Tysiak. After harvesting the wolf bones, she'd helped the woman carry them, secretly, into the city. It had been a long walk, and every step of it, Magia had thought of Tata, and how much she wished she could hear his voice, sharing with her the ways of the Puszcza. Instead, she was forced to listen to Miss Grand's grating words.

"It's been months now, my dear," said Miss Grand. "Years, even." Her fingers, studded with fat pink jewels, tapped against a rose-encrusted table. "I understood your reluctance in the early days, but this is sheer stubbornness." Her fingers casually moved from the table to the caged white flute awaiting a customer.

Magia didn't answer. She didn't want to delay her achingly long walk home with an argument. But Miss Grand unlatched the cage and picked up the flute. It quivered, as an arrow does before an archer sends the barbed shaft to its target.

"Don't you want to be more than a butcher of wolves?" Miss Grand said.

Heat drained from Magia, leaving her shaking with cold. It was true. She was a butcher. Eighteen wolves were dead at her hand. And still—

Magia owed more.

As Miss Grand brought the flute to her lips, Magia closed her eyes. She hadn't known how long paying the debt would take. Each wolf had to be harvested exactly as Miss Grand specified, in a manner according to the old Story, which preserved the magic deep in its bones. Now, pierced with holes, those bones moaned with pain or delight or whatever else Miss Grand desired.

Ay-yiiiiiih! Ay-yiiiiiih! Ay-yihhhhhhh!

Magia tried not to be swayed as Miss Grand pulled from the flute a shrill, fearsome song. Tried not to give Miss Grand anything to keep her here. If she was a killer, it was because the wolves had killed first! She wouldn't give in to Miss Grand's torture. She would not think about—

It was no use. The flute's music drew from her mind unbidden images of Tata, torn by wolves. She cried out in fury and terror.

Miss Grand immediately ceased playing and reached a hand to Magia. Magia wanted to shove the woman's knobby fingers away, but her strength had been consumed by the flute's song.

"I know it hurts," said Miss Grand, her fingers tightening on Magia's arm. "Losing my family hurt, too. But it need not hurt forever. You've already seen how my Stories draw magic from the Puszcza, and make it sing in these bone flutes. Think of what else I could teach you! If you will let go of the past, we can make a new future. Then the whole world will howl with longing for what only we can provide."

Magia took a long breath through her nose, but she couldn't speak, for her tongue felt dried to stiffness. Miss Grand's cheeks were flushed as she steered Magia toward the bookshelf between the windows. She swept an animated hand toward the garish row of books Magia had once longed for Mama to see. "Behold what I have collected! All the Old Stories of the Puszcza! What could we do together, with such riches at our command?"

Magia stared at the tomes, neatly bound in leather. The only Story that mattered to her was the one Miss Grand had woven two years ago. The one Magia was trapped in.

She was saved from answering by the rapid, repeated sound of the front door knocker. As the old lady hurried to answer it, Magia walked to the piano. As before, the china pig sat there, its brass bar rigid in its back. Magia knew Miss Grand didn't teach lessons anymore—she didn't need to—so why did the woman keep the thing? She pushed the bar to one side and let it go.

Tik tak.

Tik tak.

Magia watched the rigid bar clack out its rhythm, and heard Miss Grand sweep open the door in the hallway and greet the man waiting there.

Tik tak.

Tik tak.

Magia gazed at the pig's fat porcelain body, which rocked as the rod in its back kept up its hypnotic rhythm. Her gaze lingered on its broken right ear.

Tik tak.

Tik tak.

The sound made Magia feel numb. Once she'd been a girl who sang in this parlor. Now she was a woodcutter, doing what the debt demanded and her family required. Nothing more. But as her eyes returned to the thick spines of Miss Grand's books, she could feel that lie unravel. As of today, she'd delivered thirty-six perfectly shaped foreleg bones to Miss Grand's pantry. She was part of the Puszcza's darkness now.

There was always a poor girl who longed to have what she didn't. Always a girl, from near village or far, who reached for the cape and listened to its lies. Even when Magia rescued her from the wolf, it did no good. The girl either went mad or disappeared forever—claimed by the Puszcza, Miss Grand said.

Magia heard the front door close once more. The man would've taken the cage with the promised instrument in it. A musical rarity! A marvel! To be given to his wife, or his daughters. But not a one of them had any idea of the true horror of how the thing had come to be—they knew only that it made them shiver with delight, then hooked them on the forbidden taste of the dreaded, dangerous Puszcza, captured and tamed for their pleasure. Worse than that, those rich girls never gave a thought to who paid the true price for such magic, for they didn't disappear into the forest. Instead, Miss Grand lured only poor girls who could never own such a musical treasure. Thus, all of Tysiak believed that the flutes worked, that they kept their owners safe. No matter what the cost.

Miss Grand was back beside Magia. "So will you cling to your stubbornness?" she chided as she silenced the beat of the metronome. "Or will you let me teach you what the Puszcza has taught me—the things my mother couldn't? Stay here tonight."

Magia felt too tired to form sharp words. Instead, she thrust her fingers into her pants pocket, where they met the cold, ragged edge of a shard of pink china ear. To her satisfaction, she could still see a faint scar where the pig had gashed Miss Grand's forehead. Miss Grand might've fixed her precious metronome, but the scar and this broken bit were reminders that once Magia had been able to keep her own time. If she was patient, if she was prepared, if she was not like those poor mad girls, she would keep her own time again.

She said simply: "I have a home, and it's a far walk from here. I will not stay."

Biggest brushed off the straw he'd dislodged from the floor. He walked back to the table and seated himself across from Martin. Martin kept his eyes on the pig, but his nose was filled with the scent of the girl, which lingered in the air.

"Let me explain," Biggest said. He began to stack the empty dishes, one by one, on the tray. "Wolves are in short supply these days. At least, they are here." *Clink, clink.* Biggest gathered up the forks. "We were forced to apprehend you. For our abruptness, I apologize." Now he stopped his straightening and looked earnestly at Martin. "But we have a desperate problem. You see, our mama had an arrangement with an acquaintance. She was to work for this person — temporarily, you understand — while we were to establish a — a bed-and-breakfast here . . . for lost animals. But, as you've probably discovered, the chimney in this place is malfunctioning. It has done so since that girl visited. How can we host guests without a fire?

"That silly human girl! She wrecked everything! We've had no income for quite a while, and have been forced to wander about and scavenge our meals from wherever we could. Worst of all, our mama—poor Mama!—had to keep working, far away." Biggest looked genuinely distressed. "We haven't seen her for *years*. We can't afford to bring her back. Not since the girl ruined things!"

"How do you know it was her?" said Martin. "It could've been anyone."

Biggest reached down and picked up the battered book Martin had almost forgotten was beside the table.

"She was wearing red!" said Biggest, as if this settled it. The book's pages seemed to crackle with menace as he turned to the picture of the hooded girl overshadowed by a fanged, drooling wolf. "We found bits of red yarn in the straw! This must be her." Biggest tapped his hoof on the page, near the cowering girl's head. "It will be easy!" he said, almost begging. "You're already familiar with her smell from your stay with us. In fact, you could call up her scent in your dreams, could you not?"

Biggest was wrong. The girl in this book wasn't the same girl who'd rescued him. She wasn't the one who'd left blood and sweat in this place. She wasn't the human whose smell now permeated his world. This one was wearing a lacy dress and a cape. This one had a blank expression in her eyes; she probably smelled of nothing at all. This one didn't look like she would ever make him feel safe. This one, thought Martin, was not his Little Red.

Yes. That was a good name for her. He'd never learned her real one.

Biggest took his lack of words for refusal and rushed to speak again. "Look," he said. "I know this is difficult for you, but we're animals! We should stick together against humans, should we not? Don't you know what humans do to wolves?"

Biggest turned to another page in the book, and Martin recoiled. He'd seen this structure before! A cottage with the door ajar — and a tiny cake near the opening.

Suddenly, Martin could taste the sticky, soft crumb of the thing in his mouth. How leadenly sweet it had been, masking the bitterness beneath. Before Martin could stop him, Biggest turned the next page. In the picture was a human bed with human sleeping cloths on it. Beside the bed, a human candle for light. But, on the floor, blood poured from a four-legged body. As it had from his mother.

Martin twisted to one side and retched. There was nothing, however, in his stomach to throw up. His insides burned with emptiness.

When he turned gingerly back to the table, the book was closed. It was resting under Biggest's hoof.

"We would like our mama to return," said Biggest firmly. "I believe you would like to find the human who hurt yours." He tapped the book. "We cannot go into this Story. There are no pigs there. But you can. All you need to do is find the girl. Bring her back here. We need her to fix our chimney; make it work again. When she does, we'll give you this book. If you destroy it, humans will never use this Story to kill wolves again."

Martin felt dizzy. He had thousands of books, but he'd never destroyed one. What happened if you did?

Did the facts inside them die? Martin doubted this; but Stories—Stories might be different. *En Garde* would probably tell him to parry the pig's words. To feint and distract the brute as long as Martin possibly could, until he could figure out a way to escape.

Still, Biggest was offering Martin something the books in his tower never could. For all his reading, he still didn't understand why some humans were good and some were bad. And there was one he'd never, ever forgive. If he could go into this Story, and find *that* human . . . the one with the bone-buttoned shoes . . . the one who murdered his mother . . .

Martin had run out of things to consider. And his stomach was so empty he felt he might never be full ever again.

"Could I have time to think about it?" he said to Biggest.

Funny. This feint felt more like surrender.

Six wolves later, Magia once more stood in the pink parlor, exhausted from yet another bloody trip into the Puszcza. Before her, Miss Grand was seated primly on one of the twin sofas. She nibbled at a triangle of toast, shearing it of its sharp edge.

"Congratulations, my dear," the woman said. "You've worked hard to repay the debt—and you're close—only one more wolf!"

Magia hardly paid the woman mind. She'd counted every wolf and every bone and every step to the forest and back again. She didn't need Miss Grand to keep score, or delay her with false promises. Instead, she picked up her axe. Made sure her red hat was in her pocket. Squared her shoulders for the long walk through Tysiak.

"Of course, once you've paid me, you'll want time to see your family," Miss Grand nattered on. She took a sip of tea before continuing. "But once they are awake again . . . how will you live? How will you survive, peddling . . .

kindling and logs?" She said those last words as if they were stony pits she'd found in her rosy gooseberry jam.

Magia laughed. How would she live? Why, as she pleased! As soon as she paid the debt, Magia would leave the Story. Miss Grand would give her the key to the clock. She would wind the hideous timepiece, and Jan and Dorota and Mama would wake. Then Magia was going to smash the clock—and they would be free of Miss Grand's influence. Forever.

"If you want to keep getting swallowed by wolves, please do," she said. "I won't be there to release you." She turned toward the hallway. "I'll pay the debt. No more."

Miss Grand's teacup clinked as she set it down, and her skirts rustled as she rose. "Don't you want to know the truth about your tata before you decide to leave me for good?" she said calmly.

Magia stumbled, her boots bumping together. Turned to face Miss Grand. "What do you mean? Tata's . . ." After all these months, she still had to be careful with his name. It was like a tree branch that, pushed too hard, could whip back and slap her face. "He's . . . gone."

Miss Grand glided over her pink rug. "Oh, my dear, think!" she said. She gestured to Magia's restless hold on her axe. "You have a weapon! Didn't you wonder why your tata didn't use his? Why his axe and red hat didn't protect him against wolves? Don't you wonder what happened that day I found you, alone, deep in the woods? Why the Puszcza let *you* go?"

Magia shivered. She remembered how her feet had burned with cold when she woke to her toes in an icy puddle. How weak her legs had been. How strange her head. She remembered racing home, and the horrors she found there. But she hadn't thought to wonder why she'd been able to leave the forest, why she didn't end up in a wolf's belly like the other girls who donned the cape. She'd only wanted to go home. Like today.

"When you went missing, your tata came to me for help," said Miss Grand.

Magia nearly lost her grip on her axe. "You said . . ." She choked on the words. "You said . . . you said there were wolf tracks and blood . . ."

"There were. Because, like you, your tata was a woodcutter. There were always wolf tracks and blood when he was in the Story."

Magia had to dig her fingernails into the axe handle to keep from shaking. She knew it was true. Tata had not been himself the last few weeks of his life. Miss Grand, though, wasn't finished.

"At first, he accused me of luring you into the Story. I told him, on the contrary, that you — *you!* the littlest and most hungry — had resisted my cakes! Still, this time, you had poked your nose into my basket. Donned the cape. The Puszcza had you, ripe for the spoiling. Your tata begged for you to be spared that horror. He told me you were brave, smart, and an excellent woodswoman. He even showed me the hat you'd made —"

She flung out her hand, indicating the red hat dangling from Magia's pocket, and her voice gained volume. "I told him, yes, you were brave, yes, you were smart, and yes, you could be, one day, an excellent woodswoman. Sadly, on that day, however, the Story already had the woodcutter it needed: him."

Magia felt dizzy.

"What a father," said Miss Grand. "The Puszcza claimed him quickly, once he removed his red hat."

What was she saying? What had happened to Tata?

"Without his hat, he soon lost his way. So you could find yours."

Miss Grand gave a low whistle. From out of the rose-colored sofa cushions, from the depths of the pink yarn on the shag rug, from the painted cream pitcher on the mantle, from underneath the gem-edged plates set at the inlaid dining table, crawled an army of spiders. They quivered on their eight legs, and turned their eyes upon Magia.

"He became one of the many who have been lost in the Puszcza. I try to recruit those I can. Poor hungry souls. They go wherever I tell them to. And do whatever I ask."

Magia's knees wobbled, threatening to fell her. She'd *killed* spiders! Hundreds of them, as they'd poured into her house. She thought of the webs covering her family's faces, of the ghost webs in the forest, of . . . yes . . . the lost girls who had never come back. Never made it out of the Puszcza, mad or otherwise.

All of them . . . lost souls? Tata couldn't be . . . he wasn't . . . one of *them* . . . was he?

Miss Grand continued: "After he gave himself up for you to take his place in the Story, I uncaped you, of course.

I do keep my bargains. But I thought it best you didn't know the full extent of his sacrifice. Not then."

"I don't believe you!" said Magia furiously. It was as if each spider had invaded the nooks and crannies of her spine, until her entire back was a column of bristling fear and anger. "You always lie! Lie, and take, and cheat and—"

She stopped. From a fold of her long skirt, Miss Grand had withdrawn a simple red shape. The spiders crept closer, as if to see.

Tata's hat.

"Change him back!" cried Magia. "Change him back or I'll . . ." In her hand, she felt the weight of her axe. "I'll . . ." She'd never hurt a person before. But . . . this woman . . . she . . . she deserved it.

Miss Grand gave a melodramatic sigh. "Don't bother making threats," she said. "I don't have the power to change him back. I'm only a music teacher who sometimes sells flutes and clocks. Did you think I was more?"

Words failed Magia. All she could do was feel. And she felt like a raging fire, capable of exploding at any moment. She raised her blade.

"However," said Miss Grand, as if Magia hadn't even moved, "if you were to carry your poor spider-tata *out* of the Puszcza, then you might have a chance. You might return his red hat to him . . ." She pawed Tata's hat in her gnarled hands, kneading and poking and twisting it. ". . . and outside the grip of the Puszcza, he might be one of the few who could find his way again."

Magia's heart pounded; she thought it might snap her ribs.

"You will show me," she growled. "Show me where he took off the hat. Where he might be. *Now.*"

Miss Grand swiftly tucked Tata's hat back in the waistband of her long skirt. "Ah," she said. "That would require a new bargain, now, wouldn't it? I'll tell you what: I'll bring the hat with me into the Story tomorrow." She took a rosy crystal glass and popped it over one of the spiders. "Then, after you kill the wolf . . . after you release me from its belly . . . after we take its bones . . . then we'll discuss where you might look for your tata."

After. After. After.

Magia thought she might choke, thinking of the wolves she'd killed, how long she'd already waited for her time with Miss Grand and the Story to be finished. Her hand, without thinking, gripped the thick, rough fibers of the red hat in her pocket.

Then she watched as the spider crawled up the sheer sides of the glass and fell back again. Over and over and over.

As Magia had slain wolves, over and over and over, thinking they had been Tata's killers. All along, it had been a lie.

She lowered her axe. It would do no good to hurt this woman; Magia needed the knowledge that she had. "You're worse than a liar and a thief," she cried. "You're a *kania*, stalking traps for blood! You feed on the hurt and the dying!"

Miss Grand's face darkened. "Hurt? Dying? Look at me! What do you see? Everything fades! Everything loses its color!" She pulled at her hair until a steel-gray clump came off in her hand. "That. That was once gold." She held up one skinny arm. "This flesh—it was once tender and pink. In the end, every Story's the same. Everything turns gray. And then you get eaten!"

A pinch of color had formed in her dull cheeks, angry dots that glowed like a second set of eyes. "Don't you see?" she said. "The world is waiting to devour you. As it tried to devour me! Why should you let it? The Puszcza, and all its magic, will give you everything you need. Everything you desire. So no one can make you feel poor and alone again!"

Magia buried her fingers in the dull yarn of her hat. She had never felt poor and alone, not when she had her family. She couldn't take her eyes off the spiders, all the lost souls, as they brushed their legs together in an eerie dance.

The Puszcza had only one thing she needed: Tata. *Tata*! Somewhere, in the Puszcza, Tata was alive. To find him, she would do what she must.

Biggest escorted Martin out the door of the brick house. Then he called for his brothers, who came, their noses rippling and snuffling, to stand beside him. Martin knew what the pigs thought of him. They saw him as the picture in their hideous book. But he was nothing like that wolf, with its claws extended, its teeth dripping with saliva, and its eyes large with desire. Even if his stomach, starved of food, was pinching and clawing at him, even daring him to attack these foolish pigs.

The four animals reached the edge of the clearing, where the forest began. Martin blinked in the sunlight—his first in weeks.

"You know what to do?" said Biggest. "You have no questions?"

He shook his head—but of course, Martin had questions. Earlier, when he'd pressed his nose into the straw and inhaled one last heady smell of Red, it had made him dizzy. How had the girl's scent managed to stay strong for almost two years? More importantly, why did she have such a hold on him? Was she all things sweet and good, as he remembered, or was she part of the Puszcza's treacherous magic? After all, she was human.

Martin shook these doubts from his fur. He might not have all the facts, but he had the memory of Little Red. She'd helped him once. If he could find her, she would make everything right again.

He could think of no other way out.

Biggest put one cloven hoof on Martin's paw. He leaned in, and his breath hissed over Martin's face. "Find the girl," he said. "Bring her to us. That is your only hope of knowing the truth about your mother's murder—and destroying these human Stories forever."

Martin jerked away. How dare Biggest talk of his mother! And what did he care about the truth? The truth was that Martin had been too little to do anything about his mother's death. If only he'd been bigger! If only he'd been able to eat the human who had dragged her away! If only he'd been . . .

A full-grown wolf. As he was now.

Martin was startled by the vicious way this truth bit him. He was a wolf.

A WOLF.

If he stopped using his brain, and started using the hunger that was eating him up from the inside—if he let the desperate cries of his starving belly lead him—he could scent the girl.

Slowly, steadily, Martin drew in a parcel of air through his nostrils. He held it inside his warm body and closed his eyes. At first, he detected only the sharp scent of Snapped

Grass Blades where the pigs were trampling the earth, and the delicate traces of their Shed Skin Cells. Soon, however, he could detect other animals nearby, too, and the droplets of Sweat or Drool that they carelessly emitted. Their scents were laced with the pheromones of Fear and Love and Violence, each one a story of what had happened moments or days before.

My, what a big nose he had.

With each gulp of air, his blood grew hotter, ran thicker beneath his fur, and made his tongue swell inside his mouth. Soon, the meaty edges of his tongue pressed into the sharp points of his teeth. Soon, his ears—even the one that had been slashed long ago—pricked up, and between the lacerated pads of his toes, his claws flexed.

Then he leapt away from the braying pigs. He began to thread himself through the grasping limbs and thick underbrush of the forest. For, far off, in the deepest of the darkest places, he'd caught a whiff of Rich, Raw Blood. Her Blood.

"I am a wolf," he chanted to himself as he ran. "Wolf, wolf, WOLF!"

Biggest opened the warped and stained cover of the book he'd used to lure the wolf into the other Story. "Stop your squealing," he said to his brothers. "And I'll read the words to you."

Littlest and Middlest couldn't contain themselves. Middlest pointed to a picture and said, in a high-pitched voice, a voice he imagined would belong to a foolish girl: "Why, Grandmamma! Your hair is so wiry and thick!"

Littlest giggled violently until he fell over.

Biggest sighed. Sometimes, he wished he had no siblings. "Quiet!" he ordered. He turned to the page he'd carefully kept hidden from the wolf, and began to read.

The Girl eyed the barely visible path. "It will get me to Grandmamma's house?"

The Wolf nodded.

"You promise I'll be safe?"

When he nodded again, she left the marked path for the animal track. Once on it, her feet plunged into the darkest trees, her pace quickening to an urgent beat. She didn't notice one cake was missing from her basket.

The Wolf, meanwhile, dropped his nose to the well-traveled path and ran to Grandmamma's house, which he knew to be around the next curve. He knocked at the door with a gentle rapping of his paw.

"Who's there?" cried a thin voice.

Instead of answering, the Wolf held the iced pink cake to the window, his paw concealed beneath its wide sill.

"Oh, granddaughter!" Grandmamma cried. "You're here! Let me unlock the door."

The Wolf stood to the side so the old woman would have to open the hinges fully before seeing him. Then, with a rush of teeth and claws, he pushed his way inside the cottage and swallowed her whole.

Afterward, he opened the small chest of drawers and looked in horror at the tangle of clothing inside. The nightgowns were so tatted up with lace that his claws caught when he tried to remove one. So, instead, he secured to his hairy head a single crocheted cap, wincing as he tucked each large ear under it. Then he slid himself under the bedcovers to hide the rest of his hairy body. And he waited.

By the time the Girl arrived, the Wolf was hungry again. When a rap! rap! rap! came at

*the door, the Wolf heard in reply the thudding
rush of blood between his camouflaged ears.*

*"Come in, my dear!" he called, casting his
voice higher and lighter.*

*The Girl rushed in, tumbling over herself
with apology for her lateness.*

*"The path wound so trickily, Grandmamma!
There were false ends! Narrow places! Hidden
twists and turns! And I've lost my basket."*

*The Girl groped closer to the figure under
the covers. On the bedside table was a brass
plate, smeared with the waxy stub of a candle.*

*"My, what big teeth you have, Grandmamma!"
the Girl said as she leaned forward in the flicker-
ing light.*

"I wish my teeth were that big," interrupted Middlest.

"No, you don't," said Biggest, "for then they wouldn't
fit in your little head." He sighed. "Anyway, you don't
have to eat a girl, so it's not a problem."

"He's going to eat the girl?" squealed Littlest. "How
brave!"

"I think he's stupid," said Middlest. "Girls can't taste
very good."

"Brave!" shot back Littlest.

"Stupid!" said his brother.

Biggest closed the book. "Brave. Stupid," he said.
"What does it matter? As long as he plays his part."

Middlest got a funny look on his face. "Wait a minute," he said. "If the wolf EATS the girl . . . how will

she come back *here*? How will she fix our chimney? How will we get enough bones to pay the witch and get Mama back?"

Biggest smiled. "Oh, we don't need the girl at all. We only needed the wolf to go looking for her. Once he enters the witch's Story . . . ah . . . let's say: It doesn't end well for him."

Middlest and Littlest stared at him. Biggest coughed. "It will end well for *us*," he clarified, "because with his death, our debt to the witch will be paid. In lieu of bones, she demanded we send this particular wolf to her—alive. Now that we've sent him, Mama, our mama, will finally come home."

Someone was touching his right forepaw.

Martin kept his eyes closed. He could feel that he lay not on straw, as he had in the pigs' house, but on a bare wood floor.

The touch moved to his left ear. Rubbed the old scars there. Martin groaned and resisted coming fully awake. Was this a dream? He'd been hungry. Now he was . . . full.

Small fingers cupped his muzzle gently. Blooms of Red scented the air. "Is that you?" a voice said. "Is that really you?"

Martin let light spill into his eyes. If it was a dream, so be it. He had to know.

In front of him knelt a wild-haired girl. She was wearing pants that were too big for her, a coat that was too small, and a hat that was the ugliest specimen of millinery that Martin had ever seen. She was taller, broader, solemner than when they last met. But she smelled exactly the same. It was her. His girl. Little Red.

"Pleased to see you," Martin said. For some reason, he felt tears come into his eyes.

Little Red inhaled sharply. "You *can* speak! I thought I made up that part!"

Martin struggled against the lethargy spreading from his belly to his limbs. "Yes, I'm proficient in my speech," he said. "Books, you know." At her blank look, he moved on to more important things. "I didn't mean to leave you," he said. "I—" Martin floundered. He had words, but none of them were capacious enough. "I've missed you," he finally said.

"Oh," said Little Red. She bent her head and stroked his lame paw, over and over. "I've missed you, too."

Why had her voice lost its vigor? She was whispering. Martin tried to see around her to the rest of the room, but everything was foggy. A ponderous weight in his torso held him against the rough boards. Where was he? He remembered leaving the pigs. He remembered their frantic pawing and cacophony of squeals as he headed into the forest. After that . . . he wasn't sure.

"What's wrong with me?" he said. "Why can't I get up?"

Little Red's head remained bowed over his body. Her roughly knit cap glowed dully.

"We have to go," Martin said urgently, trying to quell the queasiness in his brain. If only she would look at him! "I told them I would be back soon. I told them I would bring you, too. I don't think we . . ." Twisting, hideous pangs gripped his stomach like iron bands. He forced himself to finish his sentence. ". . . have much time."

Little Red rested her hand on the swollen skin of his extended belly. Still, she said nothing. He thought everything would proceed smoothly once he'd found her. Now . . .

"Please?" he said. He was aware that he wasn't explaining things well. Inside his belly, a fresh agony of swelling pain began. He ignored it. "The pigs promised that if you will—"

Little Red raised her head. "Pigs?" she said.

Martin was relieved. She needed more facts. "I know it's improbable," he began again, "but there is an uncommonly sizable pig—who, oddly, drinks tea from a cup . . ."

A cascading wave of pain shook his stomach. Martin squeezed his eyes shut. He was babbling, but giving a good explanation was difficult when one felt like a seam ripper was being used on one's intestines.

"The damper in this pig's chimney doesn't open," he whispered, trying to hurry his tale. "I know; I've tried. He said you have to fix it. But be careful of the spiders."

"I don't understand," said Little Red. "Where? What pigs? Where are the spiders?"

Now a wisp of the repeated sound he'd heard inside the chimney was flitting to and fro inside Martin's head. He tried to bat it away. It was a gurgle. A murmuration, nothing more. Little Red needed the facts; if she had them, she would come with him.

But he couldn't lift his head from the floor. A terrifying

wave of fear flooded him. This wasn't how he thought it would be.

Once, he had been held. Once, he had been warm. Once, he had been . . .

Martin fought to open his muzzle, to describe the brick house where she'd held him. To his horror, all that floated out was one sticky strand of the melodious hum he'd heard for days.

Little Red cried out at the sound. "Where? Where did you hear this song?"

A song? That sound had been a song? With enormous effort, Martin formed the words she needed. "Where you kept me safe," he said. "In the house made of bricks."

He forced his eyes open. Little Red was bent to the ground at his belly, sobbing. Over her prone body, Martin saw an unmade bed, sheets spilling in disarray. A lace cap crumpled beside it.

As if he'd been tossed in a fire, Martin remembered in searing detail how he'd come to be here. And what he'd done.

He'd used his large nose to track Little Red. He'd used his alert ears to listen for the Story she was in. He'd used his sharp teeth to . . .

Oh, bewilderment, tumult, and despair!

Martin remembered the taste of the old woman's toe joints, the toughness of her weathered skin. He remembered the jaunty angle at which he'd set her lace cap over his enormous ears. He remembered the cottage door opening, the swish of a soft cape, and a voice calling out, "Why, Grandmamma! Your hair is so wiry and thick!"

Then the candle's flame had illuminated his large eyes, his large teeth, and his large ears, which bulged in lumps beneath the lace cap. He had raised himself up on his large white paws. With precision, he had clamped his large jaws about the girl's extended arm, and used it to pull her, whole, into his very, very large belly.

Then the candle, at the limit of its wick, had gone out.

· ◆ · ·

Little Red lifted her head from the floor. She'd ceased weeping.

"That chimney smelled of death," she said, her words deliberate but soft. "So I tied the damper closed. I thought I could change the Story. I couldn't. I can't change this one, either."

As Martin watched, she removed her ragged hat. Tucked it neatly under his torso. Then she picked up a well-oiled axe.

Martin didn't move. Beyond the girl, he could see the unmade bed. The space underneath it was large enough for a trembling pup to hide. He remembered crouching there as human feet approached, and how he'd been unable to smell anything. Now, with sudden clarity, he realized that the floorboards, although scrubbed over and over, reeked of Something Dark on the Floor. He was back in the house where his mother had died.

Hope left him as quickly as tendons snap from bone. Little Red had told him why the pigs' chimney didn't work. But she would never come with him to fix it.

"I'm sorry," Little Red said. "In this Story, I am the Woodcutter. And you are the Wolf."

She put her blade to his belly.

Miss Grand screeched as she rolled out of the wolf's belly. "You idiot! What kept you? I was suffocating!" She grasped the dangling bedsheet and dabbed entrails from her knobby chin. "Do I have to remind you that without me, you have no way to save your family or your father?" She picked up her fine pink silk clothes and tossed the filthy bedsheet at Magia, who gathered it to her chest as she turned away from the wolf.

Don't look at him, she told herself, *don't look.* And yet it was impossible not to smell the odor of anguished death in the room. The wolf's fur stank of it; the floorboards beneath him were heavy with blood. Her forehead was damp with a nauseous sweat, and she had to breathe in tight, short breaths to keep herself from vomiting. Had he understood why she had to do it?

How mournfully he had looked at her at the end. As if he knew what was coming.

Miss Grand, now dressed, grabbed Magia by the top of her hair. "What's wrong with you?" she demanded. She wrenched Magia's head upward and searched her face with shrewd eyes.

Magia could feel a scream forming as her head hung from the old woman's wiry hand. She pressed her lips closed. Miss Grand couldn't know. Couldn't know what this kill had done to her. Couldn't know how bitterly she despised her; hated the Story; hated her role in it. Magia had to choke that hate into quiet submission.

Her silence only made Miss Grand more suspicious. "And what did you do with your hat?" she said, her voice as biting as her grip. "Do you want to lose your way as your tata did?"

Magia resisted the fierce urge to grab her axe, which lay, still bloody, near the bed. "Of course not," she said. "I thought I was done with it. I threw it in the fire. May I have Tata's hat now? Now that I've done as you've asked? Please?"

Miss Grand yanked her to standing. "Is that why you took ages to release me?" she said. "You think I'm a fool? You left me in the wolf's belly while you searched for your father's hat! You thought you could take it from me and waltz away through the Puszcza with it!"

Magia choked back her anger. She'd hidden her own hat under the wolf, so she needed Tata's. All she had to do was form words in her mouth, sweet as cakes. "What good would that have done? I wouldn't have the faintest clue where to begin looking for him," she lied. "Only you know that."

"That's right, my dear," said Miss Grand. She dropped Magia abruptly and marched to the bed. She fished underneath the mattress. There was a flash of red as she waved Tata's hat in the air. "Think about that the next time you don't trust me!"

As Magia looked at Tata's red hat, a terrible wave of sorrow nearly took her feet from under her.

"You shouldn't have burned your hat, you foolish girl," Miss Grand scolded, but her anger seemed to have abated. "What if I don't give you this one? How will you find your way out of the Puszcza then?"

"Why, of course you will give it to me," Magia said, keeping her eyes on the hat and her voice determinedly calm. She humbly crept to Miss Grand's side. "I'm your woodcutter, the best there is. I know this Story inside and out. And, more than that . . ." Her stomach twisted in disgust at being close to this witch. Still, she made her eyes tilt to meet Miss Grand's. ". . . you know you want me by your side."

Miss Grand's colorless face flushed. "I don't know what you're going on about."

"Why, our terms, of course. This wolf fulfills the original fifty-bone bargain. If I agree to keep working for you, we should make a new bargain, shouldn't we?" said Magia.

Miss Grand was studying her, her face twitching. Never had Magia seen her look so hungry. Magia couldn't hurry this part; she would sound weak.

"It's not just for Tata," she continued. "It's that . . . I thought about what I'll do after my family wakes. My mother hated the Puszcza. And axes. And being far from Białowieża. She had big dreams for me, and she still will,

when I wake her. You—you're—different. You understand the work I was born to do. You know where I belong."
Magia was shocked to feel her chest quiver with excitement as she spun this sentence. How strange that being
powerless had made her good, at last, with words. If only
they were sweet enough . . .

Magia raised her palm to the hat that Miss Grand was
dangling, until its soft shape draped over her fingers. "I'll
continue to work with you if you give me this hat. And . . ."
She pushed forward, as if what she was asking was nothing at all. "And I need you to show me, today, where you
last saw my father. In return, I promise to stay and work
alongside you—just the two of us—until I find him and
return him to human form."

"The Puszcza is vast!" Miss Grand said, her voice
tinged with both hope and suspicion. "Even if I show you
where I last saw him, he's surely crawled from that spot!
How will you ever find one nit of a spider? You could . . .
be with me . . . forever . . ."

Magia's teeth clamped down at the thought of forever.
That wasn't going to happen. She knew where Tata was. The
wolf had told her. She shrugged, as if she were not selling
her soul. "It's better than not looking at all. And it won't
be wasted time, for you have much to teach me about the
Puszcza." She forced her lips to say the honeyed words.
"You see? I'm not as foolish as I was when I turned down
your fine cake, and your offer."

Miss Grand's lips creased into a bemused smile. "Don't
think I don't see how you're trying to feed me what I want
most to eat, my dear!" Her eyes searched Magia's as she

hesitantly stroked the girl's cheek. "I'm impressed. Your skill at reading me only proves what I knew at our first meeting: We're alike, you and I." Gradually, her fingers cupped Magia's face. "We're two peas in a pod. Two coins from the same pocket. Two roses, plucked from the same garden."

"Yes," said Magia. She couldn't bear the woman's fingers against her flesh a second longer. But she had to finish this. "We are so alike that I could become your daughter. And a *wiedźma* like you."

Miss Grand's breath caught once and held. Magia held hers, too. She forced herself to smile, and as she did, she could hear their two heartbeats align. Then the hat dropped into Magia's waiting hand.

It was a bargain. A good bargain.

"One more thing," Magia said. "You may show me Tata's last location after we harvest the wolf's bones, but I'd like the key to the clock now. I want to settle my last debt before I begin a new one." She made herself look at the dead wolf on the floor. His side gaped open, revealing the red-caped girl—an unmoving lump of sweetness like an undigested cake within. "Or aren't you happy with my work?"

Miss Grand didn't even glance at the body. "That's my girl," she said, a spark of admiration in her eyes. "Don't let anyone take advantage of you. Make them pay, immediately. Of course, I can't give you the key until we get home to Tysiak."

Magia ripped her eyes away from the wolf. No key? Had she done all this for—

"I hope you're not upset," Miss Grand said, smoothing her dress and smiling coyly. "You have to understand—anything can happen out here, and I wouldn't want to lose something precious. I keep the key close to my bones. We'll get it when we go home together. There's plenty of time for that, and more, now that you've realized what I can give you."

Go home. Together. The words cut into Magia.

"Now," said Miss Grand. "I assume you've laid the fire—expertly, as usual?"

"I did," said Magia, collecting herself, "but it may have lost its heat. Shall I go outside and attend to it, or do you want me to tidy up this beast first?"

"Of course you should tidy up," said Miss Grand. "I know that animal was dear to you." She jerked her head in the direction of the wolf. "But since I hoped you and I would be making a new start, it seemed time to cut your ties to the past."

She waited long enough to enjoy the shock that registered on Magia's face before moving toward the door. As she neared it, she said over her shoulder: "My spies are everywhere, my dear. They tell me everything you do in my Stories. Don't ever think you are alone."

As the door swung shut behind her, sealing out the sun, Magia slid to her knees at her wolf's side. Miss Grand had known! She'd known this was her wolf! And she'd sent him to be killed! The evidence of the woman's new cruelty was bitter in Magia's throat, but she couldn't dwell on it now. She'd wasted time! And words! Would it all be for nothing?

With halting breath, Magia fumbled for the ribbon that tied the cape about the girl's neck; latching her fingers firmly into it, she eased her out of the wolf's body. As usual, the mad creature couldn't acknowledge she was no longer in darkness, but she would survive. She always did in this Story.

Would the wolf?

Magia buried her face in the unbloodied fur of the wolf's neck and slipped her hands beneath his motionless body. He was cold. Had she thrown away her whole life for this one life? It could be so.

Then her trembling fingers touched a ridge of coarse, swollen stitches; her hat, where she'd tucked it under his wound, pulsed with blood. The wolf's blood. As she'd hoped.

With haste, Magia pressed the fiercely throbbing, vividly red hat upward, into the cut her blade had made. This was where she had no path to follow. She'd remade her hat once with the help of her own blood. Could she reknit a wolf's belly from his? Could she reweave this Story?

She was only a girl. A girl, hungry as all girls are, for the wild, wide darkness of the Puszcza. She, too, had once been tempted by the red cape; she was as much of a fool as the girl she'd released. The only difference was this wolf. They had been fire to each other in the cold of the cavernous fireplace, in the depths of a storm, in the darkest night of the Puszcza. He'd looked at her then with wide eyes, and she'd seen her own magic reflected in them. She had once kept him — and herself — safe.

If he was lost now, a piece of her would also forever be lost. Magia thought only of this as she drew the saved piece of pig's ear from her pocket. With its jagged edge, she cut her red hat to pieces, and used the blood-soaked yarn to pluck and lift, knit and knot; until the thirsty fibers of her hat, having gorged themselves on the wolf's blood and bone, held fast.

Then she whispered to herself a prayer. Opened the wolf's muzzle. Gave him breath after breath after breath. Until, with a shuddering gasp, he held on to the rhythm that she'd made for him — in and out, in and out — and his lungs took up the task on their own.

Magia sat back. He lived. Her wolf lived! Every inch of him, as battered and thin as he was.

The door to the cottage opened. "What's this?" shrieked Miss Grand. She loomed at Magia's shoulder, staring at the wolf as his chest rose and fell with new breath. "You've undone everything!"

This time, Magia didn't have any use for words. She took her axe by the blade end and thumped the sturdy handle backward into the old woman's forehead. Miss Grand keeled over, neatly, onto the bed.

A thimble-sized spider crept over Martin's muzzle. Its eight appendages made a hushed hissing as they steadily ascended his large nose. Behind the spider trailed a length of sticky silk, which draped softly into his fur. Martin couldn't bring himself to care. He'd swallowed two humans, and the girl he'd hoped would keep him safe had put an axe to his belly.

An *axe*. The blade had parted his skin. Its keen edge had cleaved him in two. One glint of metal, and now he was dead.

Wasn't he?

A throbbing ache consumed his belly, from his fore-paws to his tail. Oh, he was weak! And, honestly, *hungry*. If only a mouse would scamper by and faint at his feet! If only a plump bird would pop in the door and tumble, beak first, into his mouth!

Martin grunted again. What illogical thoughts he was having. Of course food wasn't going to drop by and visit him. He should open his eyes. He should rise. He should leave this place, dead or not.

And yet . . . something was amiss. He remembered being pinned to the floor by a prodigious weight. Pains had wracked his belly. Now, he felt oddly light. Now, his stomach pulsed with a gentle, throbbing sensation. With enormous effort, he opened his eyes and gazed at his torso.

Holy fur! His underbelly was crisscrossed with a patchwork of bumpy stitches!

Martin's breath quickened; he felt dizzy. He was alive, and someone had committed highly irregular surgery upon him. Who?

The fibers looked like the ones in Little Red's hat—but it couldn't have been her. She'd soberly placed an axe to his belly. And then, clearly, she'd abandoned him.

That pained him the most. He almost understood why she'd turned her blade against him—he'd devoured two of her own kind—but why hadn't she stayed to mourn him, if only a little? It was as if he were nothing more than a dead . . . *animal*. Why had he thought she would help him? She dallied in dangerous human Stories like the rest of them. "A Story can swallow you whole," his mother had warned him. "It can suck you in for days at a time. It can make you change who you think you are."

Exactly.

What he needed now, desperately, was to return to the life he knew—to go back to being alone in the safety of his tower. Then he could forget that Stories ever existed.

That the girl ever existed. He'd been wrong to think it could be different this time.

Awkwardly, he arched his aching neck. Slowly, he stumbled to standing. The room swirled about him, smelling of Danger and Distress. One paw at a time. One paw at a —

Martin halted. Not five paces from him, on the bed, was a human body. Frantically, he shook himself unsteadily from head to tail, trying to regain his mobility. He'd had enough of humans. He had to flee. Now! And yet, as he shakily padded toward the door, and freedom, a thought swelled to the forefront of his brain.

That wasn't *her* on the bed, was it?

Maybe she hadn't left him. Maybe she needed him. Maybe she—

He hobbled back toward the bed. The body's upper limbs were secured to the bedposts with bands of bright red cloth. When he peered over the edge, he saw that the eyes gazing calmly back at him weren't hers. They were those of the old woman he'd eaten.

Martin's stomach clenched as the fibers woven into his belly roiled and pinched. He shifted unsteadily on his paws. The old woman was *also* not dead?

The woman struggled against the bonds that were neatly knotted at each of her hands. He couldn't see her feet because a dingy blanket was twisted about them, as if she'd flailed against her bonds and only succeeded in tightening them. More of the cloth formed a slash over her mouth, preventing her from speaking.

Slowly, he reached a paw to the woman's face. Her eyes widened. For a full moment, the two of them stared at each other. He was alive. She was alive. Where was the truth in this Story? Martin ignored the increased prickling in his belly and tugged the gag from the human's mouth.

"Greetings," said the woman immediately. She wasn't as frightened as Martin thought she might be. "I'm Miss Grand."

Martin tilted his head to take in more of her appearance. Grand? Before, when . . . when he'd swallowed her . . . she'd been barefoot, and worn bedclothes; now she wore a fancier dress and shawl, but there was nothing grand about her. Except for the fact that she wasn't dead.

"I can see how civilized you're trying to be," said Miss Grand, if indeed that was her name. "That's not how it usually is when wolves meet humans, is it?" She struggled to sit up, but her bonds were too tight. "Would you mind . . . ?" she said, nodding at the cloth tying her hands. "I'm not comfortable."

Martin hesitated. He wanted to make up for behaving in a beastly manner, but he needed more facts.

"I'm sorry," he said. "I've recently found that my corporeal state wasn't as I expected. I'm having trouble assessing my current situation."

"Oh, my," said Miss Grand. "Such big words for *I was dead, but now I'm not*." She chuckled, then eyed him with curiosity, from his scarred ear to his lame front paw. Her gaze lingered on the patch on his belly. "Would it help if I told you how this Story usually goes?" she said kindly.

Martin was baffled. Why was she being pleasant? Still, she might give him what he wanted: the truth. He nodded.

"You are a wolf," said Miss Grand, settling back against her limp pillow. Her voice was soft and hypnotic. "I don't expect you to understand humans. Even you, though, can see this forest should make any decent child afraid." She purposefully tilted her head toward the dense trees visible through the open door.

Martin nodded again. Logical. The woods were frightening to *him*. And to his mother, who had repeatedly warned him against going into them. If only he'd listened.

"But . . . ," said Miss Grand, "there's always one girl who thinks she knows better. Who ignores the warnings and the rules. Not even the look of the place gives her pause—not the shadows, nor the heavy underbrush, nor the lack of established paths. Oh, no. She ignores all that, and prances into the forest, swirling her basket of cakes and twirling her cape, sending bursts of sugar into the air. What does she think will happen? The wolf tries to behave, he does. Until the besotted girl tells him exactly where she is going." Miss Grand's eyebrows drew together in a disapproving line. "She sends him directly to my house! Can you believe it?"

Martin could. He'd also been tricked. Lured. Led.

"I know, when he comes, I shouldn't let him in," Miss Grand said, her voice catching with a sob. "I know it's foolish! But . . . but . . . he shows me a cake! I think it's my granddaughter come to see me! I miss her terribly! Out here, I'm alone."

Martin was shocked at the amount of emotion pouring from this human. Before his eyes, she seemed to grow more fragile and helpless. He gently brought the edge of the blanket to her cheek and dabbed at the tear that threatened to roll into her mouth.

"Thank you," said Miss Grand. "You're a decent sort. As most wolves are, when not in the thrall of the Story. By the time the wolf gets to me, the poor thing is wild with hunger." She paused and looked away delicately. "You know what happens."

Martin did. He appreciated her not mentioning the details.

"Before long," Miss Grand continued, "the silly girl arrives, and lo and behold! She's eaten, too. If only she had half a brain! If only she would see, before it's too late, the trouble she's causing! She never does. We're both trapped. All we can do is wait in the wolf's belly for the woodcutter to rescue us."

Martin's ears quivered. "The woodcutter?"

"Why, yes," said Miss Grand. "The woodcutter always waltzes in, at the last minute, to save both the foolish girl and myself." She gazed at him sympathetically. "Unfortunately, her rescue usually costs the poor, duped wolf dearly."

Martin felt unsteady. "And this time?" he prompted her. "What happened this time? Why didn't I die?"

A wicked smile played on Miss Grand's lips. "I finally got the better of that last-minute heroine," she said, with coy satisfaction in her voice. "This time, I saw that you, my brave wolf, weren't . . . expired. So I snatched the wood-cutter's hat from her head, and I used it to dress your wound."

As the old woman studied his belly, Martin winced. It was as if the fibers were biting him! He knew wounds itched and burned as they healed—his anatomy book had told him so—but this was more than that. It felt like *bees*! He concealed his discomfort from Miss Grand.

"That was . . . sensible of you," said Martin. He hated to be stingy with his gratitude, but he needed more facts. "And how, then, did you end up secured to this bed?"

Miss Grand's words were smooth. "The other girl—the one with the bewitching cape—wasn't happy that I was aiding the wolf that had eaten her. I told her that we were all victims of the Story. She would have none of it. I managed to shred the cape so she couldn't use it again—but alas! She was younger and stronger than I. She tied me up with that cape, and left me here to rot."

"And the woodcutter?" Martin said carefully. "What happened to her after you took her hat?"

"I don't know," said Miss Grand. Her tone was weary, and redolent of defeat. "She left without looking back."

Martin's heart wrenched in his chest. It was as he'd thought: He'd been left to die alone. He could hardly stay upright against the surging pain.

"I doubt she lasted long without her hat," Miss Grand went on cheerfully. "I know this is hard to believe, and I

risk you doubting my word if I tell you this . . . but . . ."
She heaved an extended sigh, and then gazed directly
into his eyes. ". . . but . . . humans who work in woods as
deep as these can lose their way. To stay safe, they often
wear red hats. Red reminds such humans of the fires of
home, and the beating hearts of those they love. If they
lose the hats' protection, they can also lose their human
form. Have you not noticed the spiders that infest the
Puszcza? How they cling to you and beg for connection?"

Spiders? The forest could turn humans to spiders?

Little Red had spoken of spiders. She'd wanted to know
about the one he'd found in the chimney. The spider who
sang. Could that spider have been human once?

Suddenly, Martin remembered the sick girl he'd seen
disappear outside the cottage the day his mother died. When
Martin had sniffed the snow, all that he'd found was . . . a
spider. A spider scurrying into a lone patch of dry leaves
in the rapidly rising snow.

This woman could be telling him the truth. Which meant
that . . . Little Red . . . without her hat, she, too, could be,
at this moment . . .

Martin couldn't hold all this truth in him. He fled
outside.

Sure enough, there was a deliberate set of boot prints
marching away from the cottage. Little Red had left, and
not turned back. Could she even now . . . be a spider?

Why did he care? She'd put an axe to him, and then
abandoned him.

As Martin stood there, dizzy with change and loss, the
smell of smoke filled his nostrils. The cottage had no

fireplace. Instead, outside, there was a fire circle, in which flames dimly glowed. Over the embers hung an enormous cooking pot.

Martin raised his bent head. Was that pot . . . hadn't he seen such a pot . . . at the pigs' house, the night Little Red had rescued him? What was one old woman doing with such a large pot?

He inched closer. Near the pot was a stack of firewood for stoking the flames. And leaning against the wood was an instrument. It was pierced with holes. Carved with elaborate curlicues and dramatic totems. Martin recognized the squiggles from his music-theory book: Those markings were music. And the object was a flute.

Martin reached out a paw, and then drew it back again. A tremor shook his body. He didn't need a book to tell him what the flute had been made from. Beside it was a neat pile of bones. Achingly white, gracefully curved, infinitely strong, and devastatingly beautiful wolf bones.

Miss Grand had left out a piece of her sad tale. So had the pigs.

Martin padded, every hair bristling, back into the cottage. The old woman had been struggling against her bonds again. The blanket about her feet had fallen to the ground. She stilled when she saw him, but it was too late. Martin saw her boots. They were sewn from the delicate pelts of animals and buttoned with hooks of bone. Wolf bone.

It was her. The human who had dragged away his mother.

Martin had thought he'd been angry before, but now he recognized what anger truly was. It was as red as love, and as powerful. Once, he'd been too small to hold such anger. Now he was big.

"What did you do to my mother?" he growled.

"Oh, dear." The woman heaved a prolonged sigh. "I don't think we have time for another story."

"No stories," snarled Martin. "I want facts. There are wolf bones in your yard. What do you do to the wolves who die here?"

"Facts? You want facts?" Miss Grand's mouth wrung out a false smile. "Here's a fact. When the foolish girl without her cape runs, mewling, back into the forest, and the woodcutter departs, stuffed full of brave heroics: Who's left to pick the bones but me? Me, alone in the night.

"I could feel sorry for myself," Miss Grand said. "But I do not. Because . . . ," she went on, her voice gaining a lilt to it, "a wolf also knows the night, and the darkness, and the ache of fear. A wolf is everything we give it to swallow. We kill it and it comes back. We fight it and it never dies. It stalks us. We humans write stories to kill it, to defeat it, to boil it alive, to slice open its belly, but none of that works."

Her voice grew teeth.

"Because you can't truly kill a wolf. He's the wildness without which the world would be a pale shadow of itself. He makes us feel alive. He reminds us of the magic in our tame and failing human bones!"

The flush in her face spread to all her flesh. She pulsed with the urgency of what she was telling him.

"Who can resist that? No one! So I make beauty from loss! I carve flutes from the bones I take. Beautiful, wild, and magical flutes. It turns out that humans will pay the most astonishing amount of money for a taste of something truly alive. And with that, they stay safe from that aliveness . . . from the real world."

Martin saw again the instrument leaning casually against the stack of wood.

"You murdered my mother . . . AND my father . . . to sell what made them most alive?"

Miss Grand's voice subsided to a measured softness. "Oh, my poor dear, of course I did. I'm as hungry as you."

At her words, Martin's wounds bloomed with renewed fierceness.

"A story is nothing but trouble, is it not?" Miss Grand said, too kindly. "Opening things we'd rather had stayed closed."

The pain in his belly wouldn't let Martin move. He dropped his gaze. The fibers that basted his wound were brilliantly pulsing. Why had this woman sewn him up, only to cut him open again with her words? He wanted to rip out the stitches, rip out his own flesh if need be, to get rid of the pain, so he could devour it, and Miss Grand, for good.

"The truth is," Miss Grand was saying melodiously, "no one wants to change the Story. Its lies suit them. You and I, on the other hand . . ." As Martin looked back at her, her lips curved in a beauteous smile, even though a spider had begun to ascend the slope of her neck. "We don't want to be deceived ever again. We believe we can do better. Why don't you release me so we can?"

More spiders began to pour out of the cracks of the house and move toward the bed. Martin looked down at Miss Grand. *You and I?* The woman thought she could bind them both together with those words?

"Release you?" he said. "Never. That's not how it is when wolves meet humans."

He bared his teeth. Drooled on her fine clothes. Made her shake in her horrible, fancy boots.

Then, as a phalanx of spiders surged over the woman's body, Martin leapt out the door, away from the dank smell of the cottage.

As he did, he felt new strength surge through his limbs. That horrible human wasn't worth another second of his time, but he hoped those spiders would take hours to wrap her tightly in their webs and make a tasty meal of her and her lies. He wouldn't stay to find out. He inhaled the dangerously wild air of the Puszcza.

Little Red had said she'd thought she could change Stories—but that she'd failed. He wasn't going to fail. Not while there was a bone left in his body.

All Magia needed was time. Miss Grand had told her where the key to the clock was: near the bones at her house in Tysiak. And the wolf had told her where Tata was hiding when he'd sung a wisp of Tata's song: in the chimney of the brick house. She would follow the wolf's paw prints back to that house; she would scoop Tata's spider form to safety. When she brought him out of the Puszcza, she would return his red hat to him, and then she could only pray that he would be Tata again.

For now, though, Tata's hat was over her ears. The blood that flowed up to meet it warmed her scalp and tinged her cheeks a glowing pink. As she hurried on her way, Magia began to sing:

My wood feeds the fire
The fire feeds the pot
The pot feeds my family
And my family . . .

Magia's stride didn't slow, but her voice caught in her throat. She loved her family, desperately and dearly, even more now that she'd lived without them for two years. She also knew that she needed *more* than her family. She was alone in the Puszcza, and the Story had grown beyond her strength to control it. She might never get home.

So, as Magia followed the wolf's tracks, she added a new verse to Tata's song.

The fire feeds on wood
The pot feeds on bones
My hat feeds on blood
But I — I must walk alone . . .

Magia had sung this verse three times when two pigs spotted her.

She'd sung it three and a half times when they knocked her knees out from under her, sending her axe flying.

And after they bound her limbs, she wasn't singing at all. She was howling with fury.

"**W**hy didn't Biggest tell us that girls bite?" said Middlest.

"And kick!" said Littlest.

"And howl!" they both said together.

Why, if they hadn't knocked the axe from her hands, she would've chopped off their springy tails! For the girl they had captured wasn't like the picture in Biggest's book.

Oh, how she squirmed and tried to claw her way upright! But Littlest pushed her back, keeping a watch on her teeth. Middlest wrapped vines around the girl's wrists. Then they both shouldered her body against a tree. Biggest had said they didn't need a girl after all. Why had she come into their Story again?

Perhaps if they looked at her belongings, they could figure it out. Middlest went to pick up the girl's axe. Biggest would be pleased when they brought him a new tool. Next to the axe was something that had fallen from the girl's pocket. It was shiny.

EEEEEEEEEE!

Littlest trotted to his brother's side.

EEEEEEEEEE!

There, on the forest floor, lay their mama's ear.

"It's cold," said Middlest, his snout quivering as he nosed the ear. "And hard. *Soooo* hard."

Both pigs looked fearfully at the bound human, and then at the axe and the ear they were holding. What had this biting, kicking, howling girl done to their mama? What would she do to *them*?

Biggest had said the girl had been in the brick house before. That she'd broken their Story. That if they sent the wolf back to the witch, he would eat the girl, and everything would be fixed. As they stood, paralyzed with fear, the girl twisted against her bonds and gnashed her teeth. Then, when she realized she couldn't free herself, she snarled words at them.

"Take me to the brick house!"

Middlest and Littlest couldn't move a hoof.

"Or ELSE," said the wily human.

Middlest and Littlest knew what *or else* meant. Biggest said it all the time. Clutching the girl's axe and their mama's ear, they backed away from the girl where she lay, bound and furious. Then, with two flips of their tails, they turned and ran off.

When they got to the brick house, the two pigs were astonished at how quickly things happened. No sooner had they closed the door — and even before they could present Mama's ear or the axe to Biggest — than they heard what they had waited to hear for months and months and months:

Paws pounded at the door. A gravelly voice called out: "Let me in! I know what's wrong with the chimney! I can fix it! I can fix it!"

To be sure, it wasn't: *Little pigs! Little pigs! Let me come in!*

It was, however, a wolf!

"How will he fix our chimney?" whispered Littlest. He was so confused by the way their Story had been unraveling that he was glad to have one thing go right.

"I have no idea," said Biggest. He refused to whisper; his voice boomed. "If he does, we'll be ready for him."

Together, they heaved their massive iron pot closer to the fire. They rolled extra logs into the grate, and readied a match. Then, oh! How they squealed and carried on and ran about the house with frantic hoofbeats, simulating panic. But each move was choreographed. Planned. Prepared. No matter how hard the wolf pounded at the door, there was only one way he could come into this house.

Martin wasn't stupid. As he gazed into the dim maw of the pigs' chimney, he knew he should go home to his tower. What he didn't know, he'd learned. What he didn't have, he'd found. And what he didn't understand, he'd sniffed, and sniffed, and sniffed again and again, until he was filled with facts. Facts that made his whole body heavy, as if he'd swallowed rocks.

Fact: Little Red had told him that the pigs' chimney—*this* chimney—stank of Death.

Fact: On the night he'd been in this house as a pup, there'd been an enormous pot in the pigs' fireplace. The same kind of pot he'd seen at Miss Grand's.

Ergo: Between the evidence of the chimney's odor and the pot's diameter, it was highly likely that . . .

Fact: These pigs boiled wolves for their bones, too.

Martin's stomach roiled. His head ached. His eyes stung.

A story is like a spider, his mother had said. *It throws out one gauzy strand, and then another. You're intrigued.*

You watch as a pattern develops. Ooh! So pretty! And then you're stuck!

But how could he have foreseen this pattern? Martin put a paw to the knobby stitches of his wound. The pigs wouldn't let him in. It was true he hadn't brought them the girl, as he'd agreed, but . . . she . . . once she had . . . if only she would . . . again . . .

No. There was no point in going down that path. At this thought, Martin's wound ached fiercely; his brain felt fuzzy; and most of all, his heart hurt. But:

Fact: Little Red was gone. He could no longer count on her help.

Fact: If he wanted his paws on that dreadful Storybook the pigs had promised him, and the chance to destroy the Story once and for all, he would have to fix their broken damper himself.

Fact: If he did so, they would be able to use their chimney and their fireplace and their pot again, perhaps to boil more wolves for their bones. Even *his* bones. Still . . .

They had to catch him first, didn't they? He wasn't going to let himself be tricked into eating any more humans, and becoming slow and heavy again, was he? He was wiser now.

So — he would let the pigs believe him ignorant of the facts. At least until he had that evil book in his paws. Then . . .

Fact: He would devour that monstrosity. Down to the last distasteful page. Destroy every Story in it. For he was a wolf. All he needed was a way in.

Cautiously, Martin put his forelegs into the brick shaft of the chimney, bracing his claws against the rough sides. His heart pounded in his throat. The chimney was narrow! No wonder the pigs, with their ponderous porcine haunches, hadn't been able to investigate what obstructed their heat source.

He, on the other hand, was tapered and sleek. He excelled at squeezing and slinking. He put his head into the meager passageway.

Urrrrrgh. In the dim light, Martin's keen eyes registered substantial clumps of singed lupine hair in the nooks and crannies of the brick. A rank odor of Doom and Loss assailed his snout, and made his throat sting with its acidity. Little Red had said the chimney smelled of death. She hadn't been precise. The chimney reeked not of Death, but of the Death of Countless Wolves.

Martin seized his tongue in his teeth to keep from wailing. The last time he'd scented this smell, he'd been a pup. He'd thought he could run from it. So he had. He'd run and he'd run and he'd run. All the way back to the loneliness of his tower.

This time, he wouldn't flee. This time he would make sure this smell, and all those like it, would never clog his nostrils again. Martin slipped his upper body into the chimney. His forepaws trembled with the effort of keeping himself from plunging to the bottom of the shaft. His torn belly bumped against the jutting bricks. His breath came in irregular gasps. He was terrified, plain and simple.

Martin lowered himself another few feet into the darkness. He wedged each of his hind legs against the chimney walls, digging his claws into the brick and cursing his weakened state. If only he had a rope or some—

Urrrrrrrrgh. Martin recoiled, nearly catapulting himself out of the chimney. His eyes now saw what his nose hadn't. The walls of the chimney crawled with spiders. Hundreds of them! They dangled from webs, which spread thickly from nook to cranny, cranny to nook, across the breadth of the chimney. Not one of them was singing. Or susurrating. Or humming. Or speaking . . .

In fact, Martin believed they were hissing at him. What had Miss Grand called them? Lost souls? He wished they would be lost somewhere else. At least he had plenty of experience in combating the tickly things. One had to claim one's space.

"Move over," he muttered as his claws tore through the cloying strands. "Give way; get out of here; DISSIPATE!" Exactly the words he'd used on the interlopers whose webs blocked his way as he descended his tower stairs each morning. Only those spiders hadn't clung to his muzzle and descended with him into the darkness.

Soon, displaced spiders swarmed his ears, jamming his auditory canals with their plump bodies. Martin's head seethed with their sibilance. He wanted to howl. He was afraid, however, they would take that as an invitation to enter his mouth, too. Instead, he gritted his teeth and wiggled himself, spiders and all, into the belly of the chimney.

Deeper and deeper and deeper.

At last—near the bottom of the narrow passage-way—he saw the hard metal edges of the jammed damper. One final spiderweb was woven across it, but this one—

Layer upon layer of silk strands were twisted into bands as thick as rope. It was a creation as wonderfully wrought as the lacelike arteries and veins in his anatomy book! And at the center—

The strands that bound Martin's wound together contracted in a shudder of recognition. That wicked woman had told him that red reminded humans of the fires of home, and the beating hearts of those they love. No wonder the lost souls swarmed this chimney. Nestled in the heart of the spiral was a solitary piece of yarn.

Red yarn.

For the first time in his life, Martin knew he was truly seeing a color. It wove through the interlocking layers of the spiderweb like the sun-streaked clouds Martin had often seen of a morning from his tower; it reminded him of those days long ago when he'd woken, warm, his nose against a book, and knew that he need not stir from his snug bed, for his beautiful, resourceful mother would be there soon, to dangle a slender mouse tail before him. And then they would read a good, long book together.

Martin's eyes swam with tears. And yet, as he gazed at the web, he felt a stirring of joy, too. Little Red hadn't known what would happen when she tied the damper shut. She hadn't had all the facts. And yet—beauty had grown from her act of kindness.

The Little Red-Hearted One *had* changed this Story. What else had she changed?

Carefully he tucked his muzzle to his belly and contemplated the knitted web there. Why hadn't he died? Why hadn't the Story that devoured his mother devoured him?

The old woman had said that after Martin had been cut open, she'd snatched the woodcutter's hat from Little Red's head. Used it to repair his wound.

Martin recalled, with sudden clarity, that this wasn't correct. Little Red had taken her hat off BEFORE she'd raised her axe over him. Tucked it neatly under his belly. As if she'd planned all along to do something with it.

A rush of hope swelled Martin's heart. It was possible that Little Red hadn't left him to die. It was possible she'd closed his wound and saved his life yet again. Helped him find his way. Martin reached for the final, ropy tangle of spiderwebs sealing the damper. Maybe Little Red hadn't been able to change the Story that had killed his mother, but she'd changed *him*. And he was going to get that hideous book from the pigs, and destroy every Story in it.

Martin snapped, sliced, and slew each thick strand of spiderweb that blocked his way. The spiders resisted, of course, but although they swarmed, and bit, they were no match for a wolf. Soon, there was nothing left but the last crimson wisp of Little Red's hat, tied firmly to the closed damper. Delicately, Martin took the bit of yarn in his mouth and tugged it loose.

There.

Now he could go back to the pigs' door like a civilized animal and tell them that he'd fulfilled his part of the bargain. If they didn't honor their half . . . well . . . they couldn't stay inside their brick fortress forever. And if they stonewalled him . . . he now had a clear way in.

Exiting the chimney was harder, for Martin had to inch his way backward. Limb by limb by limb. *Up and out*, he told himself. *Up and out.*

He'd wedged himself halfway up the chimney, his back stiff against a particularly uneven piece of masonry, when the shaft around him darkened.

"We're grateful that you've fixed our little problem," said a familiar deep voice from above.

Martin didn't like having his backside to Biggest. Calmly, he called over his shoulder, "That is correct. I was unable to bring you the girl, but I have solved your dilemma nevertheless. I look forward to you keeping your end of our agreement."

"Certainly," said Biggest. "We're prepared to do that." He shifted away from the opening a moment and called out: "Brothers! The wolf is at hand!"

At his words, a scraping sound filled the chimney. Below him, Martin saw the long-dormant damper creak open! Through the opening, he saw a book—THE book—as it was tossed onto the waiting logs. Then he heard the sound of a match striking stone—and then—the lit match touched paper.

Pffft.

Smoke billowed up the chimney. It stung Martin's eyes and filled his throat. They were destroying the book! As he'd wished. All the Stories would die! But . . .

Below him, Martin saw the hook over the fireplace swing back into place. A giant pot of water filled his vision.

"I'm sorry," said Biggest. "I regret to inform you that we cannot let you leave this chimney."

Oh.

Martin squeezed up the chimney as fast as he could. "You let me go before!" he called out. "Why are you trying to kill me now? Now that I've done what you asked? I won't hurt you! This whole thing makes no sense."

"Of course it makes sense," said Biggest, "if you know that in the Puszcza, wolves do not die easily. You cannot die in our Story at all . . ."

Martin coughed and choked. He certainly felt like he was dying. The smoke was making him dizzy. His claws began to lose purchase on the walls. The spiders, too, were fleeing his body. They scurried over his hindquarters, heading for clear air.

". . . unless you willingly climb into our chimney," Biggest finished. "That's the way our Story ends."

Martin's head felt funny — as if, for a moment, his mother had nudged him with her snout. He could distinctly hear her telling him, again, about the stickiness of Stories.

And then you're stuck, she'd said. *You struggle, but you cannot get out. It's a trap!*

One spider hadn't fled the chimney. It was clinging to Martin's heavy—oh, so heavy—head, and—singing? He didn't know. He couldn't be certain. He didn't have all the facts—and there was no time to find more.

Martin had reached the top of the chimney, but Biggest was waiting for him.

Magia's mouth tasted of blood. Those loathsome
pigs! They had taken her axe and given her a potato-sized
bruise on her forehead, and the smelly vines they used to
cinch her wrists and ankles had scraped her skin raw as
she wriggled out of them. Worst of all, when she'd finally
managed to free herself, she was surrounded. The forest
floor swarmed with spiders. Thousands of them.

They had bitten her, of course. And now they obscured
the wolf's paw prints—the trail she'd been following to
find him. She couldn't see any marks in the swaying, rolling
sea of hissing legs. Nor could she find the pigs' hoofprints.
Soon, the spidery legs, like a broom, had swept away every
tread Magia might've followed to the brick house.

Magia spat out the blood that had gathered on her
tongue. She resisted scratching at the huge, swelling spider
bites that dotted her arms, and instead pulled Tata's hat
tighter over her ears. It made her horribly anxious and sad
to think of her father, waiting for her in the chimney and

singing. He could be close, so close! But she was running out of time.

Magia scanned her surroundings. She could name each and every tree:

The always-green *świerk* with its four-sided needles.

The sweet-smelling *sosna* with plump cones and needles in clumps of three.

The sturdy-trunked *dąb* from which the handle of her axe had been made.

And everywhere, the hard and heavy *buk*, which Tata said could live for hundreds of years, and whose low-limbed branches sheltered their home.

Oh! Home! The thought of it pierced Magia's heart. But which way was it?

Tata's red hat could tell her.

Magia cleared her mind of the pigs, and the spiders, and even of her wolf, alone with his wound. She prayed her stitches in him would hold, and if they did, that he would flee as far from the Story as he could. Then she concentrated on what her true story was. And where she wanted—no, needed—to go.

Slowly, her feet turned away from the deepest reaches of the Puszcza, away from her lost Tata, her lost axe, and her lost wolf. Even away from her home.

For there was no time to go there now. If she didn't get to Miss Grand's house and snatch the key while she still could, then she might never get it. Never wind the clock. Never free her family. If she did manage all that—then—well—Dorota and Jan and Mama—they would help her return for Tata. If he could survive that long. She said another prayer for him.

Don't worry, little one, she'd once told her wolf. *I'm going to make us somewhere to be safe.*

Magia didn't think there was any safe place left. She only thought that it was a long way to Tysiak, and she had to get there before Miss Grand did.

Smoke filled Martin's lungs. Above him, Biggest's hoof lifted, ready to send him to his death. Martin stared down at the waiting pot.

How long did water take to boil? According to his books, a liquid boils faster or slower depending on the size of the pot, the altitude at which it is placed, and, of course, the intensity of the fire underneath it, not to mention—

The bulging fibers in Martin's belly contracted. When he looked at them, they were as red as the flames under the pot. Why, it was as if he could hear his gut talking to him.

You don't need to take into account every variable, it seemed to say. *You don't need to use your brain at all. You know how long this water will take to boil. Know it for a fact.*

Martin couldn't believe it. His belly was right. He did know when this pot would boil—

Never.

Because he wasn't going to allow it to.

Martin allowed himself a brief moment of quiet glee. Then, as Biggest slammed his hoof down toward his head, Martin let go of the sides of the chimney.

The water, as he predicted, was only uncomfortable, not yet scalding. And when, instead of struggling to get out of the giant kettle, he used his weight to rock it back and forth until it tipped off the hook and crashed onto the hearth, Littlest and Middlest were so frightened by the noise and the flood of hot water that they didn't hit him with the pot lid, or try to tie him up with vines, or even bite him. They stood in front of the door, whimpering, and clutching a strange, shiny piece of pink porcelain.

Oh, how fascinating! Martin found he could see pink, too. Pink, of course, being a fainter kind of red.

Then the sudden squeals of Biggest echoed from the roof: "HELP, MY BROTHERS! I'M STUCK IN THE CHIMNEY! HELP!"

The two pigs scampered from the house.

Martin, his fur soaked, shook himself briefly. He hadn't planned for Biggest to lose his balance when his hoof only struck air, but if he had, that wasn't his concern. Martin stumbled free of the confines of the brick structure. He blinked and coughed in the fresh air.

Above him, Biggest yelled again: "NO, YOU DIMWITS! GO BACK IN! PUT OUT THE FIRE FIRST! THE SMOKE WILL KILL US ALL!"

The younger pigs rushed back into the house. Martin ignored all this. His work was done. He'd seen the Story that had killed his mother burn to ashes. He could go back to his tower. If that was what he wanted. Did he?

As if in answer, the fibers in his belly contracted again. They burned and twisted and chewed. This time, he was sure he heard words.

Once, he had been held. Once, he had been warm. Once, he had been loved.

If only he could be . . . again.

Martin tilted his muzzle to the breeze. Perhaps if he took a tiny — no — minuscule — no — infinitesimally insignificant sniff of air, he could know if Little Red's scent was anywhere still in the Puszcza. That couldn't hurt anything, could it?

But it could. It could hurt a lot. For when Martin did indeed scent Little Red, it turned out she was heading rapidly out of the woods.

Martin hesitated. Fear rose in his throat at the thought of going beyond the Puszcza, beyond everything he knew. Nor was he up to full speed, not yet. He had to be careful of his repaired belly. The same belly that was still talking to him. Was he going mad?

Once, he had been held,

it said.

Once, he had been warm,

it cried.

Once, he had been loved,

it sang.

Soon, the gloriously brilliant hat in his belly was beating out a rhythm so rich, so raw, so red that Martin knew he would reverberate to it forever. With a dazed clarity, he looked down at his repaired wound. He was a changed wolf.

Once, he had been held. Once, he had been warm. Once, he had been loved. If he wanted to, he could be, again. If—

If he would follow the girl. Wherever she was going.

So he did.

Magia trembled, her pulse rocking in her ears. Her legs, weary from the long walk to Tysiak, were as stiff as the pikes of the guards she'd avoided. The spider bites had itched and swelled, making her clumsy, slow, and exceedingly ill-tempered. She hadn't eaten in hours and hours.

Still, in the predawn darkness, she'd arrived at Miss Grand's house. The parlor had been eerily quiet, and no fire glowed in the maw of the fireplace. Magia had managed to grope her way carefully to the kitchen, and the thick shelves of the pantry. With desperate, shaking hands, she'd searched and searched and searched through the cages and the stacks of knobby, dry bones waiting to be carved into flutes.

The key wasn't there. Not anywhere! And now—

Tik tak.

Tik tak.

From down the hall, Magia's ears filled with the familiar sound of the metronome clicking steadily. Who had set it moving? Had someone come in the front door while she'd been in the gloom of the kitchen?

Magia crept down the hall, making her footsteps as soft as if she walked in snow. Cautiously, she craned her neck into the parlor.

There stood Miss Grand. She had escaped her bonds. She was gleefully listening to her pig metronome, and tottering, in her sleek, pink animal-skin boots, along to its rhythm.

Then Magia saw something else. Something that made her stop breathing.

Ow. Ow. Ow. Martin's eyes burned as they skittered from the rosy fuzziness of multiple rugs to the glowing pink swags of silk cloth that draped the pink-tinted windows to the pink piano that commanded the space between twin pink sofas. He had followed Little Red. This was the right place, his nose told him. But where was she? And what was that sound?

Tik tak.

Tik tak.

There on the piano was a fat china pig. A brass rod was stuck into its painted back, and the metal piece swayed from side to side, making a clicking sound.

Tik tak.

Tik tak.

Martin blinked his eyes to clear them. Was that a metronome? He recalled the page in his music-theory book that showed how such a timekeeper worked. But—

Blessed Jawbone of the Mother Wolf!

Leaning against the instrument, placidly regarding

him, was the woman who had killed his mother. In her hands was an axe.

Martin felt his hind legs gather into a knot of fury. He exploded from the doorway toward the human—and—

—stumbled, his body sluggishly staggering on four paws. Back and forth, back and forth, he swayed, barely able to stand.

Tik tak.

Tik tak.

Martin gazed with horror at the metronome. What was wrong with his limbs? Was that thing—the hideous piggish thing—*controlling* him?

Tik tak.

Tik tak.

The beat of the metronome grew louder. Martin felt groggy and weak. Yes. Something was definitely wrong. It wasn't his wounded belly, for as he'd traveled out of the forest, the red fibers had settled down. But now—he could feel that even his heart rate had slowed to the rhythm of the brightly painted pig.

"How—how did you get here?" he said.

Miss Grand laughed at his struggles to remain upright. "Come now. You know my friends would never leave me tied up in the forest. And this—this is my home. We all welcome you, most delightedly."

She gave a low whistle. From all corners of the parlor crawled a slow wave of spiders. They quivered on their eight legs and turned their many eyes upon Martin.

"Poor lost souls," said Miss Grand. "They will do anything for a chance to change their fate. And I have much to promise them." She smiled thinly. "Besides, if they hadn't helped, I would've simply waited for the Story to end. For time to run out."

Martin was dumbfounded. He stared at the axe glittering in her hands. He'd seen it before. That was Little Red's. But what could this woman mean? Time couldn't simply run out.

"Think about it," Miss Grand was saying. "Would I let myself be eaten if I wasn't sure I could escape? Sometimes, the woodcutter doesn't hear my screams. Or . . . he doesn't want to do his duty anymore. Or . . ." Her pale blue eyes were hard as they considered Martin. "There is an educated wolf. It happens. In that case, all I have to do is wait for the Wolf Hour to come again." She indicated the pinkish light that had begun to steal its way through her heavily cloaked window. "Then the Story starts over. Begins again, as I have written it."

At Martin's blank look, she twitched a thin arm toward a shelf above the rosy piano. Between the bookends, which were glossy-cheeked china girls with shepherds' staffs and blush-colored full skirts, perched a row of different colored tomes. Martin squinted to see the spines. Each of them, he noted, was authored by an "M. Grand." One of them, though, looked familiar. It was horribly stained, and well-used. And it was pink.

"The pigs *burned* that book," Martin said weakly, staring at the distressed cover. "I saw them!"

"Oh, my dear," said Miss Grand. "You don't think burning a book destroys a Story, do you? The pigs tried that before. It never worked." Then she hefted the axe in her hands and stepped toward him. "But we mustn't waste any more time on these explanations. The important thing is that you're supposed to be dead. And yet—here you are."

"I—I don't understand," said Martin. It was hard to think with that metronome pounding in his head. "Why do I have to be—dead?"

"Oh, my dear!" she said again. "It's simple. The girl promised me your bones. She promised me them in exchange for people she *really* loves—her family. It would be a horrible shame if she lost such a treasure for the likes of you."

Martin stared at the old woman's hideously pink shoes, and then at her weapon, which was coming closer and closer. He couldn't move a single limb. Had this whole long journey been nothing but an invitation to a trap? Why had he thought he could escape Stories, if his mother and father hadn't been able to?

"A bargain is a bargain," said Miss Grand, as she sidled closer. "You and that girl may think you can rewrite my Stories, but you cannot." She grasped his scarred ear with her clawlike fingers. "I am owed one more wolf. One more wolf and its bones."

Desperately, Martin tried to remember every book he'd ever read, searching for a fact that might save him. But there was none. Little Red had promised this woman his bones? But hadn't she tried to change the woman's Stories, too? What was true, and what was lies? He could no longer tell.

"Why not?" he parried, to hide his distress. "Why can't someone rewrite them?"

Miss Grand cackled, and drew his neck to the surface of the piano. "Because, you *beast*—a Story is nothing more than a sequence of events arranged in time. *My* time. And when I say it ends, it ends!"

Martin couldn't look at the axe anymore. He closed his eyes. He could picture thousands of ways these events could have been arranged differently. He could imagine a world of *good* endings. But no matter how hard he thought, the beat of the metronome was relentless and brutal. It struck each rational thought from his mind before he could catch it. Instead, it seemed to say:

You are a wolf. A wolf. A WOLF.
You should be dead.

*T*ik tak.

Tik tak.

Magia swayed on her feet at the sight of Miss Grand. She felt as helpless as if she'd been transported back to the day she'd first seen the evil woman. How Magia had struggled — right there! — to sing scales to make Mama happy. How bitter the fear that had squirmed into her throat when, instead, the china pig had spiraled off the edge of the piano. And how viciously Miss Grand had slammed the piano lid on Magia's fingers, leaving bruises that thrummed to this day.

Tik tak.

Tik tak.

But now there was no Dorota to defend her. No Jan to coax laughter from Magia's pain. There was only a wolf Magia had saved, and then lost. Saved, and then lost. And he was about to be killed again, for the metronome's beat was sucking the will to move from him.

Magia understood why Miss Grand thought she wouldn't interfere with this kill. Her debt—the one she owed for the clock—wasn't fully paid. If Magia didn't honor the bargain for fifty bones, the witch wouldn't honor it, either. There would be no other key. No chance to restart the clock that held her family in its spell.

The witch cackled.

"A bargain is a bargain," she was saying. "You and that girl may think you can rewrite my Stories, but you cannot."

"Why not?" the wolf blurted, his voice fuzzy and strange. "Why can't someone rewrite them?"

Miss Grand pressed the wolf's head against the piano. Quietly, she positioned Magia's axe over Martin's neck.

"Because, you *beast*—a Story is nothing but a sequence of events arranged in time. *My* time." She looked directly at Magia. "And when I say it ends, it ends!"

To Magia's horror, the wolf closed his eyes. Accepted his fate. Nothing but the sound of the ticking metronome filled the vastly pink parlor.

Magia was pierced with a dreadful, helpless sorrow. Miss Grand had her axe—and everything else Magia treasured. What could she do?

She knew only what she would *not* do. She would not let her wolf die alone. So, she opened her mouth—

And she howled.

The wolf's fur stood on end. There was a gleam of his bright teeth as his muzzle parted in astonishment. And then Magia saw his eyes snap open and lock on to hers.

Oh, my wolf! she sang. *You know this melody! Sing with me! Sing!*

For what was a howl but a song? A song of hunger, and a song of love.

Martin's eyes swam with tears. He knew this song. It wasn't the tender one she'd charmed him with in the brick house, but it was one he had heard before, wailing though the Puszcza. Little Red had sung then of blood, and things breaking; of an angry flaring of fire, and a sudden, desperate darkness. But he'd never answered her. He'd never told her how hungry he was, too.

The wolf shifted his muzzle against the piano. Then, to the ends of the pink parlor, he loosed the most beautiful sound he'd made in two years.

Ah—whoooo! Ah—whooooo! Ah—whoooooooooooo!

The garish books on Miss Grand's shelf wobbled. The rose-decked teacups shivered. The pink curtains swayed. The stiff arms of the twin sofas quivered.

Now that he'd started, Martin couldn't stop. Everything he'd lost. Everything he'd found. All the things, good and bad, that had happened to him. They were all there, entwined in his howl, along with Magia's. It was no wonder, then, that the piano, with its raft of strings locked under its shiny pink top, quivered under his muzzle—and began to echo their song.

Ah—whoooo! Ah—whooooo! Ah—whoooooooooooo!

From the depths of the stiff instrument, a new aching, pulsing cry!

If Martin had been able to show Magia his *Encyclopedia of Musical Oddities* at that moment, he could have told her why such a cry had arisen: because the strings of the piano were vibrating at a different frequency than the notes he and Magia were singing.

Magia would've said: *What are you talking about?*

And then Martin would have explained further that when two frequencies interact, they can produce a third note, different altogether. That note, which sounds like the howling of an animal, is sometimes called a "wolf tone" or more plainly, a "wolf."

No, Magia would've said. It wasn't frequencies or vibrations or tones that did it; it was all her bitter days working in the Puszcza. They had shown Magia what she wanted: not just to be a woodcutter, but to know how to find her own way. Even when—*especially* when—in darkness and filled with hunger.

And now, most of all, Magia wanted to go home. She wanted her family. And she wanted Martin—her wolf— to be part of that family, too.

Whichever theory was correct, the result was the same: The longer and higher Magia and Martin howled, the more the piano strings howled with them.

The witch tried to steady herself, to swing the axe down on the wolf's neck, but underneath her hands, the piano swayed and shuddered. Over and over, the *wiedźma* had assailed its sturdy strings with the keening of her wolf-bone flutes, but this! This was a real wolf, and a real girl, both filled with the wildest magic there was.

Mama Pig tried to steady herself, too. She was tired of keeping time for someone else. Tired of the stiff rod in her back. Tired of dancing to someone else's tune. She knew this girl; this girl had let her jig once. This girl had almost helped her escape.

And now this girl was singing about family and love and wanting what you couldn't have. Mama Pig knew this song, too. She wanted her three sons! Her ever needy, ever silly, ever proud and yet precious piglets! Inside her hard china body, something began to pound.

Throughout the pink parlor, Magia and Martin's howl built to a glorious, shattering crescendo. It shook every book off Miss Grand's shelves. It toppled her rosy tea set. And it broke the rod clean out of her metronome's back.

Suddenly, where a delicate, always controlled china pig had been, stood a flint-hoofed, barrel-chested, righteously furious, enormous mother sow. The piano, unable to bear the weight of the transformation, buckled. Its strings pinged with anguish. Then it, too, crashed to the floor.

"My babies!" Mama Pig cried fiercely, her voice chewing into the pink parlor like a saw against glass. "Where are they?" She tossed her massive head through the pile of broken piano pieces and then glared at the three of them. "I swear, if you've hurt a hair of their skinny-skin skins—"

"Stupid hog," said Miss Grand, with a stomp of her bone-buttoned pink boots. "Your dumb piglets let this girl ruin their Story! Now you've ruined everything, too!"

With one flip of her snout, Mama Pig removed the axe from Miss Grand's hands.

"No one calls my children dumb," she said. She cocked a triangular hoof threateningly.

"No!" cried Magia. "No! Wait! I need her to tell me where the key is!"

Too late. Mama Pig placed her hoof squarely in the old woman's chest and shoved her with all the weight of her pent-up anger. Miss Grand toppled, her pink boots flying up briefly before thudding to the floor. Then Mama Pig lumbered out the front door, heading for the Puszcza and her piglets.

Magia flung herself to the carpet near Miss Grand's motionless form. The witch's face was stiff. No breath came from her lips. Where was the key? Miss Grand couldn't die, not without giving Magia what she'd promised! Could she?

But thanks to the triangle-shaped hoofprint embedded in Miss Grand's silk dress, she didn't move again. Not when Magia turned out the woman's lace-edged pockets. And not when she tugged off her buttery-soft boots. Not even when Magia pulled out her jewel-encrusted hairpins, one by one by one. The key was nowhere. Nowhere!

Magia, on the verge of collapse, gripped the rosy fibers of the carpet under her hands. She wanted to scream. How could Miss Grand keep what Magia wanted from her, even in death? She stared at the woman's wretchedly pinched mouth and wished she could make the witch live again, if only so she would spit out all her secrets.

Then Magia sucked in her breath. Miss Grand, for all her evilness, never quite lied; instead she twisted the truth. That's how she got people to do what she wanted. With her flutes, she fed the townsfolk a taste of the Puszcza, but not real wildness. With her metronome, she offered students hollow lessons, but no real teaching. And with her glorious cape, she'd tempted each girl who found it—even Magia—with a taste of what they hungered for most. But never, not once, did she feed them anything that would last.

Miss Grand had said the key was with her bones. Not the ones in her pantry, because Magia had searched through every last, dry one. But if you took the witch's words as a morsel of the truth, there were other bones in this house. Human bones.

Gingerly, Magia pried opened Miss Grand's rigid mouth, and shuddered as she ran a finger along the woman's gums. Neatly tucked against her teeth—yes, next to her jawbone—was a slender white key.

Magia sat back on her heels, clutching the key. Her heart was full of the thought of her family waking again. She looked up at Martin, ready to share with him the whole truth of why she'd done what she'd had to do in the Story.

Martin, though, was looking at a spider that had fallen from his fur. When Little Red had thudded to her knees beside Miss Grand, it had plopped into the crushed pieces of the piano. Now, as it crossed the tedious expanse of rug toward the girl, Martin observed that its body was a plain sort of *dąb*-bark brown, and the short bristles on the spider's head were quivering rapidly from its effort to push forward. And audible only to Martin's large wolf ears, it emitted a faint rhythmic sound.

Martin had heard this sound over and over inside the brick house. He'd repeated it, in the cottage, to Little Red.

Still, he was unprepared for her reaction when she followed his gaze to the spindly, tiny dot approaching her, and she finally heard the sound, too.

She tore the red hat from her head and placed it directly in front of the spider. It buried its body in the closely knitted fibers. Little Red, hovering over the hat, bent even more closely over it, her breath pulsing into the room with long shudders. For several long seconds, Martin could only breathe with her.

Then they both gasped. Instead of a tickly-legged spider, suddenly a large human male crumpled, pale-skinned and battered, against the carved leg of one of the pink sofas. The man didn't move.

"Tata!" cried Little Red. She reached for the rose-blotched blanket on the sofa and covered his shivering body to warm him. "Tata, it's me! Magia! Your little nut! Your songbird! Your daughter!" She shook his arm, and stroked his cheek, and called his name, over and over.

The man twitched and fumbled as he sat up, clutching the ridiculously fringed blanket about him. One hand reached for and patted his two legs, which stuck out from the cloth at a stiff angle. Then he spoke in a hoarse voice, his eyes clearing.

"Magia . . . is that you, my *siekierka*?"

"Yes, Tata, yes!" cried Magia. She slipped her warm hand into his cold one. Her throat was raw from howling and her voice scraped out raggedly. "It's me. Your little axe."

"I didn't know . . . ," said Tata, looking at her with haunted eyes. "I didn't know when I agreed to pay for the clock . . . how many girls . . ." His voice trailed off as he choked, and then began again. "In the end, I could . . . I could only save you . . ."

Magia said nothing. She put her arms around her father and held him.

As for the wolf, he smiled from one scarred, large ear to the other. He'd never seen a happy ending before.

"That hat is uglier than a sheep's tongue," said Dorota.

Magia sighed. Her sister was pristine in her city clothes; even the tidy bundle of books she'd claimed from Martin's abandoned tower was precisely stacked in order of size and tied with a strap. The cover of the human anatomy book fairly glowed from her polishing of it. Magia would never be as put-together as her sister.

Still. Dorota had tucked a slab of not-quite-tender beet between slices of not-too-blackened bread for her. The juices stained Magia's fingers as she wrapped the slipshod lunch in a cloth to stow in her coat pocket.

"Yes," Magia told her sister. "I agree. It's a good thing the best healers don't faint at the sight of ugly."

Dorota's shoulders squared, and she blushed. Magia suppressed a grin. With her newfound books, her sister was going to be the best healer Tysiak had ever seen. And if Dorota would never say it, Magia would. As many times as it took for the whole world to know.

"Go on," said Mama. "It's a long way to walk." She kissed Tata, and then Magia, before offering them each a fragrant canteen of *kwas chlebowy*. Then they were out the door, and on the path to the forest.

If only Jan were here to see us off, too! thought Magia. But he'd apprenticed himself to a real soldiers' unit in town, not the one manned by the bullying gate guards. The world still needed help to keep it safe.

For yes, people in Tysiak still whispered about the Wolf Hour. The hour between darkness and dawn. The hour when it was said that more folk are born into this world and more people leave it than any other. They said that if you were lost in the Puszcza at that hour, you might never come home.

That had been true for some unlucky girls, thought Magia, as she and Tata approached the Puszcza. But not for her. And now—she had work to do.

Magia pulled her red hat firmly over her forehead. The fibers bit into her skin, taking blood in payment for her safe passage. Beside her, Tata did the same. As they threaded their way, two flames, deeper and deeper into the forest, a wolf joined them. He limped slightly but walked jauntily, his belly flashing with the richest of crimsons. And when light began to pierce the canopy of trees, he sang the loudest of all of them.

The melody they wove, these three, as darkness lifted from the Puszcza, was haunting, and lovely, and as red as red as red could be.

ACKNOWLEDGMENTS

Tina Wexler, my agent, believed in this story from Once Upon a Time until The End. For that, she deserves a talking wolf pup of her own, although she probably prefers a cat. Cheryl Klein, my editor, wields powerful plot magic; this book might've lost its way without her; thankfully, with her, it did not. Thank you for fearlessly asking the right questions, and for patiently listening to my answers. Likewise, I'm indebted to my writing group, who took my pigs, wolves, spiders, and little girls seriously, and who sent me owls as needed. I also owe special thanks to Liza Parfomak, who read the manuscript with an eye to the Polish language. Her linguistic advice was invaluable; any errors, however, remain my own. In addition, I'm ever grateful to my parents, Jim and Mary Lewis, who not only taught me to read, but read to me, long after I was no longer small. Listening to Lloyd Alexander's Chronicles of Prydain put me under the spell of stories for life. And as always, my heart and love to Mike, who is everything.

ABOUT THE AUTHOR

Sara Lewis Holmes is the author of *Operation Yes*, which was named to the Kids' Indie Next List and nominated for seven state awards, and *Letters from Rapunzel*, which won the Ursula Nordstrom Fiction Prize. Thanks to her husband's service in the Air Force, she has written stories and poems in eleven states and three countries, as well as her current home of Washington, DC. She loves both the city and wild places, and has found magic in both. Please visit her online at www.saralewisholmes.com and @SaraLewisHolmes.

This book was edited by Cheryl Klein and
designed by Carol Ly. The text was set in Sabon
MT Std., a typeface designed by Barcelona EF.
The book was printed and bound at R. R. Donnelley
in Crawfordsville, Indiana. The production
was supervised by Rachel Gluckstern, and
manufacturing was supervised by Angelique
Browne.